# Twilight of the Dead

APRIL 1945. RETREATING German troops mount a valiant rearguard action against the mighty Red Army, and it's only a matter of time before Berlin falls, especially as the undead Rumanian vampyrs have become allied with the Russian forces. Unless Lord Constanta and his undead army are stopped, their plan to enslave all humans will succeed. Soldiers from each side must put aside their mutual hatred to target the true enemy. As the war for Europe reaches its brutal climax, a bloody fight for the future of mankind is about to begin!

**FIENDS OF THE EASTERN FRONT**
Created by Gerry Finley-Day and Carlos Ezquerra

Fiends of the Eastern Front

# Twilight of the Dead

## DAVID BISHOP

**BLACK FLAME**

*To Gerry and Carlos, who started it all.*

## Historical note:

This novel is a work of fiction set during the Second World War conflict between Germany and Russia. As far as possible the historical details are accurate, but the story takes liberties with reality for narrative effect.

## A Black Flame Publication
## www.blackflame.com

First published in 2006 by BL Publishing, Games Workshop Ltd., Willow Road, Nottingham NG7 2WS, UK.

Distributed in the US by Simon & Schuster, 1230 Avenue of the Americas, New York, NY 10020, USA.

10 9 8 7 6 5 4 3 2 1

ISBN 13: 978 1 84416 384 7
ISBN 10: 1 84416 384 9

A CIP record for this book is available from the British Library.

Printed in the UK by Bookmarque, Surrey, UK.

# PROLOGUE

"In these hours, the whole German people look to you, my fighters in the East... thanks to your resolution and fanaticism, thanks to your weapons, and under your leadership, the Bolshevik assault will be choked in a bath of blood.

At this moment... the turning-point of this war will be decided."

– Adolf Hitler

SOMETIMES THERE IS little difference between fiction and reality, a narrow margin between the truth and a lie. One person's fervent belief is another's falsehood, one man's recollection merely propaganda in the eyes of a different witness. When it comes to telling the story of the Great Patriotic War between Russia and Germany, such differences become even more blurred, such distinctions even more meaningless.

Much of what happened in that fateful conflict is a matter of public record, as proven by military documents and eyewitness accounts. But the whole truth about what happened remains secret, hidden from the light. I believe it is long past time the truth was told. I was there, so I will tell it – whether or not you believe my version of events is up to you. But everything I am about to tell you is true, no matter how fantastical it may sound.

My name is Victor Danilov Zunetov and I was a soldier in the Red Army during the Second World War. At first I was a kommisar, a political officer charged with ensuring the rank and file showed due deference to our masters in Moscow. My father was an important man in the Communist Party and did his best to ensure I remained safe. But I was determined to fight the fascists who invaded Mother Russia in the summer of 1941. Eventually I secured a posting to Leningrad (now known as St Petersburg), arriving at the besieged city in January 1942. It was there I first met Grigori Eisenstein, a disgraced former officer who served with a shtrafroty, a penal company. These small squads were given the deadliest, most dangerous jobs within the blockade, undertaking suicide missions no sane soldier would attempt.

Fate and my own stupidity conspired to have me join Eisenstein's company of the cursed. There I discovered the war's greatest secret, the truth that remains buried to this day. It is a well-established, documented, historical fact that German armies posted along the Eastern Front were supplemented by soldiers from other countries, such as Rumania and Italy. But one of the war's dirtiest little secrets is that among the Rumanian warriors was a squad of sinister soldiers from the region of Transylvania. These men were inhuman; a troop of undead parasites who sustained themselves by drinking blood from living humans. German soldiers found themselves caught in an unholy alliance with a cadre of supernatural creatures, monsters they called vampyr. Not all the Germans were happy to fight alongside these fiends. During my time in Leningrad I met a squad of enemy troopers hellbent on deserting to our side, rather than become thralls of the vampyr. Twice I heard tell of an attempted mutiny against the Rumanians in 1941, led by three brothers named Vollmer. Such tales gave me hope when I came face to face with the bloodsucking fiends.

The leader of the vampyr was an austere, aristocratic figure called Constanta. He wore the uniform of a Hauptmann, yet seemed to have a power and command over

German troops far in excess of his rank. Constanta's fate became inextricably linked to that of Eisenstein's when the two fought behind enemy lines. The vampyr attacked my commander, tainting Grigori with the vampyr lust for human blood. But Eisenstein used the power of his Jewish faith to delay the infection's spread, forcing a Star of David emblem into the wounds left by Constanta's fangs, and cauterising the flesh. I helped him stave off the infection, becoming his unofficial second-in-command. Together we discovered a terrible truth: Eisenstein would never be free of the inhuman taint while Constanta lived. But the Rumanian was one of the most powerful vampyr to walk the earth, created by the father of all the vampyr, a creature known only as the Sire. The discovery of this fact cost the lives of everyone else in our squad, including the woman Eisenstein loved, Sofia Gomorova.

By the end of January 1943, the blockade of Leningrad had been broken. Many hundreds of miles further south, the brutal German attack upon the city of Stalingrad was finally defeated. The tide was turning in the Great Patriotic War; the German Blitzkrieg had been blunted. For the first time, the Russian people truly began to believe we would prevail against the Nazis. But Eisenstein and I knew there was a menace far greater than Hitler and his cronies abroad in this conflict. All of mankind faced a foe that bullets and bombs would not defeat. Until we all recognised the vampyr as our common enemy, the war between nations would continue.

I told the story of my time at Leningrad in a previous volume, a book my publishers entitled *The Blood Red Army*. Now I will finish the story of my involvement with the vampyr, of how it took me to the streets of Berlin and the terrifying interior of Transylvania. The fact I'm writing these words proves I survived – would that I could say the same of my friends and comrades from those final, fateful months of the war. I have pieced together the story of what happened on both sides of the conflict, thanks to what I saw and what others have told me. I cannot claim to be the most reliable of narrators, but what follows is as accurate a record of events as my limited skills can create. Most of all, this is the story of my friend Grigori Eisenstein and the sacrifices he made for us all.

Now, I must choose where best to begin my narrative. There is much I could tell you about the events of 1943 and the early months of the following year, but I suppose the beginning of the end came in August 1944, when we invaded Rumania. It was there we first encountered Karl, Gunther and Ralf, and where I first set eyes on my beloved Mariya. Yes, that is as good a place as any to begin. You may choose to believe that what follows is fiction, but I know the truth. Read on and judge for yourself…

# PART ONE: BETRAYAL

## One

I KNEW OUR mission was in trouble when Ryazanov's head exploded. He was on my left as our unit crawled up the hill towards a ramshackle farmhouse. I had caught sight of a muzzle flash in the distance and a moment later half of Ryazanov's face was gone, turning the air between us to a fine pink mist. I pressed myself into the mud-strewn hillside, one hand reaching across to my comrade's shoulder. I knew no living soul could survive such a wound but I still had to check. Ryazanov's corpse rolled over and a lifeless eye stared past me at the darkening sky. The right half of his head was gone, glistening white bone protruding from the remnants of his shattered skull. I spat out a curse and pushed the body away. Ryazanov had been a brave soldier and fearless vampyr-hunter, a valuable addition to the ranks of our unit. Replacing him would not be easy, but that was a problem for another day – we still had a mission to complete. Our target was meant to be waiting in the farmhouse atop the hillside, unaware of our approach. But an enemy sniper inside the derelict building was

9

now targeting us and Ryazanov was the first casualty. In less than the time it took to draw breath, the hunters had become the hunted.

Five of us were hugging the hillside, our position halfway between the settlements of Tirgu Frumos and Jassy in north-western Rumania. To my right was Gorky, a dark-haired youth from Moscow who'd joined our unit less than a week earlier, the sole survivor of a vampyr attack on a Red Army outpost three days before. Gorky remained unproven in battle and it was my duty to watch him, and see how he reacted under the pressure of a life and death mission behind enemy lines. Eisenstein had been against offering Gorky a place in our ranks, but I had volunteered to be responsible for the pale-faced private. As we lay on that muddy slope, pinned down by the sniper, I could see Gorky gasping for air, timorous breaths betraying his terror. Eisenstein had been right, as usual – the newcomer would not last long in a real fight.

Beyond Gorky was Komarov, a hardened veteran from Stalingrad who'd joined our unit six months earlier. Bald, belligerent and battle-scarred, he had saved my life on several occasions but accepted no thanks for that. His only interest was vengeance against the fiends who had murdered his men, turning them into undead monsters. Komarov was not one for exchanging anecdotes over a flask of vodka, no matter how black or humorous the subject matter. He lived to kill and killed to live – end of story.

Eisenstein was furthest from me, his grizzled face turning to inquire about Ryazanov's fate. I shook my head, drawing a finger across my neck. Eisenstein grimaced, his bloodstained fingers tightening their grip on his PPSh submachine gun, one hand clasping the circular magazine of ammunition. He was not yet thirty then, but his grim features had the careworn aspect of a man twice his years. The war was aging all of us at an accelerated pace, but that was doubly true of Eisenstein. His ongoing battle with the taint of vampyrism was wearing him down, as if he was fading away from the inside out, becoming a shadow of the man he had once been. Unlike the undead monsters he hunted, Eisenstein could still walk in daylight. But everything else about him was slowly, relentlessly being consumed by the creeping black cancer of his infection.

Huddled beside Eisenstein was a terrified Rumanian soldier, a prisoner of war we had captured earlier in the day. He was the one who'd led us to this location, promising that the farmhouse contained one of our most sought-after targets in this war of terror and attrition. Judging by the terror in the Rumanian's eyes, he was as surprised as anyone by the presence of a sniper overlooking our position, and so had not deliberately led us into the line of fire. But that didn't change the fact that we were pinned down on open ground and time was running out.

I shifted my attention back to the farmhouse. If our quarry was inside, why had they only fired once? Were they running out of ammunition or simply waiting for a clear target before shooting again? Whatever the answer, we did not have time to play games. The sun would set in less than an hour. Once that happened, our advantage over the target would be lost. I gave a low whistle to the others then crawled forward over the churned-up soil towards the farmhouse. A bullet whistled past my left ear and thudded into the mud behind me. Another shot followed, then another and another, each round missing us by the slightest of margins. It took a brilliant marksman to keep five men pinned down with only a handful of bullets.

"He's toying with us," a familiar voice whispered in my ear. Eisenstein had crawled across to lie beside me in the mud. "He's marking time, waiting for reinforcements."

"If we try to storm the farmhouse, we'll be cut down before we can get close."

"Agreed." Eisenstein glanced across to our Rumanian POW. "Horezu soiled his uniform when the first shot was fired. He's even more scared than Gorky, if that's possible."

"Do you think Gorgo's the shooter?"

Eisenstein shook his head. "He'll be safely in his coffin, waiting for sunset so he can join the retreat. Until then he's trapped inside the farmhouse. No, I'm guessing it's one of his thralls. You know how the vampyr like to keep their cannon fodder close by."

I nodded bitterly. In the nineteen months since Eisenstein and I escaped the blockade around Leningrad, we had learned many lessons about the behaviour of Transylvanian bloodsuckers and their servants. Rarely did a senior vampyr like Constanta venture anywhere without a cadre of thralls as bodyguards. This had been increasingly true since the Red Army decided to reform many of its penal companies into vampyr-hunting units known as smert krofpeet – death to the blood-drinkers. Constanta and his kind were all but invulnerable, yet they guarded their undead bodies jealously. Having sacrificed their souls to achieve a kind of twisted immortality, they had no intention of letting that status be snatched away from them.

"So what do we do?" I asked Eisenstein.

"We'll have to–" he began, but fell silent in the middle of his reply. An unearthly cry split the air, stabbing at our minds like daggers. It was a sound I'd heard before, a sound that chilled the blood in my veins. Eisenstein's eyes shifted from me to the farmhouse, the colour draining from his features. I twisted round to follow his gaze and gasped in dismay. A dozen dead German soldiers were lumbering from the building towards us, their arms outstretched, fingers clawing the air. All were walking corpses, resurrected by their undead master's cry. I glanced over my shoulder and saw a similar horde emerging from the ground behind us. That explained why the hillside was so churned up. The corpses had dug their own graves and then lain beneath the surface, waiting for the signal to rise up.

"It's a trap!"

Eisenstein spat out a disgusted curse. "Not if I can help it!"

FOUR HOURS EARLIER most of the Axis forces had been fleeing from this same area, racing to stay ahead of the Red Army's rapidly advancing Second Ukrainian Front. The retreat had been a chaotic affair, without proper transportation or support. Anyone unable to make their way south was left with a handful of ammunition and orders to delay the oncoming Soviets as long as possible. Most of the abandoned had fought to the death, no doubt terrified by propaganda tales of the fate awaiting anyone taken prisoner by the Russians, but some surrendered or were overwhelmed.

Horezu was among those we captured. He had crawled unarmed from an empty trench, waving a white flag and calling for sanctuary. I recognised a familiar terror haunting his eyes and took him aside for interrogation. Horezu spoke only broken German, his sentences littered with untranslatable Rumanian phrases, but I understood enough of his words and gestures to interpret what he was saying. I sent Ryazanov to find Eisenstein and bring him back. Once my commander appeared, I made Horezu repeat what he had told me while I translated.

"Please, you must protect me," the hollow-eyed Rumanian begged. "If the nightwalkers know I am talking with you, they will come, they will bleed me dry. One of their leaders is not far from here, waiting until dark for his chance to retreat. You must protect me!"

"One of their leaders?" Eisenstein asked, his eyes glinting in the harsh August sun. "Victor, ask him if it's Constanta."

Horezu paled at the mention of the vampyr lord's name. The Rumanian soldier's quivering hands made the sign of the cross before his cracked lips kissed a silver crucifix he had hidden inside his shabby uniform. "Not him, Gorgo."

"Sergeant Gorgo?" Eisenstein demanded.

Horezu nodded in response.

"Scheisse," I heard myself whisper. "That's Constanta's second-in-command!"

Between us, Eisenstein and I had hunted down and slain seven members of the Rumanian vampyr lord's inner circle, along with dozens of their unholy acolytes and hundreds of thralls. But the leader of the vampyr horde and his second-in-command had always eluded us. Intelligence reports passed to smert krofpeet units indicated that Constanta and Gorgo were busy spreading their undead taint in other theatres of the war, fighting alongside the Japanese forces in the Pacific or strengthening the resolve of German U-boat crews in their battle for control of the Atlantic. Wilder claims suggested that Constanta had been sighted alongside Rommel in North Africa, or had been smuggled into England on a covert mission to assassinate the British prime minister, Winston Churchill.

To us it did not matter whether these tales were true or not. All we cared about was destroying Constanta. Eisenstein would remain forever tainted until the vampyr lord was no more, and I had seen too many good men and women die at the hands of Constanta's underlings to rest until the monster behind this campaign of terror was destroyed. The news that Constanta's second-in-command was so close came as something of a shock. Eisenstein and I had heard much about Gorgo's loyalty and his murderous methods of enforcing the will of

Constanta, but neither of us had ever encountered the Rumanian sergeant. Now, if our informant was telling the truth, Gorgo was within our sights.

"Where is he?" I asked Horezu in German. "Where?"

The frightened private rattled off a set of directions in his native tongue. I had spent several years as a student in Berlin before the war, something that had saved my life on more than one occasion, but the Rumanian language was completely new to me. I asked Horezu to slow down, but was still unable to interpret his words. Finally the youth asked me in German for a map. Eisenstein cautiously produced his field map and Horezu pointed to a hilltop less than twenty kilometres away from their position, in the no-man's-land between our troops and the retreating Axis forces.

"How many vampyr?' Eisenstein asked through me.

"Only Gorgo," Horezu replied. He frowned. "You want more?"

"No. He'll do." Eisenstein glanced across at me, his eyes alive with excitement.

We needed no words. Both of us knew the significance of Gorgo's presence in this area. If we could interrogate him, the information gained would be invaluable. But capturing a creature capable of turning itself into a bat, a wolf or a translucent mist was no mean feat. We would need every skill we'd gained since Leningrad, all the luck we'd ever possessed, and the element of surprise.

I GRIMACED AS the resurrected German soldiers advanced on us from two directions. So much for luck and the element of surprise. Whoever was inside the farmhouse knew we were coming and had sent these corpses to kill us. All we had to combat them were our skills, our weapons, and our courage.

Eisenstein was in a crouch, facing downhill. "Concentrate on those coming up towards us," he shouted at the rest of our unit. "Aim for the head!"

Komarov responded first, dropping three of the enemy with shots from his Moisin rifle by the time I'd twisted round to open fire.

"What about the corpses coming down from the farmhouse?" Gorky asked, his voice a high-pitched whimper of terror.

"Those corpses are keeping us alive," I shouted. "They're between us and the sniper!" I glanced sideways and realised Horezu was missing. "Komarov! Where'd the prisoner go?"

"I don't know and I don't care," he snarled, taking aim at another of our slowly shuffling enemies. "The little bastard fled when he saw what was coming for us."

A scream of pain answered my question better than Komarov. I glanced over my shoulder in time to see Horezu struggling among the resurrected. One of the dead was biting the Rumanian's right thigh while another was gnawing at the private's throat. The screaming stopped when the corpse ate through Horezu's vocal chords, blood spurting from the wound. I put a bullet through Horezu's forehead and he slumped to the ground, his torment at an end – for now.

Eisenstein and Komarov had finished off the resurrected below us and turned to face those above. Several of the walking corpses had stopped to feast on Horezu's body, but most were still advancing on our position.

"We should fall back," Gorky bleated, his PPSh trembling in his hands. "There's too many of them... We should fall back!"

"Haven't you been listening to Comrade Stalin's pronouncements from Moscow?" Eisenstein asked. "Not one step back is permitted for the Red Army. No retreats, no surrender."

"But we–"

"Are you questioning our orders?" I snarled at Gorky. The fearful newcomer shook his head. "Good. Then you stay here with Komarov and keep the resurrected

occupied while we circle round to the farmhouse."
Gorky opened his mouth to protest but thought better of
it.

"Try to keep a few of the enemy between you and that
sniper," Eisenstein advised, "otherwise he'll realise
we're trying to outflank him."

"Get moving," Komarov urged. "We've less than an
hour to sundown."

Ten minutes later Eisenstein and I had circled round
the eastern slope of the hill and had come up alongside
the farmhouse. It was little more than a dilapidated log
cabin, the thatched roof badly in need of repair and most
of the windows covered by wooden shutters. One of the
shutters hung open and the barrel of a rifle protruded
from it, aiming at our comrades down the slope. We
couldn't see the sniper from our position, but occasional
shots were still being fired at Komarov and Gorky
through the shambling crowd of resurrected corpses.
Eisenstein tapped me on the shoulder and jerked a
thumb towards the back of the farmhouse. We crept
silently round the structure, our weapons ready to fire,
fingers tensed over the trigger. On the northern side of
the farmhouse was a closed door, apparently the only
entrance. As we got nearer to the door, a woman cried
out a Russian curse from inside the building.

Eisenstein and I took up positions on either side of the
entrance, suddenly uncertain of our ground. What the
hell was a woman doing inside the farmhouse, and a
Russian woman at that? Female soldiers were a common
enough sight in the Red Army among medical, communications and transportation staff. Women had also
proven themselves adept as snipers during the battle for
Stalingrad, thanks to their patience and capacity to with-
stand great personal discomfort. But men were still the
frontline troops of the Great Patriotic War, and the first
choice for specialist units like ours that often went
behind enemy lines. Eisenstein was particularly resistant

to having women in his smert krofpeet squad after what
had happened to his lover Sofia in Leningrad.

We listened at the farmhouse door, straining to hear
what was happening within. A low, guttural voice was
hissing and snarling, demanding answers in a mixture of
Russian, German and what sounded like a dialect of
Rumanian. But no reply came and after a few moments
I heard the unmistakable sound of a fist striking flesh,
the crack of bone breaking and a female cry of pain.
Again the questions were asked, this time loud enough
for me to hear them clearly. I whispered a translation to
Eisenstein, careful to keep my voice low enough to
escape detection.

"He wants to know why she came here, how she knew
about this place, who sent her. What's her connection to
those soldiers outside?"

"All good questions," Eisenstein muttered under his
breath. "I wish she'd answer them."

Another voice spoke inside the farmhouse, harsh and
sibilant. I recognised none of the words, but the accent
was all too familiar: Transylvanian.

"That's one of Constanta's men. It could be Gorgo, if
he's still inside."

"Good, then let's join him," Eisenstein replied,
switching the magazine in his submachine gun to one
loaded with silver-tipped rounds. I retrieved a small
crossbow slung across my back, slotting a clip of five
sharpened wooden stakes into position and making sure
the weapon was primed and ready to fire. My spare hand
reached for the antique silver flask held in a clip on my
right hip, fingers quietly loosening the lid with its black
enamel cross. I never drank from the flask, keeping the
holy water inside it for those who would find its touch
far more corrosive. Consecrated liquid would not kill a
vampyr unless you drowned them in it, but a single drop
of holy water was like acid to the undead, a valuable
tool during interrogations. Finally, I pulled a string of

garlic bulbs from inside my knapsack and slipped it over my head like a necklace.

Eisenstein smiled. Both of us knew we could be dead within moments.

"Ready?" he asked.

I nodded before smashing the heel of my boot hard against the brittle farmhouse door. It shattered inwards like so much kindling and Eisenstein burst through the space where the door had been, firing silver-tipped death in a horizontal spray across the room. I followed him in a second later, loosing off three bolts at smears of movement on the other side of the room, always expecting to feel the final, fatal stab of death at any moment. All around us the air was filled with screams and pain and ashes, a sure sign of the undead being exterminated. Vampyr exploded into a cloud of dust when destroyed, a fact that hid their true form from sceptics.

When no return fire came, I let myself relax long enough to take in our surroundings. The sniper at the open window was dead, his body punctured by two bullets and a wooden bolt from my crossbow. He must have been an ordinary German soldier, since his corpse remained intact. Nearer the centre of the room floated a cloud of dust where one of the interrogators had been standing. His captive was tied to a wooden chair, her face blackened by bruises. One of her eyes was swollen shut and blood dripped from her broken noise. Her dark brown hair was pulled back from her face, revealing pale skin that provided a stark contrast to all the blood and bruises.

Even through the pain and suffering, I could see she had a simple, striking beauty. Like Eisenstein and me, her Red Army uniform bore the insignia of the smert krofpeet. She, too, was a vampyr hunter. The bodies of four male smert krofpeet were splayed across the farmhouse floor like broken, discarded rag dolls, each of them with savage wounds evident on their necks, and a pool of blood spilling out from beneath their bodies. All four had been brutally murdered, no doubt by the creature standing next to the captive. It took no great wit to realise this was our quarry.

Gorgo was a powerfully built figure clad in the uniform of a Rumanian soldier, the rank of sergeant evident from his insignia, pain and anger etched into his malevolent features. Two dark eyes gleamed at us with an animal's cunning and his lips were drawn back in a snarl, revealing elongated fangs. He had snatched one of my wooden bolts out of the air, no doubt aided by the lightning fast reflexes vampyr possess, but two smoking holes were visible where Eisenstein's silver-tipped bullets had torn through the Rumanian's tunic.

I did not need to see the insignia of a bat clutching a swastika in its talons over a mountain peak to recognise the creature as one of Constanta's inner circle; only the strongest of vampyr could sustain such injuries and yet live. Like all his kind, Gorgo was careful to stay away from the sunlight spilling in through the window. He hissed at us through bloodstained teeth, cursing in a variety of languages and dialects.

"You must be Gorgo," Eisenstein replied, aiming his PPSh at the vampyr's heart. "Don't even think about trying to escape or transform yourself. We know all your tricks, fiend."

"Who are you?" the monster sneered back at us in Russian.

"An old acquaintance of your friend Constanta. We met him near Leningrad."

Eisenstein pulled aside the collar of his uniform to expose the area where the vampyr commander had bitten him two years earlier. The wound was heavily bandaged but infected blood and black pus had still soaked through the bindings. In the centre of the malodorous mess was a void, a patch in the shape of a six-pointed star where the bandage remained clean. Eisenstein possessed a silver Star of David emblem which he kept pressed against Constanta's bite marks. Though it burned and tormented him, the icon also held the vampyr taint in check.

"He did this to me," Eisenstein said.

"The Jew," Gorgo breathed, chuckling under his breath. "Lord Constanta told me about you. How you gave yourself to him, but then tried to fight off the bloodlust. Your feeble attempts to deny his dominion over your body are pitiful indeed!"

"Really? I'm surprised the mighty Constanta even bothered to mention me if I'm as insignificant as you say." Eisenstein stepped closer to Gorgo before speaking again. "Where is he? Where's your lordship hiding himself these days?"

"I do not answer to you, mortal."

"Haven't you heard? I'm not a mere mortal anymore. I'm a daywalker. I have all the strengths of your kind, but none of the weaknesses. Holy water and silver mean nothing to me. You hide from the sunlight but I bask in it, and I welcome its warmth upon my face."

"You lie," Gorgo sneered.

"We'll see," Eisenstein said. "Victor?"

I moved closer but was careful to stay beyond Gorgo's reach. I retrieved the flask from my hip, fingers brushing across its engraved surface as I unscrewed the crucifix lid. Eisenstein opened his lips and I tipped a mouthful of holy water inside.

"Hmm, tastes good," he said with a smile. "Would you like some?"

When Gorgo didn't reply, Eisenstein spat the liquid into the vampyr's face. The monster howled in agony, skin sizzling as it was burned away by the holy water. While Gorgo convulsed with pain, I slipped the necklace of garlic from my shoulders and draped it over his head instead, before hurriedly moving away once more. The Rumanian tried to pull the bulbs away but his fingers burned whenever they touched the garlic. Curls of acrid smoke rose from the seared flesh where holy water had burned its way down to the bone. Eventually Gorgo gave up trying to escape the necklace, preferring to glare at us with venomous rage.

"What do you want, Jew?"

"The name's Eisenstein. Remember that. And I've already told you what I want: answers. Where's Constanta? Where is the ruler of the vampyr?"

"He is our lord, but not our ruler," Gorgo snarled. "The Sire, the creator of us all, is the true ruler of the vampyr. Lord Constanta is his emissary, his ambassador to the outside world. In your human terms, Constanta is the Sire's general on the battlefield."

I tipped some holy water into my left hand and flicked a few droplets at the fiend. "Where on the battlefield, djavoli? Where's Constanta?"

Gorgo flinched, twisting his head from one side to the other, trying in vain to keep the holy water from striking his face. When he finally stopped thrashing about, utter hatred and contempt were all too evident in his scarred, scorched features.

"Enough!"

Eisenstein smiled with satisfaction. "Well?"

"Sighisoara. He's at Sighisoara," Gorgo said. "Constanta has gone home to prepare for the next phase of our glorious crusade."

"There, that wasn't so difficult, was it?"

"Don't trust him," another voice croaked. Gorgo's prisoner had been silent since we burst into the farmhouse, but now she stirred. "He's a liar. They all are."

"All of them?" I asked. "Gorgo's the only one here."

"Not for long," she replied, blood bubbling from between her lips. "That cry you heard earlier, that was their summoning call. This place will be crawling with the undead and their thralls soon. We'll be dead less than an hour after sunset unless we leave now."

"Untie her," Eisenstein told me. As I moved to cut the captive's bindings, footsteps became audible outside the farmhouse. Eisenstein and I spun round, ready to fire, but relaxed when we saw it was our comrades Komarov and Gorky in the shadows by the doorway.

"I was wondering when you'd get here," Eisenstein said. "Have you dealt with all the walking dead?"

Komarov lurched forward into the light, revealing a gaping hole where his right eye had been. Gorky looked just as bad, with most of his throat torn out and intestines spilling from a gaping wound where his stomach had been.

"The resurrected must have got them," I whispered.

"Now it's your turn," Gorgo announced, a throaty chuckle resonating in his chest. "Take them, my children. Feast on their flesh! Drench yourselves in their blood!"

At Gorgo's command the corpses of the smert krofpeet soldiers on the floor rose up, hissing and clawing at us, their lips drawing back as if to smile, revealing freshly grown fangs. Komarov and Gorky lurched forward to join them, trapping us in the centre of the farmhouse.

Eisenstein spat a curse at Gorgo before opening fire with his PPSh, sweeping round in a complete circle. I threw myself at the female prisoner, knocking her to the farmhouse floor. Once we were both beneath Eisenstein's line of fire, I took aim at the nearest vampyr and emptied my remaining wooden bolts into its heart. The creature exploded into dust while Eisenstein's silver-tipped bullets accounted for two more of the bloodsuckers. The last of the smert krofpeet threw itself between Eisenstein and Gorgo, shielding the Rumanian with its body. The newly converted vampyr exploded into ash as silver-tipped bullets punctured it, but the delay gave Komarov and Gorky enough time to attack Eisenstein, preventing him from finishing off Gorgo. Meanwhile the Rumanian was ripping the garlic necklace away from his neck and burning his fingers to the bone in the process, the stench of charred flesh suffusing the farmhouse. Screaming in agony, the vampyr staggered towards an internal door.

Cursing myself for not using the crossbow on Gorgo, I pulled my Nagant pistol from its holster and fired at the retreating monster. Both shots just missed his head as he dived through the doorway. Shifting targets, I put two shots through Komarov's head, sending the reanimated corpse over backwards. Eisenstein used the butt of his submachine gun to smash Gorky's skull to a bloody pulp.

"What happened to Gorgo?" Eisenstein gasped once the last of our attackers had stopped moving.

The prisoner tilted her head towards the side door. "Through there."

Eisenstein glanced out the window. The sun was sinking ever closer to the horizon but it was still daylight. "He can't have gone far. One step outside and he'll be burned alive."

"Don't be so sure," the woman said. "My squad was lying in wait here two days before Gorgo arrived. We searched the building, didn't find anything. But that bastard appeared out of thin air and slaughtered most of my men in under a minute."

"How'd you know Gorgo was coming here?" I asked her.

"Untie me and I'll tell you."

"That can wait," Eisenstein snapped. "Victor, reload your weapons and wait here. I'm going to see what's through that door."

I pulled a fresh supply of wooden bolts from my knapsack and slotted them into place on the crossbow while Eisenstein edged across the room. Once I'd nodded my readiness, Eisenstein kicked open the door and tensed to face Gorgo. But nothing came from beyond the door: no sound, no movement, no attack. Eisenstein crept inside and a long, agonising silence followed before a fresh curse echoed in the air. Eisenstein emerged from the bedroom as a vehicle's engine roared in the distance.

"Damn it!"

"What's wrong? Where's Gorgo?"

Eisenstein ignored my question, racing out of the farmhouse. A few desultory gunshots followed before silence fell upon the dilapidated structure once more.

"You were going to untie me?" the prisoner prompted.

"Yes, sorry, I forgot," I muttered, pulling a silver-edged knife from inside my left boot to slice through the ropes binding her. Once cut free she rolled aside, hands rubbing her joints and massaging the places where the cords had cut into her arms and legs.

"How do you feel?" I asked.

She gave me a withering glare of disdain. "Like I've been bound, beaten and battered. How do you think I feel?"

"A little gratitude wouldn't go astray," I pointed out. "We've just saved you from having your throat ripped out by one of the most powerful vampyr in this bloody war."

"I didn't ask you to save me. It was *your* blundering that got my men killed!"

"How do you come to that brilliant conclusion?" I snapped.

"One of your squad must have tipped off Gorgo about the trap we'd laid for him."

I couldn't help but laugh at her twisted logic. "Gorgo was the one laying the trap here, not you. He had dozens of German corpses buried around this building waiting to be resurrected. He must have known smert krofpeet units were operating along this section and decided to see how many of us he could lure into an ambush. Had you considered that possibility?"

The woman frowned. "No. No, I hadn't..." She looked round the farmhouse, taking in the corpses and the clouds of ash still hanging in the air. "What a mess."

Eisenstein returned, his face black with cold anger. "Gorgo got away. There was a hidden tunnel in the bedroom leading down the hill to a waiting German staff car. The bastard must have planned this whole thing – a ruse to lure both our squads here – and we fell for it."

"Have you got any water?" the woman asked. "I haven't had a drink for hours."

"Only holy water," I said, offering my little flask. "We were in a rush to get here before sundown, to make sure Gorgo wouldn't make an easy escape."

She took the flask and drank gratefully from its contents, wiping her lips dry with the back of one hand. "My name's Charnosova, Mariya Charnosova."

"I'm Victor Zunetov and that's Grigori Eisenstein," I replied, pointing at my comrade.

"We should get back to our own lines," Eisenstein decided. "It'll be dark soon and I don't want to be out in the open when the sun sets. Especially now we're inside Rumanian territory."

"Agreed," Mariya said, getting to her feet with some difficulty. She looked about the room, searching for something. "Gorgo's men took my weapons when they overwhelmed us."

I strode across to the bedroom and glanced inside, spotting a black knapsack with a red star symbol on its side. A handful of sharpened wooden stakes protruded from within. I brought the knapsack out to Mariya who smiled at me in thanks. Her eyes were striking, warm and comforting despite her injuries and her bruises, despite her harsh words and accusations earlier. I found myself staring into her eyes, unable to tear my gaze away. In a war so ugly and brutal, it was a shock to be confronted with such beauty. In my experience, few survived the company of vampyr, and yet Mariya had withstood torture and interrogation at the hands of Constanta's second-in-command. It was clear that she had remarkable reserves of courage and strength, making her a valuable addition to our decimated unit. Convincing Eisenstein of that would be another matter entirely.

# Two

HANS AND RALF Vollmer never knew whether it was fate, chance or happenstance that reunited them on one of the war's most decisive days. August 23rd was a Wednesday and the battle for Rumania was changing from a rout to capitulation. The Red Army had launched its offensive three days earlier with a dawn artillery barrage followed by armoured spearheads stabbing deep into German-held territory. Within thirty-six hours the Rumanian positions between Jassy and Tirgu Frumos had caved in, and Russian troops were streaming down the Prut River valley. Many of the Axis companies in eastern Rumania were outflanked and encircled, cut off from supplies, and all hope of retreat was vanquished in a matter of hours.

For the Vollmer brothers and their friend Gunther Stiefel, these events were merely the latest in a long line of reversals. All three of them had entered Russia as part of Operation Barbarossa in June 1941, the Wehrmacht's Blitzkrieg tactics tearing through the ill-prepared Red Army defences. But much had befallen the invaders since then: the harsh, early winter of 1941 that halted the German advance twenty kilometres from the Russian capital, Moscow; the bitter Siege of Leningrad, where a city and its defenders somehow held their own against unspeakable terrors; the battle for Stalingrad, where Hitler's mightiest warriors could not dislodge a tiny army from the banks of the Volga, no matter what devastation was brought upon that once mighty city; the mechanised Armageddon that was the Battle of Kursk, where tanks died screaming in a clash of titanic proportions; and a dozen other reversals, each contributing another fracture to the once all-conquering Wehrmacht machine.

All that was history by August 1944, the backdrop to an army slowly, painfully retracting its claws from territory first claimed three years before. Of all the lands Hitler did not wish to give up, Rumania was among the most vital, for it provided the Third Reich with oil. Without fuel Germany had no hope of victory, though few on the front line still believed victory was possible. Should Rumania fall to the Red Army, the writing was on the wall for Hitler and his cronies in Berlin. It would be merely a matter of months before the Thousand-Year Reich was wiped away, destroyed and discredited in a dozen years. But for Ralf, Hans and Gunther, the end of the war could not come soon enough. Each had seen enough death and suffering to last them a thousand lifetimes, and none of them wished to witness anymore.

Hans was the youngest of the Vollmer brothers, a new recruit fresh from the Hitler Youth ranks when Operation Barbarossa had begun in 1941. Back then he'd believed every word the Nazi propaganda machine fed him. He swallowed all the lies and justifications and tyranny without question, his thoughts guided and shaped by what Berlin wanted him to believe.

To Hans's young eyes, the Eastern Front was a holy war aimed at stopping the Bolshevik taint spreading across Europe, an anti-Communist crusade to secure new territory for the Fatherland. But his eyes were opened to the terrible truth behind the lie when he discovered that the Wehrmacht had bound itself to creatures of the night, loosing undead horrors upon the battlefields of Eastern Europe.

Ralf had had none of his younger brother's illusions, even in 1941. The eldest Vollmer was a veteran Panzer commander then, with a crew of four ready to obey his every word without question. The five men inside the metal behemoth had fought not for some mythic greater glory, but because it was their job – they were soldiers and this was what they'd trained to do. Nazi propaganda had no place inside a Panzer, as far as the crew was concerned.

Like his men, Ralf wanted to do his part in the battle for the Ostfront and then go home, with his personal code of honour satisfied. But Berlin had other ideas. The Wehrmacht was required to conquer the Soviets by any means necessary, even if that meant forming an unholy alliance with vampyr from Rumania's Transylvania region. Ralf, Gunther and the others found themselves sharing a tank with a vampyr, and later fighting mechanised battles alongside creatures whose only motivation was bloody victory. The Panzer crew tolerated this for as long as it could, but after three months it could take no more of this hypocrisy and chose to rebel against the undead.

There had been a third Vollmer brother stationed on the Ostfront in 1941. Klaus was a Stuka pilot with the Luftwaffe. Like his siblings, Klaus became aware of the horrific alliance the generals back in Berlin had formed. All three brothers pooled what they had learned about the vampyr, assessing the weaknesses and vulnerabilities of the undead enemy.

The Vollmers planned and executed a mutiny against Constanta's Rumanian Mountain Troops, ambushing the bloodsuckers near an abandoned settlement called

Ordzhonikidze on September 27th, 1941. More than a thousand vampyr were wiped out, but Constanta escaped to wreak vengeance upon the surviving conspirators. Klaus was not one of the survivors, having sacrificed himself to save the others. In the years that followed, Hans and Ralf often wondered whether their dead brother had not chosen the wiser course of action. Perhaps it was better to die in battle for a cause you believed in, rather than to survive and be forced to fight alongside monstrous creatures of the night.

All the human survivors of the ambush at Ordzhonikidze were court-martialled. Those that escaped execution were busted down in rank and scattered along the length of the Ostfront. The mutiny cost Ralf and his men their tank. All five men were demoted from Panzer crew to Panzergrenadiers, and were forced to run alongside the vehicle in which they had once ridden so proudly. The demotion cost three of the former crew their lives. Radio operator Helmut Richter perished in the cold outside Stalingrad, while gunlayer Willy Buchheim and loader Martin Schmid were blown apart by Red Army artillery at Kursk.

Like other survivors of the mutiny, Ralf and Gunther learned not to speak of what they had seen and done with the outsiders. The penalty for a German soldier caught talking about the vampyr was death by firing squad, though the order prohibiting such talk was never made official. The presence of the undead among the Wehrmacht's allies was the Eastern Front's dirty little secret, something to be kept from the history books.

Hans spent most of 1942 trying not to freeze to death near the Arctic Circle. His penance for helping organise the mutiny was a posting to Finland, where he joined local soldiers and other German troops in besieging Leningrad from the north. Both sides had entrenched positions by the time Hans arrived, so his greatest enemy was fighting off the bitter cold. Later he heard rumours that Constanta had visited the siege and left a dozen Rumanians behind to augment the war of terror and attrition. Hans tried to convince others about the threat posed by the vampyr, but most of his comrades thought him insane.

When the blockade began to crumble early in 1943, Hans was reallocated to a scratch unit further south, which was used to plug gaps in the established companies along the Ostfront. It was such an operation that took him and two others from his unit to the outskirts of Ploesti on August 23rd, fifty kilometres north of the Rumanian capital, Bucharest.

Hans and his two comrades, Ganz and Berkel, were ordered to join a Panzergrenadier squad trying to stem the Soviet advance. They found the beleaguered soldiers a few kilometres north-east of Ploesti, waiting by the remnants of a railway line while a squad of engineers tried to restore telegraph communications with headquarters. The screams of Stalin's Organs – the Red Army's famous Katyusha rocket launchers – were all too audible in the distance. To Hans's eyes, the Panzergrenadiers looked like broken men. Their uniforms were shabby and in need of repair, while most of the soldiers were carrying at least one injury.

The perpetually hungry Ganz volunteered to see what rations were available while Berkel went in search of the unit commander. Hans moved among the men, hoping rather than expecting to see a familiar face among the dour, listless troops. It had been more than a year since he'd last had any letters from home, and even longer since he'd heard from his elder brother. For all their ideological disagreements in the past, Hans missed Ralf. But he walked right past his sibling nonetheless when they came face to face.

It was Gunther who recognised the younger Vollmer, his friendly features splitting into a broad smile. "Hans?

Hans, is that you? God in heaven, what are you doing here?"

Hans stopped and stared at Gunther's mud-smeared face, trying to recognise him. There were more lines than before and the eyes possessed a sadness Hans had never previously seen in them, but those smiling features were still unmistakable.

"Gunther? Gunther Stiefel?"

"One and the same! Scheisse, when did you grow up so fast?"

"Three years in hell will do that to you."

"Ach, tell me about it." Gunther cupped a hand by his face and shouted at a shuffling, solitary figure who was wandering on ahead. "Ralf! Ralf, come back here!"

The figure stopped and slowly turned round. Bronzed by the sun and heavily wrinkled around the eyes, Ralf looked every one of his thirty-three years and more. A scratchy, ragged beard grew across much of his face, evidence that he had long since given up caring about his appearance. Added to this was a slump in his shoulders and a despairing stance that spoke of utter weariness and resignation.

"Gunther, I need a piss and I need it now. Unless you've got something of crucial importance to the war you need to say, let me empty my bladder."

"How about a family reunion, old friend?"

Ralf strode back towards Gunther, his face a murderous scowl. "I swear, if you're…"

But his words died away as Ralf caught sight of the person standing next to Gunther. "Hans? What in God's name are you doing here?"

"I've come to help your sorry company," the younger Vollmer replied. "And from the looks of this lot, you could do with all the help you can get."

Ralf embraced his brother, the two men clapping each other joyfully on the back, both grateful to see a familiar face after so long away from home, fighting in foreign lands. Eventually they extricated themselves and stepped back to look at each other.

"You've lost weight," Ralf commented, "and some hair, too. Going bald already, eh?"

"Runs in the family," Hans retorted cheerfully, rubbing a hand across his elder brother's close-cropped scalp. "That beard doesn't suit you at all."

"Least I can grow a beard," Ralf said. "You're twenty-two and you still haven't got any stubble!"

"My birthday's not for another month. I'm still twenty-one."

"Yeah? Well, I feel closer to a hundred these days." Ralf clapped a hand on Gunther's shoulder. "Where did we put that confiscated vodka? This calls for a celebration."

"I thought you were going for a piss?"

"Ach, that can wait. It's not every day your little brother comes to visit!"

"This is more than just a visit," Hans interjected. "I'm part of a relief team sent to help fill out the gaps in your unit."

"Good. We've been more than two dozen men short for weeks, and now HQ has got us babysitting these engineers while the Bolsheviks are blowing seven kinds of hell out of the poor bastards trying to hold the front line. How many men did you bring with you? Twenty?"

Hans grimaced and shook his head.

"Ten?" Gunther asked hopefully.

"Three, including me."

"Three?" Ralf snapped, letting an angry curse fall from his lips. "Well, I suppose it's better than nothing. These men of yours, are they any good?"

"Ganz is fonder of eating than fighting, with the waistline to prove it, but he's a crack shot. Berkel's a tough little bastard. We should be glad he's on our side. Don't make any jokes about his height... He's liable to react badly."

"Sounds promising," Gunther said brightly.

"We'll see," Ralf grumbled.

Berkel appeared in the distance, his eyes lighting up when he caught sight of Hans. The short, curly-haired figure pushed his way through the Panzergrenadiers to reach him.

"Hans, I can't find the bloody commander. Seems the last one got killed and this lot hasn't had a replacement assigned to them yet. Nobody's sure who's in charge, but they suggested I should talk to a guy with the same last name as you – Vollmer."

"I'm Vollmer," Ralf volunteered.

"He's my brother," Hans explained to the baffled Berkel.

"Then this is for you," the diminutive soldier said, handing a sealed pouch to Ralf. "HQ told me to deliver it to the unit's commanding officer. It's for his eyes only."

"Typical headquarters paranoia. God forbid the soldiers fighting this way should be told what's going on." Ralf pulled a dagger from inside his right boot and used the blade's edge to slice open the pouch. From inside he removed a single sheet of instructions and a blood-stained map that had been folded over several times. Ralf skimmed the typewritten page, swearing under his breath before handing it to Gunther.

"Read it out loud. Let everyone hear what they want us to do."

Gunther glanced down the page, the colour draining from his features as he did so. After a moment, he called for the surrounding Panzergrenadiers to pay attention. "The following is a direct order from our commanders in Bucharest. We are to proceed north-west towards the mountains for five kilometres to a particular map reference, where we will rendezvous with a consignment of equipment for the Rumanian Mountain Troops. We are required to escort the convoy over the Alps into

Transylvania. Our liaison with the Rumanians will be an Obergefreiter Cringu."

The announcement brought murmurs of disquiet from several of the Panzergrenadiers. Berkel was also dismayed, having fought with Hans alongside a company of Constanta's thralls near Leningrad. He avoided being drafted into their ranks thanks to a timely intervention by Hans and Ganz, both of whom were all too well aware of the threat posed by the Rumanian lord and his underlings. Dark muttering moved quickly through Ralf's unit as word spread about the new orders and their significance. Hans took his brother and Gunther aside, speaking to them in hushed tones so as not to be heard by the others.

"Your men know about the vampyr?"

"We encountered them a few times over the years. Constanta even turned up in Stalingrad while we were there, but he was busy with another Panzergrenadier unit, trying to capture the northern factory district." Ralf retrieved the orders from Gunther and peered at them. "Hans, didn't you tell me once about meeting a collaborator called Cringu who worked for Constanta?"

"He's a servant responsible for transporting coffins around the battlefield to ensure the most senior vampyr have somewhere safe to sleep during the hours of daylight."

"This equipment he's taking to Transylvania... It's probably a truckload of bloodsuckers."

"Could Constanta himself be in one of the coffins?" Gunther asked, fear chilling his voice.

"Perhaps, or members of his inner circle of vampyr," Hans suggested. "Why choose us as guards to make sure it gets home safely? And all the way back to bloody Transylvania?"

"It can't be a coincidence we were given this mission," Ralf scowled. "Constanta seems to enjoy taunting us. He probably thinks it's funny to make us do this; payback for what we tried to do to him and his underlings at Ordzhonikidze."

Gunther nodded. "We've been keeping tabs on everyone who survived the mutiny. You, me and Ralf: we're the last ones still alive and still here on the Ost-front. The rest have been invalided back to Germany or are lining a grave somewhere in Russia."

"So what do you suggest we do?" Hans asked his brother.

"Follow our orders," Ralf replied. "If this is a trap, I plan on taking some of the vampyr with me when I die. If it isn't, travelling into Transylvania gets us that bit closer to Germany. The nearer we get to Berlin, the better our chances of going home alive and in one piece when this bloody war ends. I haven't come this far to die in some country I couldn't care less about!"

THREE HOURS LATER the Panzergrenadiers reached the map reference stipulated in Ralf's orders. Twice on the way there they'd been attacked by Soviet dive-bombers and forced to scramble for cover. The Luftwaffe was a shadow of its former glory and the skies over Rumania were all but contested territory by this point in the war. It was possible to shoot enemy planes out of the sky if they swooped close enough to the ground, but such successes were rare.

By the time Ralf's men had reached the rendezvous, the sun was already past its apogee and shadows were starting to creep across the landscape. The road from Ploesti towards the brooding mountains ahead was little more than a dirt track, winding its way up a shallow valley alongside a small river.

For the first time in days the Russian artillery was out of range and out of earshot, but some of the soldiers found the silence tougher to take, Gunther among them. Like most of the Panzergrenadiers, he had become used to having a constant barrage at the edge of his thoughts, day and night. When that background noise was removed, it made the wary soldiers all the more aware of their surroundings.

The rendezvous site was halfway along the valley, where undulating hills of green rose up on either side of the river. In some of the fields rapeseed was coming into bloom, the yellow blossom forming startling blocks of colour against the verdant slopes and azure sky overhead. Farmhouses were few and far between in this area. All the civilians had long since fled to the cities, hoping to avoid being caught up in the fighting. Most of the nearby buildings had been destroyed by passing armies, such devastation typical of the scorched earth policy employed by both sides in this brutal conflict. There were no farm animals to be seen since they had been slaughtered years earlier to feed hungry soldiers. Nor did any birds fly between the trees, a fact that made the silence all the more eerie and oppressive. Crops rotted on the hillsides, neglected and forgotten, while grassland grew ever taller, waiting for a harvest that would not come.

There was no sign of Cringu or the convoy of equipment, so Ralf posted six sentries up and down the valley, and sent out a dozen more men into the surrounding hills as patrols and lookouts. He put the rotund Ganz to good use, appointing him company cook with orders to fix a meal from whatever could be foraged or found. Berkel was given control of the radio and sent up into the hills in the hope of getting a signal back to HQ. The rest of the soldiers were told to clean their equipment or rest, whichever they thought more useful.

That left Hans and Ralf alone, at last giving them a chance to talk through all that had happened since they'd seen each other last, nearly three years before. The two brothers were still deep in conversation more than an hour later when Berkel came running into camp, calling breathlessly to them. At first his words would not come, such was his exhaustion from sprinting with the bulky radio strapped to his back. Eventually he was able to gasp out part of a news bulletin he'd heard while scanning through frequencies.

"The Rumanians..." Berkel panted. "They've surrendered!"

"They've what?" Ralf exclaimed.

"Surrendered! There's been some sort of... coup... in Bucharest... The king's had the Rumanian government... arrested... and he's called a... a ceasefire!"

"If all the Rumanians lay down their arms, the front line will collapse within a matter of days instead of weeks," Hans said. "Army Group South is no match for the Russians."

"Berkel, did you hear anything else?" Ralf demanded.

"King Michael is giving an address by radio this evening to the Rumanian people and the outside world. They didn't say what it would be about, but you can guess the rest."

Hans and Ralf said nothing for a few moments, letting the news sink in.

Eventually it was the younger Vollmer brother who broke the silence. "The ceasefire is only the first step, not the last. I wouldn't be surprised if the Rumanians switched sides and declared war on Germany before the end of the week. Once that happens, we're all living on borrowed time in this country."

"We've got more immediate troubles," Ralf pointed out. "The Rumanian forces made a limited impact on the war when they fought with us. They'll make even less difference if they join the Russians. Our problem is Constanta and his kind. If they switch sides also, and if Stalin and his generals in Moscow decide to use the vampyr against us..." Ralf stopped speaking, his eyes widening. "Scheisse! For all we know Cringu could be bringing Constanta here – now! If he's heard about the Rumanian ceasefire..."

Hans nodded hurriedly. "Berkel, how strong was that radio signal you picked up?"

"Not strong at all. It kept fading in and out. Why?"

"If we're lucky, Cringu won't have heard the news from Bucharest yet."

Ralf arched an eyebrow. "Since when have we been lucky in this cursed war?"

"We're still alive, aren't we?" Hans asked rhetorically. "If Cringu hasn't heard the news, we still have one advantage: the element of surprise." He glanced at the sun slowly sliding towards the Transylvanian mountains. "If the convoy gets here during daylight, we can destroy whatever it is Cringu is transporting."

"*If* he doesn't know about the ceasefire, and *if* he gets here before sunset... There's a lot of things that can go wrong with your plan," Ralf said.

"Do you have a better suggestion?" Hans looked at his brother and Berkel. Both men shook their heads. Before they could speak, a loud whistle cut through the air. One of the sentries in the hills was waving to them with one hand and pointing down the valley with the other.

"Two trucks!" the sentry called down. "Rumanian markings!"

"Cringu," Ralf decided. "And he's brought a friend."

"Or a fiend," Hans said.

Ralf frowned, his mind made up. "Berkel, rouse the others. We haven't got time to call the rest back from patrol, so we'll have to make do with the men we have nearby. Tell them to break out the special ammunition. They'll know what I'm talking about."

Berkel turned to Hans for confirmation, provoking Ralf's ire. "I've got seniority here, you young fool. Now do as I say!"

"You heard him!" Hans snarled. "Move it!"

Berkel scurried away, moving among the slumbering soldiers and kicking them awake. Some cursed in protest, but Ralf's two-word phrase quickly shut them up.

"Special ammunition?" Hans asked, smiling ruefully.

Ralf pulled two clips for his MP38 machine pistol from a knapsack and tossed one to his brother. Hans nodded admiringly at the silver-tipped rounds slotted into it.

"Let's just say I've been stocking up," Ralf explained, "in case of emergencies. After we were all but wiped out by the Bolsheviks at Stalingrad, I figured the Rumanians would turn on us eventually. So we've been looting silver from every city, village and farmhouse we've gone past since, getting ready for the inevitable." Ralf pulled a clip of standard rounds from his MP38 and stowed it away, shoving the silver-tipped ammunition into place instead. "Looks like the inevitable is already here."

By this time the nearby Panzergrenadiers were assembled and ready, their faces tense, fingers resting on the triggers of their weapons. Several had bayonets fixed to their rifles, a gleam of silver visible above the tip and edge. Others had slid necklaces bearing crucifixes over their heads, making sure the silver crosses stayed visible atop their clothing. Each of the men knew exactly what was at stake, and none had any illusions about the enemy they were facing.

Hans collected a fistful of special ammunition clips from his brother, using one of them to replace the regular rounds in his MP38. The two trucks were still not visible, hidden by a bend in the river valley, but the sound of their labouring engines was now audible.

Hans made sure his weapon was ready to fire before turning to Ralf. "How do you want to handle this?"

"Nobody starts shooting until I give the signal. We want to get both drivers out of their vehicles and on the ground where they'll be more vulnerable. But Constanta is no simpleton and I doubt he suffers fools among his minions either. If Cringu gets any hint of something being amiss, we're all in trouble."

Ralf looked round the faces of his men, fixing each of them in his gaze, one by one. "Stay back and follow my lead. Your chance will come, men."

The first of the trucks rumbled into view, black fumes belching from its tailpipe, a surly-faced creature at the driver's wheel. The vehicle was a battered relic with a heavy tarpaulin slung over its tray shielding the cargo from daylight. The second truck followed along behind, no different from the first. Hans squinted to see who was at the wheel of both vehicles.

"That's Cringu at the front. I remember him from the first day of Barbarossa. We almost came to blows at a bridge crossing into Reni. He caught me trying to sneak a look at his cargo."

"Better if you stay back out of sight," Ralf said from the side of his mouth. "He probably won't remember you but it's best if we don't take any chances."

Hans nodded before slowly moving to the back of the gathering. Berkel moved forward to take his place.

"You ready for this?" Ralf asked, his voice steady and casual.

"I think so," the younger man replied, his voice trembling.

"Don't be afraid of being afraid. A little fear keeps you on your toes. Just follow my lead." Ralf smiled and waved at the lead truck as it approached.

The driver brought his vehicle to a halt, leaning out the window to glare at the gathered soldiers. He was sour-faced with dark, greasy hair spilling from beneath his cap. The insignia of an Obergefreiter was prominently displayed on the collar of his uniform.

"Who's in charge here?" he sneered.

"Who wants to know?" Ralf replied, gentle mockery audible in his voice.

"I'm Obergefreiter Cringu," the driver snarled.

"My apologies," Ralf said, smiling insincerely. "Your accent's so thick, it's hard to understand your German."

"My German has not been a problem before," Cringu fumed. "Now, answer my questions you insolent dog. Who's in charge here?"

"When you didn't arrive on time, our commander went on ahead to scout the route. He should be back soon."

"We would have been here sooner but the accursed Bolshevik bombers blew apart one of the bridges from Ploesti!"

"How unfortunate. Well, as I was saying, our commander should be back soon. In the meantime he left us with orders to check all your equipment. Apparently there are Red Army commandoes operating in this area, called deep knife units, trying to smuggle themselves behind our lines." Ralf turned to his men and gestured for them to come forward. "All right, let's get this equipment unloaded and checked! The sooner we get this done, the sooner we can move on."

"No, I forbid it!" Cringu bellowed, rapidly opening his door and climbing down from the driver's seat. "You have no right to interfere with my Lord Constanta's equipment."

"Sorry, Obergefreiter, but orders are orders," Ralf shrugged. "Get to it, men!"

The other soldiers surged towards the back of the two trucks. Cringu shouted something in Rumanian to the driver of the second vehicle, who swiftly scrambled down from his cab. Cringu ran to the back of his truck, putting himself between it and the Panzergrenadiers. When Berkel reached past him to pull the tarpaulin covering aside, Cringu produced a pistol and aimed it at Berkel's head.

"Touch that and I execute you," the Rumanian warned, his voice shaking with fury. Hans pushed through the other soldiers, putting himself between Cringu and Berkel.

"There are more than a dozen of us and only two of you," Hans pointed out. "Have you got enough bullets to kill us all?"

Cringu's eyes narrowed as he studied Hans's face. "I know you... We've met..."

Before Hans could reply, a single shot was fired in the distance. All those clustered round the two trucks turned to see where it had come from. One of the sentries up on the nearby hills was pointing at the sky to the north, shouting something that couldn't be heard clearly. But the reason for his intervention was all too clear in the blue air above the mountain peaks. A trio of Russian dive-bombers was swooping across the sky, searching for targets. The three planes banked smoothly before accelerating down the valley, racing towards the trucks and all those gathered around them.

"Incoming!" Ralf bellowed. "Take cover!"

The Panzergrenadiers sprinted away from the trucks, some diving into the river while others scrambled off the dirt track and flung themselves against the hillside, hugging the slope. Cringu backed away from his vehicle but remained standing, aiming his pistol at the lead plane as it got nearer. He fired repeatedly at the aircraft, his bullets flying uselessly past the plane. A bomb dropped from beneath the Russian flyer, then the pilot peeled away, flinging his machine back up into the blue canopy. The other two planes also unleashed their cargo but no bombs tumbled towards the ground below. Instead a blizzard of white paper exploded in the air, thousands of printed pages falling slowly from the sky like a giant's confetti.

Hans watched Cringu, the only man still standing in the valley. Even the other driver had taken shelter, foolishly diving beneath the back of his truck. The Rumanian kept firing at the passing planes until the last possible moment before the missile from the first plane made its impact. Then the Obergefreiter dropped to the ground, using his hands to shield his face.

The tumbling bomb missed Cringu's truck but thundered directly into the front of the second vehicle. A massive fireball of orange flame mushroomed upwards, followed by clouds of billowing black smoke. But there was something else inside the explosion: an unearthly scream like the wailing of a thousand frustrated banshees, crying out in torment. Then came a rain of ash and hot metal as shrapnel showered the valley and surrounding hills. A shard of metal the size of a man's chest stabbed into the ground beside Hans's head, less than a metre away from decapitating it.

Once the howling and flames and falling metal had died down, Ralf and the others slowly got back to their feet, stumbling towards where the bomb had exploded. More Panzergrenadiers came running down from the hills, eager to see what had happened. The Russian planes disappeared over the horizon, gone to find fresh targets. As the soldiers approached the remains of the second truck, the blizzard of paper started settling over the river valley. Gunther was first to realise that the pages were a Soviet propaganda drop. One side of the page was blank, but the reverse had a message written on it in three languages: Russian, German and Rumanian.

Gunther read out loud the message dropped on them by the enemy aircraft. "Comrade Rumanians! Your King and Country will soon be fighting with Russia! We welcome you to the winning side in this Great Patriotic War!"

"I don't believe you!" Cringu said, snatching the leaflet. "Let me see that..." He read the message, his lips moving as his beady, porcine eyes moved across the words. "If this is true, I must tell my master. Lord Constanta must be made aware that–"

"I beg to differ," Ralf whispered, pressing his pistol beneath Cringu's chin. "You see, once you and the other Rumanians join forces with the Bolsheviks, we'll become prey for your vampyr masters."

Cringu was about to call out but Ralf silenced him by shoving the end of the pistol into the Obergefreiter's mouth. "Not a word or else I'll blow your brains out the back of your skull. Understand?"

Cringu nodded grudgingly.

"That's better. Now, where's Constanta? Is he inside your truck?"

The Rumanian shook his head.

"Was he in the second truck, the one the Russians bombed?"

Again, Cringu shook his head.

"Where is he, then?" Ralf withdrew his pistol far enough for the prisoner to speak, but kept it aimed at Cringu's head.

"Sighisoara," the Rumanian said. "He's at his ancestral castle in Sighisoara."

"Why's he gone there?" Hans asked, moving to stand beside his brother.

"There were rumours King Michael has been negotiating an armistice. This war could be over before Christmas if the Wehrmacht continues to retreat so quickly. Lord Constanta went back to Transylvania to prepare for the next war."

"The next war?" Gunther asked from nearby.

"The war of blood," Cringu replied, a cruel smile spreading across his repellent face. "The war that will decide the fate of us all. The war that has been coming for a thousand years."

"Humans versus vampyr," Ralf said quietly.

"The final conflict," Hans added.

"The time of revelations is almost upon us," the Rumanian continued. "The vampyr shall rise up to claim their rightful place as rulers of this continent, and then all the continents. They shall achieve their destiny, becoming the true master race, establishing a new world order."

"And where will you be in the midst of all this glorious triumph?" Gunther asked. "I notice his lordship hasn't seen fit to grant you equal status."

"What happens to mankind when the vampyr take charge?" Hans added.

"The chosen ones will be awarded places of honour in the new world order, given dominion over the human cattle, allowed to pick and choose those they wish to live and those they condemn to death." Cringu looked at the Panzergrenadiers gathered around him. "You shall be culled, your blood taken as sustenance for my masters, and your carcasses burned. It is no more than you deserve. We have tolerated your presence on our soil long enough!"

"Trust me, we can't wait to leave this godforsaken country," Ralf replied.

Cringu laughed at him. "I shall reserve a special kind of hell for you."

"The Führer beat you to it. I've already been to Stalingrad," Ralf said, and pulled the trigger. A third eye appeared in Cringu's forehead. His other eyes tried to look up at it before glazing over. The third eye appeared to blink once before a trickle of blood ran down the Rumanian's face. He collapsed to the ground, the rear of his head sporting a gaping hole. The body twitched and spasmed for a few moments, and then a wet stain appeared around the crotch as his muscles relaxed and his bowels voided themselves. Then Cringu was still, his insidious life at an end.

Ralf shoved his pistol back into its holster. "What happened to the other driver?"

Berkel pointed at the singed remains of a corpse protruding from beneath the still burning remains of the other truck. "The Russians took care of him for us, and whatever was in his cargo."

"Then I think it's time we got a good look at what Obergefreiter Cringu was taking to his undead master in Sighisoara, don't you?" Ralf peered past the remaining shower of paper still fluttering down from the sky. The sun was getting ever closer to the mountains, but twilight was not yet upon them. "Yes, while we still have time to deal with whatever's in there."

RALF SENT OUT runners to call back the remaining Panzergrenadiers from sentry duty. He told those present to form into groups surrounding Cringu's truck, ensuring they were back far enough to be safe from immediate attack but close enough to fire on anything or anyone that might emerge from the cargo.

Ralf himself went to the back of the vehicle and peered inside, counting half a dozen crates. Three of the long, rectangular boxes looked more like coffins than military equipment, while the others were stamped with Rumanian phrases. Finally, Ralf asked for three volunteers to help him open the crates and deal with whatever was inside. Hans was first to step forward, closely followed by Gunther. Ganz found himself propelled from among the others, the point of Berkel's bayonet jabbing the portly Panzergrenadier between the buttocks.

"That's very noble of you, volunteering for such a potentially hazardous task," Hans said.

"I didn't," Ganz protested. "It was Berkel!"

"Then both of you can help," Ralf decided. "Hans, I want you to stay back with the others. If this goes wrong, you're to take charge of them."

"But I want to–"

"That's an order, Vollmer!"

Fuming, Hans saluted his brother and marched away to join the others keeping watch from a distance. Meanwhile Ralf, Gunther, Berkel and Ganz carefully removed the large tarpaulin covering the rear of Cringu's truck. The four men slowly lifted each of the coffin-like crates outside and leaned them against the side of the vehicle, so they faced the setting sun. Once all three boxes were in position, Ralf used a bayonet blade to break open the heavy metal padlocks keeping each container sealed.

Finally, he had Gunther, Berkel and Ganz stand opposite the crates, each man armed with special ammunition and ready to fire.

Standing to one side of the first coffin, Ralf ripped open the lid and let the fading sunlight flood the interior of the box. Inside was a figure dressed in the garb of the Rumanian Mountain Troops, the familiar bat and swastika emblem visible on its peaked cap and tunic. The creature was human in shape but the hands and face were like nothing any of the Germans had seen before.

There were claw-like talons where fingers and nails should have been, and the skin was black and leathery with thin white hairs protruding from it. The face was closer to a jackal than any human, with elongated features and yellow slits for eyes. As the sunlight entered the coffin, the creature awoke and screamed an unearthly cry of anger and torment. The monster tried to emerge from its confinement but the black flesh was burning and boiling from its bones, hissing and spitting like so much hot fat on a griddle. The thing began to howl and thrash, its vile body going into spasms, still screaming, still raging at its own death. Most of the soldiers turned away, unable to bear looking at this grotesque spectacle as it perished.

"Finish it off!" Ralf snarled.

Gunther opened fire, emptying his magazine into the monster. When the last silver-tipped bullet penetrated its torso, the vampyr exploded, showering his executioner with green bile and seared black skin. Gunther stumbled backwards, retching and vomiting, trying to get the horrific stench from his nostrils and lungs.

By now the creatures inside the other two coffins had sensed what was happening but both were powerless to escape their fate. Ralf ripped open the second crate to reveal another monster cowering inside, uselessly trying to shield itself from the sunlight.

"Shoot it," Ralf ordered Berkel and Ganz. They both fired repeatedly at the vampyr until it exploded.

The procedure was quickly repeated for the occupant of the third and final coffin. Only when the trinity of vampyr was destroyed did Ralf stagger away to one side, the contents of his stomach violently vacating his body to coat the crushed grass. Hans emerged from among the gathered crowd of soldiers to see how his brother was doing.

"I'll be okay in a minute," Ralf gasped. A thin stream of green bile hung down from his lips and chin.

"The sun's nearly down," Hans said. "Ganz and I will open the other crates and make sure there are no nasty surprises waiting inside for us."

"Be careful," Ralf muttered. "If those things were vampyr in their true form, I hate to think what they were taking back to Transylvania with them."

Hans and Ganz clambered up into the back of Cringu's truck, both of them armed with bayonets for opening the crates. Hans prised off the lid of the first box, peering inside cautiously before revealing the contents to Ganz. Within were dozens of glass bottles, all of them carefully sealed with corks and crimson wax. Each was filled with a heavy, dark liquid that resembled thickened red wine.

"It's blood," Hans realised. "Litres and litres of it. They must have drained this from their victims and brought it with them in case they needed to feed during the journey."

Ganz tapped a foot against the second crate and was rewarded with the sound of glass bottles clinking together. "This one's the same."

Sure enough, when the lid was removed they could see that there was enough bottled blood to fill a bath. Hans removed one of the containers and threw it to Ralf who was slowly recovering from his close encounter with the vampyr.

"What do you make of that?" Hans asked his brother.

Ralf broke open the bottle and sniffed at the contents. "It's blood all right, but mixed with something else... almost a sweet smell. Maybe they use an additive to stop it from spoiling."

In the distance the last rays of light gave way as the sun dipped behind the mountains. Clouds on the horizon were becoming shades of pink and orange, while twilight was already creeping across from the other side of the sky. Ralf gave orders for the others to gather wood and start fires. With Cringu and his charges eliminated, it was safe to spend the night at this location.

Ganz didn't bother tapping the final crate on the truck and simply shoved his bayonet beneath the lid and ripped it open. "Guess we should be grateful they brought their own supplies to drink, otherwise they'd have started on us tonight."

He lifted the lid away from the crate and cried out in surprise. A small girl clad in a white nightdress was cowering inside, her body trembling with terror.

"What the hell is she doing in there?" Ganz said.

"God in heaven! She must have been their evening meal. Vampyr prefer to take sustenance from living humans," Hans replied in complete horror.

When he saw what his brother and Ganz had found in the final crate, Ralf tossed the bottle of blood he was holding to Berkel. "Hans, get away from that child. You too, Ganz."

"Why?" Hans asked, perplexed by his brother's stern tone of voice.

"Get down from the truck. Now."

Hans did as Ralf commanded. "Come on, Ganz. You heard what he said."

"But she's a little girl, nothing more," the rotund soldier protested. "Look at her! Poor thing's scared out of her wits."

Ralf drew his pistol and aimed it at Ganz. "I said get out of the truck. Do it."

Ganz waved Ralf away, crouching on one knee beside the crate to talk to the child. "You've got our big, bad commander worried! What do you think has got him so scared, eh?"

The little girl smiled at him, her eyes gleaming. "Come closer and I'll tell you."

"Why? Is it a secret?" Ganz replied.

She nodded, beckoning him nearer. "I'll whisper it in your ear."

"Ganz, you fool. Don't get any closer to her," Ralf snarled.

"Come on, commander," Ganz said, glancing over at Ralf. "You can't be frightened of a child, can you?"

He didn't notice the little girl's lips drawing back into a grin, gradually revealing the elongated fangs protruding downwards from her upper jaw. Ganz turned back to hear her secret. He was still smiling expectantly as the child bit deep into his neck, blood spurting from the twin puncture wounds. By the time Ganz fought his way free of the girl's deadly embrace, she had drained half the blood in his body. The soldier crawled away from her, one hand clasping weakly at the holes in the neck, trying to staunch the bleeding. But crimson skirted from between his fat fingers as his terrified heart pumped the blood out of Ganz's body.

The child rose up from her crate, her pure white nightdress now stained scarlet. Ralf put three silver-tipped bullets into the little girl's chest and she exploded into a cloud of ash and dust which slowly settled back into the crate where she'd been kept.

Ralf looked sadly at Ganz. The sobbing soldier was sprawled in the back of the truck.

"I told you to keep away from her," Ralf muttered, shaking his head.

He shot Ganz twice through the head and once through the heart.

"You didn't have to do that!" Berkel protested from nearby.

"Yes, he did," Gunther said. "You know what happens to the victims of vampyr. Sooner or later, Ganz would have become one of them. Better to put him out of his misery now."

Hans approached his brother, still startled by what had happened. "How'd you know?"

"Her crate didn't have any air holes in it. A normal child would have suffocated long ago if they'd been locked in there, but vampyr don't need to breathe. Not like us."

Ralf shoved his pistol back into its holster. "Let's get the camp established for the night. In the morning we'll go through Cringu's documents, see if they can tell us what he wouldn't. If the Rumanians do decide to switch sides, we'll need every advantage we can get against those bloodsucking bastards."

# Three

THREE DAYS AFTER King Michael told the world his country had surrendered to the Allied forces, the announcement we'd all feared came to pass. On the 26th of August, Rumania formally declared war on Germany and the other Axis forces. In other circumstances, Eisenstein and I would have been cheered by the news. While the addition of the battered Rumanian Army would not significantly augment our efforts to defeat Hitler's forces, every new ally was welcome to join our side. But we knew the true consequences of the Rumanians switching sides. Somewhere in Moscow the Red Army's commanders had decided to make a deal with the devil, as German generals in Berlin had done three years before. Now Constanta and his vampyr would be fighting alongside us against the Axis forces. Our most bitter enemy had now become our ally, but how could we ever trust a cadre of undead fiends?

A second announcement was made on the same day, one much less widely circulated. As a consequence of the Rumanians joining our side, the Red Army was

disbanding its smert krofpeet units with immediate
effect. Those who had fought against the vampyr
menace were given a choice. Most of them had come
from a shtrafroty, so they could return to the certain
death of a penal company for the rest of the war.

Alternatively, each man and woman was offered the
opportunity to serve a new master: the Red Army's
counter-intelligence division smert shpionam, better
known as SMERSH. The vampyr-hunter units were being
formed into new squads called gloobokee-nosh – deep
knife. These would be responsible for acts of insurgency
behind enemy lines, and preparing the way for the
rapidly advancing Red Army. In the past the smert krofpeet had been a law unto themselves, and were able to
move along the front line as each unit saw fit. But the
deep knife squads were to be operated under SMERSH's
control, with a new command structure.

Eisenstein and I did not need long to make our choice.
We had both come to the smert krofpeet from a penal
company and neither of us had any wish to go back to
the shtrafroty. If life as a vampyr-hunter was precarious,
it was even more perilous within the penal companies.
Such units were given the worst jobs, almost always suicide missions and armed only with whatever weapons
the members could scavenge from the battlefield.

Officers saw the shtrafroty as utterly expendable, often
carelessly using them as cannon fodder to test the
enemy's strength. Neither Eisenstein nor I knew what
life in a deep knife unit would be like, but we reasoned
that it couldn't be any worse than that of the shtrafroty.
Joining SMERSH was a chilling prospect. It had existed
for only a year by then, but the organisation's utter ruth-
lessness terrified even the NKVD. Despite this,
Eisenstein and I rated our chances of survival better with
a deep knife unit than as part of a lowly shtrafroty. So
the pair of us volunteered for the nearest gloobokee-
nosh, willingly handing in our smert krofpeet insignia.

We were less happy to surrender our anti-vampyr weapons, but it was a condition of acceptance to the deep knife.

Once we had been given our new insignia – a blade stained with blood – Eisenstein and I were sent to join the nearest gloobokee-nosh unit near Ploesti. Three other members were waiting for us when we arrived at the appointed rendezvous shortly before dusk: two near identical Mongolians and Mariya Charnosova. She had been ushered away for medical treatment and debriefing after our failed attempt to kill Gorgo five days before. I had been unable to make contact with her since Rumania's sudden surrender had thrown Red Army communications into chaos. Mariya's face lit up when she saw us approaching.

"I never thought I'd be grateful to meet you two again!" she exclaimed. "Are you both deep knife?"

"Yes," Eisenstein replied dryly. "Thanks for the welcome."

"Sorry, I didn't mean..." She almost blushed with embarrassment, something I found quite beguiling. "I just meant I didn't want what happened in that farmhouse... Well, you know." She fell silent, so I changed the subject to spare her further shame.

"Who are these two?" I asked, tilting my head towards the two Mongolians.

"I think they're brothers," Mariya ventured. "I can't speak Mongolian and their Russian is mostly made up of obscenities. From what I can make out, they're both called Borjigin. That could be their family name, or else they have the same first name."

"Mongolian communists outlawed first names in the Twenties," Eisenstein said. "As a protest many people switched their surname to Borjigin; Genghis Khan's tribal name."

"You speak Mongolian?" I asked, surprised by this revelation.

"Only enough to start a fight," he replied. "We had a Mongolian in the shtrafroty at Leningrad before you arrived. Don't ask how he ended up there. Didn't last long."

Eisenstein approached the two brothers who were crouched near a fire on the ground, each of them sharpening a wickedly sharp curved sword with a whetstone. He muttered something at the pair in their own tongue and they looked up in surprise. The pair began talking swiftly, words tumbling out of them like water from a newly broken dam. Eisenstein held up his hands, pleading for them to slow down. The brothers smiled and invited him to sit by the fire. Both had the narrow eyes, olive complexion, and thick black hair characteristic of their people.

Eisenstein produced a small flask of vodka and offered it to the Borjigins. One of them sniffed its contents suspiciously before tipping a single drop on to his tongue. He swallowed and smiled, pleased by the fiery liquid's effect. His brother snatched the flask away and helped himself to a mouthful. Soon the trio were jabbering at each other in a mixture of Russian and Mongolian, sign language filling in the gaps where mutually known swearwords failed to suffice.

"Looks like Grigori's made two new friends," I commented.

"Good," Mariya said. "The way those two were staring at me earlier, I didn't like to think what they had planned. The only word I did recognise sounded suspiciously like whore."

"Don't worry. I won't let them touch you."

She glared at me. "I don't need your protection."

Now it was my turn to be embarrassed. "I'm sorry. I didn't mean–"

"I survived more than an hour at the hands of that godless monster Gorgo," Mariya continued, not letting me finish my apology. "I'm sure I can handle two lust-addled Mongolians."

"Look, I wasn't try to suggest–"

"I simply meant it would be a shame if I had to kill them. Most Mongolians I've met are brave, resilient fighters. I'd rather have them on my side than in the ground."

"Right," I agreed. "Of course."

Mariya looked at me and smiled. "You'll have to forgive my tendency to rant and rave, but it isn't easy to be a woman in this war. Most men expect us to do no more than tend their wounds or mind the radio. I used to think the same until I saw for myself what happened in Stalingrad."

"You were a sniper?"

"I worked in signals, translating enemy transmissions until I was asked by the NKVD to help interrogate a prisoner of war after the Germans surrendered. It was because of him I first learned about Hitler's unholy alliance with the vampyr. I discovered my brother Josef had been fighting with a smert krofpeet unit. He was murdered by Constanta, so I vowed to avenge his death. I got myself attached to a team of vampyr-hunters as a translator. Gradually, I learned how to fight and how to kill. One by one the others in the unit got killed and were replaced by new recruits. Eventually I was the most senior member of our smert krofpeet so I became its leader."

"They were the slaughtered men inside that farmhouse," I realised.

"Good fighters, all of them. Gorgo and his minions tortured and killed them, one at a time, trying to break our spirits... But none of them talked. We didn't know anything but Gorgo didn't care. It was almost as if he was testing us, assessing our strengths and weaknesses..."

I nodded. "I've seen that before. The vampyr treat this war like a rehearsal; a fact-finding mission for them to learn about us and the Germans."

"Exactly." Mariya smiled, and it lit up her face despite its mottling of purple and yellow bruises, the lingering marks from Gorgo's mistreatment. "You know something more about them, don't you? About their reasons for fighting in this war?"

In my head I still wasn't certain I could believe in her, but my heart told me Mariya was worth trusting. So I told her about my experiences with Eisenstein in fighting the vampyr at Leningrad, and all we had learned about these nocturnal fiends since then.

"Constanta himself once told us the vampyr would always fight with the winning side in this war. When the battle for Europe is over, the Rumanians intend to launch a new conflict: for the future of mankind. In exchange for their help, Hitler promised the vampyr their own sovereign state, an undead nation. Now the tide has turned against the Germans, the Rumanians are swapping sides. I wouldn't be surprised if Stalin has cut a similar deal with them, thinking he can control these monsters by force. But Constanta's ambitions stretch far further than having a country his kind can call their own. He wants vampyr to have dominion over the continent, maybe the whole world eventually. Victory over the Germans will only be the beginning of the fighting, not the end."

After such a statement, most people would have considered me unbalanced or deluded. But Mariya's eyes showed only sadness and recognition. "Are you sure of all this?"

I shrugged. "As sure as anyone can be of anything in this war. Constanta gloated to us of his ambitions outside Leningrad. I doubt they've lessened in the months and years since then."

"Quite right," a harsh, guttural voice interjected from the shadows. I spun round to see Sergeant Gorgo emerging from the darkness, flanked by two more soldiers bearing the insignia of the Rumanian Mountain Troops. Too late, I realised night had fallen in the time Mariya and I had been talking. Instinctively I grasped for my crossbow that normally stayed slung across my back before remembering that I had given up my anti-vampyr weapons to join the deep knife unit.

Eisenstein and the two Mongolians were on their feet in an instant, hands clasping whatever weapons they had, ready to fight, to kill, to die if necessary. But Gorgo's response caught us all off guard. He began to laugh.

"My, my," he chuckled. "That's quite a welcome for anyone to face, but especially since I'm your new commander." Mariya gasped beside me. Gorgo noticed her presence and smiled. "That's right, Charnosova, you heard me right. All of you have been handpicked for inclusion in my deep knife squad. Each of you has personally tried and failed to kill me in the past, and proven yourselves to be determined, implacable and deadly opponents. Now that we're all fighting on the same side, my Lord Constanta thought it would be a delicious irony to harness your strengths and direct them towards defeating the accursed Germans." The Rumanian glared at us, one eyebrow raised imperiously. "Well, what do you have to say?"

The Mongolians spat a series of curses at Gorgo. Their words were beyond my understanding, but the meaning was plain: they meant to kill the sergeant as soon as possible.

He laughed and nodded. "What about you three? Do you feel the same?"

"Can you doubt it?' Mariya sneered.

"No," Gorgo agreed, "but I had to ask." He snapped his fingers and a dozen more vampyr emerged from the darkness to encircle the five of us. "You have a choice: either you can die here and now, knowing you have failed to stop my kind; or you can swallow your pride and agree to follow my command. In exchange for taking the latter option, you get to live and you get to help us destroy the Germans. Who knows? One day I might let my guard slip and you'll even get the chance to destroy me. Of course, I will always have my two bodyguards at my side, so that chance might never come, but it is, at least, a possibility."

He repeated the offer to the Borjigins in their native tongue, locking eyes with the two brothers. All trace of humour vanished from the vampyr's glowering, malevolent face. "Well, what is your decision?"

It was Mariya who spoke first, stepping closer to Gorgo. "I'll follow your orders – for now. But before I die, I'll see your kind driven from the face of the earth," she vowed.

"Promises, promises," Gorgo replied lightly. "And the rest of you?"

The Mongolians responded next, moving to stand beside Mariya. I looked at Eisenstein, but he betrayed no hint of his thoughts, one hand stroking the pustulant bandage round his neck.

"My patience is remarkably limited," Gorgo warned. "Make your decision or die where you stand." Eventually I moved to join Mariya and the others, leaving Eisenstein on his own. Gorgo gave a grim smile of satisfaction. "My Lord Constanta predicted as much. He said your pride would get the better of you, Jew."

Shaking his head in disgust, Eisenstein took a step towards the rest of us. "Very well, I will accept your command. But you shall not see the end of this war, fiend."

Gorgo laughed. "Such bravado! Such thwarted hatred! It will be a pleasure to make you five do my bidding." He snapped his fingers again and the other vampyr melted away into the blackness around us, all except the sergeant's two bodyguards. They remained at his side, a dark shadow of murderous menace.

"Now, gather your belongings and any food you wish to bring with you. From this point we shall march and fight during the night and sleep during the day. Before dawn we must have reached the foot of the

Transylvanian mountains. Anyone who falls back on the march will be slaughtered and used as fodder for my bodyguards. Unless the Jew wishes to partake of our crimson sustenance?"

Eisenstein shook his head, disgust evident on his features. He produced a drinking flask, the lid tightly fastened and bound with strips of thin rubber to prevent leakage or evaporation. "I brought my own to drink," he replied.

Mariya stared at him in horror, while the Mongolians looked mystified by this exchange. Gorgo translated for them, pointing at Eisenstein. The two men glared at my comrade with a new distrust, their previous friendliness wiped away.

Within a few minutes we were marching into the darkness towards the black silhouettes of the mountains just visible against the bleak night sky. Gorgo strode confidently forward at the front, accompanied by one of his bodyguards, while the Mongolians followed along behind, whispering to each other and taking the occasional furtive glance over their shoulders at Eisenstein. He walked along in the middle, his shoulders slumped beneath the curse he had carried since being bitten by Constanta.

Mariya and I were behind him, and Gorgo's second bodyguard brought up the rear. I felt for Eisenstein, wishing there was some way I could ease his burden, my yearning made worse by the knowledge there was nothing I could do.

After we'd been marching more than an hour, Mariya edged closer to me and whispered out the side of her mouth. "Was what Gorgo said true? Is Eisenstein like... them?"

"Yes and no," I replied. "Didn't you hear him talking with Gorgo in the farmhouse?"

"I kept fading in and out of consciousness. I couldn't tell what was real and what wasn't by the time you two burst in," she admitted. "Gorgo had broken me, but he never got the chance to find that out thanks to you and Eisenstein."

I explained about my comrade's unique condition, and how he had fought back the vampyr taint. "He still eats, fights and thinks like you and me, but sometimes, when he can hold back the urge no longer, he has to drink human blood. To keep those around him safe, Grigori carries around that small flask of it. He gets fresh supplies from field hospitals when he can. Sometimes, if he's close to succumbing, I'll let him drain a little from me to keep him going."

I rolled back the sleeve of my tunic to reveal a succession of scars up my arm from the occasions when I'd sliced open my skin. "Every time Grigori sucks blood from a living person, it pushes him another step closer to becoming one of them. He's been on the cusp of losing his humanity for months."

"Now we're marching towards Transylvania," Mariya muttered, "the heartland of the vampyr. What affect will that have on him?"

I looked at my friend ahead of us, his feet dragging along the ground as he battled against his unholy urges that I could never understand. What torments must he be suffering? Would they be made worse by this journey into the heart of darkness? I shook my head.

"I don't know," I told Mariya. "I honestly don't know."

# Four

It took Ralf, Hans and the other Panzergrenadiers three days to traverse the narrow pass over the Transylvanian Alps and down into the vampyr homeland below. Thankfully, Cringu's papers had included a comprehensive map showing a safe route between the towering peaks. Cringu had been under orders to deliver his cargo to Castle Constanta on the outskirts of Sighisoara, before proceeding to a nearby prisoner of war camp for a rendezvous with the leader of the vampyr shortly before midnight on August 27th. The directive also identified the Panzergrenadiers as an expendable escort, ready for sacrifice should circumstances demand it. Ralf made sure all of the others saw Cringu's orders so none of them would have any lingering doubts about Constanta. Kill or be killed, it was the nature of any war. But that was doubly true of this bloody conflict.

The journey through the mountains would have been quicker but Ralf was reluctant to leave anyone behind. Cringu's truck could only carry a dozen men, so the others ran alongside the vehicle as it clambered up the treacherous alpine track with Gunther at the wheel. All the soldiers were grateful that they were making the trip in late August, when summer had melted the snow from even the highest peaks. Such an ascent would have been unthinkable during winter. Even so, it took the Panzer-grenadiers until the 26th of August to reach the top of the pass.

When they reached the highest point, Ralf had Gunther stop the truck. All those inside spilled out, joining their comrades for the chance to look down on Transylvania. The countryside was a rolling patchwork of greens and yellows undulating away into the distance, stretching as far as the eye could see. It looked peaceful, even benign.

"Hard to believe this is Constanta's homeland," Hans muttered to his brother.

"Remember the serpent in the Garden of Eden... Every paradise has its monsters."

Berkel had been appointed navigator. He smoothed out Cringu's map on the ground, using lumps of rock to weigh down each corner against the chill breezes that rose up from the valley below. Gunther took charge of the men while Ralf and Hans studied the map with Berkel.

"What are our chances of reaching Sighisoara by midnight tomorrow?" Ralf asked.

"Minimal," Berkel calculated. "It's taken us three days to get here from north of Ploesti. We've got at least twice that distance to travel before we're close to Cringu's rendezvous."

"We were travelling uphill all the way to get here," Hans pointed out. "Going downhill should be faster, much faster. If we left most of the men behind and went ahead in the truck with a handful of our best troops..."

Ralf shook his head. "We still wouldn't make it in time. Even if we did, we'd be exhausted and under-strength for any sort of confrontation. We're marching into the heartland of the vampyr. I've no intention of leaving men behind in this terrain, and little stomach for facing Constanta and his kind without sufficient support. We continue as we have been. If his lordship is still waiting for us at Sighisoara when we get there, so be it."

"Some of the men might think you're afraid of Constanta," Berkel ventured.

"Some of the men would be right," Ralf replied. "Only a fool would not feel any fear when faced with such a foe. Constanta and his kind have lived in the shadow of mankind for centuries. They have chosen to emerge now because they can profit from the madness of this war. I don't intend to add myself to all their other victims… Not willingly, at least."

"Then why go to Sighisoara at all?" Berkel asked, a hint of desperation in his words.

"We know the truth about the vampyr," Hans said. "If they are switching sides to fight with the Bolsheviks against us, we have an opportunity to strike against Constanta and his kind before they join the Red Army. This could be our last chance. Once the vampyr have been integrated into the Soviet forces, we will not have such an opportunity again."

"Hans is right," his brother agreed. "Do or die, it's as simple as that." Ralf stood up, holding a hand above his eyes to shield them from the sun's glare overhead. "Once we move down into Transylvania, we are in vampyr territory, so we'll travel only by day. At night half the men will sleep while the others stand guard. Tell everyone to dump their conventional ammunition. I doubt we'll have much use for it here, and losing the extra weight will help us move faster. We leave in twenty minutes. Spread the word."

THE PANZERGRENADIERS MADE remarkably good time coming down the Alps, moving faster than Berkel had anticipated, and they reached the outskirts of Sighisoara

by midday on the 28th August. By then they knew that
the Rumanian armed forces had switched sides to join
the Russians, but that meant little in Transylvania. The
region had been largely ignored for the past three years,
having long since been held by the armies of the Axis,
and any able-bodied men had long since been sent away
to fight on the Ostfront.

The mountains to the east and south would slow any
Soviet thrust into the region. Transylvania remained
German-held territory, but it was a matter of time before
the local population of women, children and elderly men
grew hostile to their occupiers. For the moment, the
Panzergrenadiers were still able to move unhindered
across the countryside.

Ralf chose not to take his men into Sighisoara. Judging
by the maps found in Cringu's truck, the settlement was
built around a medieval citadel and contained a thousand dark corners where the Panzergrenadiers could be
ambushed and slaughtered. Any local resistance movement was likely to be at its strongest in such places,
where people could gather and resentment could fester.
Better to stay out of such towns and cities and keep to
the gently rolling countryside where the soldiers could
see anyone approaching long before an attack could be
made.

Instead the Panzergrenadiers made for Castle Constanta, a towering stone structure close to the outskirts
of Sighisoara. The baronial home stood on the brow of a
hill, offering magnificent views of the black, brooding
Transylvanian mountains.

According to Cringu's map, this imposing castle had
been a private school before the war. Ralf and Hans
knew it had been a rehabilitation centre for injured
German soldiers during the early months of Operation
Barbarossa because their brother Klaus had been sent
there three years earlier. The injured pilot had been visited by Constanta while a patient at the centre and heard

of a nearby prisoner of war camp where thousands of Russian soldiers were sent every week. After recovering from his wounds, Klaus had visited the POW facility and was horrified by the atrocities he had witnessed there. He wrote to Ralf and Hans about the things he discovered, although his letters had kept the details vague enough to escape the attention of censors within the Wehrmacht. It was only when the surviving Vollmers saw the outside of Castle Constanta that they realised Cringu's rendezvous was the same POW camp their brother had visited in 1941.

The Panzergrenadiers watched the castle from a safe distance for several hours before venturing closer to the daunting stone walls. There was no sign of movement from within or without the building: no plumes of smoke rising from the numerous chimneys, no vehicles coming or going, no sentries posted atop the crenellated walls or patrols guarding the perimeter, no banners or military standards hung from the flagpoles. Most curious of all, not a single bird flew within a mile of the building, nor did any wild animals approach it. Nothing grew from the ground around the castle. As far as anyone could see, the castle was utterly deserted and the land on which it stood was dead and uninhabitable.

Leaving Hans in command of the others, Ralf and Gunther drove towards the castle in their stolen Rumanian truck. Cringu's vehicle might afford them some protection from any hostiles hidden within the stone walls. If the castle was some gigantic trap waiting to be sprung, it would only capture the two of them. The others would still have time to retreat and get the hell away from this forbidding, foreboding landscape.

But as the truck rumbled ever closer to the castle, no attack came from inside the structure and there was no sign anybody was waiting for them from within. Gunther drove in through the gaping entrance, past the tall wooden gates that stood politely open, and came to a halt in the castle's gravel-covered courtyard. Slowly, cautiously, the two men climbed out of the vehicle, their weapons ready to fire.

An eerie whistling of the wind around the battlements and the banging of a wooden shutter against the castle wall could be heard. Blank windows stared down at the two intruders, offering no hint of what lay behind them. A doorway from the courtyard into the building hung open, inviting them to enter. Ralf and Gunther accepted, moving swiftly inside. They cautiously advanced through the ground floor, checking each room and corridor, each nook and cranny, each shadow and stairwell for signs of life or the undead. Inside it was cold and draughty, with high ceilings and plaster crumbling from the walls. A lingering scent of disinfectant hung in the air, no doubt a legacy from the time when this place had been a rehabilitation centre, but the Wehrmacht had long since moved such a facility nearer the Ostfront.

Ralf and Gunther crept up a staircase to the next floor. It proved as vacant as the one below, as did the one above. Finally, after more than an hour of moving through the deserted castle, both men were satisfied that there was nothing and no one to be discovered here.

"This may have been Constanta's ancestral home," Ralf muttered, "but I doubt he's been inside these walls for months, perhaps years."

He and Gunther were moving back down through the castle, making one last sweep before signalling for the others to join them.

"I've seen more life in a cemetery," Gunther agreed, cheerful as ever.

"Don't make jokes like that. Especially not in here," his comrade admonished.

"Sorry," Gunther said, looking abashed. "Should I call the rest to come in?"

"I guess so." Ralf let himself relax at last, easing a finger off the trigger of his MP38.

Gunther wandered outside and fired off three quick bursts, the signal that all was well. Ralf extracted a pipe from the bottom of his knapsack and began wadding tobacco into the small wooden bowl. He had been delighted to find a pouch of fresh tobacco among Cringu's possessions, and it was good quality as well, not the ersatz rubbish given to German soldiers. Constanta obviously made sure his thralls got the best as reward for serving him well. Exchanging your soul for a good smoke and better rations didn't sound like much of a bargain to Ralf, but he knew such choices were never consciously made. You gave yourself with a thousand tiny compromises, not one simple decision.

Ralf patted his pockets for matches before leaning back against a heraldic crest on the wall to light his pipe. He was more than a little surprised when the crest slid aside and he almost tumbled backwards down a flight of stone steps that had been concealed behind it. Ralf teetered on the brink of the staircase but regained his balance just in time. He moved away from the rectangular space where the heraldic crest had been mounted on an oak panel, hands trembling as they clutched at the stock and trigger of his machine pistol.

A mixture of stomach-turning odours escaped from the stairwell: the musky iron of spilled blood, the sickly ripeness of decomposing flesh, and something else, something Ralf couldn't immediately identify. Light danced at the bottom of the stone steps, casting strange shadows on the curved walls. Was something moving down there? Something alive?

"They're coming in now," Gunther announced from beside Ralf, startling him.

Ralf spun round, ready to fire, hissing curses at his comrade. This startled Gunther in turn, who jumped backwards in surprise, grappling at his own weapon.

"God in heaven, Ralf! What's the matter with you?" Gunther demanded once the two of them had recognised each other and relaxed.

"I might ask you the same question, fool," Ralf snarled through gritted teeth. "Are you tying to get yourself killed, sneaking up on me like that? I almost executed you."

"I'm sorry, I didn't realise that..." Gunther's voice trailed off as he noticed the open panel. "Where did that come from?"

"That's what I was about to find out!"

"Ahh. Sorry."

Ralf smiled. Despite his best efforts, he could never stay mad at Gunther for long. They had been through too much together and had seen too many horrors to take each other for granted.

"How long until the others get here?"

"It'll take them five minutes to reach the outside walls," Gunther calculated.

"Good. That's long enough for us to take a look in the dungeon." Ralf edged closer to the open panel, his weapon at the ready. "Coming?"

The two Germans crept slowly down the winding stone staircase, moving almost soundlessly, their senses straining to detect any threat ahead of them. The dancing light came from a burning torch hung on the wall. Gunther took the torch from its bracket to help illuminate their downward path, but Ralf remained in front of his friend. After descending for more than a minute, they reached a landing laid with flagstones perhaps a metre square in area. Opposite them stood a heavy wooden door with a mighty bolt closed across it.

The sickly smells were seeping through the door, leaking out from whatever lay beyond it. Ralf pressed an ear against the wood but could hear no sound. His hand slid across to the bolt, ready to pull it back.

Gunther tapped Ralf on the left shoulder. "Are you sure about this?" he whispered hoarsely. "We've no idea what's inside there. Maybe we should wait for the others. They'll be here in the next minute or two."

"Better we face whatever's inside alone. If it's too much for us, the others'll still have the chance to escape," Ralf reasoned.

With one hand still clutching his weapon, Ralf tugged on the bolt but it would not budge. Eventually he shouldered his machine pistol and used both hands on the stiff shaft of metal. After several seconds of intense effort the bolt abruptly gave way and slid aside. As it did so, the door swung inwards and Ralf stumbled forward into the dungeon. A rank stench billowed outwards into the stairwell, choking both soldiers. Light from Gunther's torch spilled into the chamber, exposing the horrors within. It took all the pair's experience not to flee when they saw what was inside the dungeon.

The chamber best resembled the charnel pit of some savage predator. Dozens of rotting human corpses were strewn carelessly about the floor, some missing limbs, others so decomposed it was difficult to know what age or gender they had once been. Tens of thousands of maggots writhed atop the bodies, crawling in and out of wounds, fighting with each other for the tastiest morsels of flesh. Pus and blood oozed from the corpses towards the flagstones of the landing, while a mass of flies were buzzing and weaving in the fetid air.

On the far wall beyond the corpses was a grisly selection of unfortunates left hanging from manacles and chains. Some were little more than skeletons, cold collations of brittle bones held together by scraps of skin and cloth. Others looked almost fresh, their naked torsos and faces still bloated by gases expanding from within them. No light other than that from Gunther's torch was visible within the chamber. Neither man could see any windows that might let a glimmer of sunshine or hope into this dank, damned place. The dungeon beneath Castle Constanta was like hell on earth, a chamber of torments and tortures, the sort of hole where even a deal with the devil could not save your life.

Ralf and Gunther gagged and choked on the foul odours escaping from the dungeon, both of them forcing their faces into the crook of an elbow, trying to shut out the stench of death and decay and despair.

"Close the door," Gunther urged his comrade. "Better that we seal this place off forever and let nature take its course."

Ralf nodded, not opening his mouth to speak lest he breathe in any more of the malodorous air leaking from the dungeon. He was about to pull the door shut when a tiny squeaking noise beyond it caught his ears.

"Did you hear that?"

"Hear what?" Gunther gasped.

"A noise from inside, as if someone was trying to call out to us but their words were being muffled... or gagged."

"You don't think anyone could be alive in there, do you?"

"I hope not for their sake," Ralf replied.

Both men stood silently, concentrating all their senses in search of the noise. After a few seconds the squeaking resumed. It was louder now and more insistent. Soon it was not a single squeak being repeated, but dozens of similar noises, as if the sounds were conversing.

"Ye gods, where is it coming from? Who's making that noise?"

Ralf peered upwards at the ceiling of the dungeon. The space above the rotting corpses was black... blacker than it ought to be. More disturbingly, the blackness appeared to be moving, shifting, flinching. Ralf took the flaming torch from Gunther's grasp and lifted it closer to the blackness, trying to get a better look at this strange phenomenon.

"Not *who*'s making it, but *what*. Look!" Ralf moved the torch closer to the pulsating darkness so Gunther could see it too.

The ceiling of the dungeon was covered in bats, thousands and thousands of black bats. They were hanging upside down from rows of tiny hooks, each of them moving and twisting about on their perch. The chorus of squeaks kept jumping from one bat to another, as if they were calling out in their sleep. Gunther took a step closer and his boot crunched a brittle piece of bone that had rolled out on to the landing when Ralf opened the dungeon door. The bone cracked loudly and the bat nearest the door opened its beady red and black eyes. The creature shrieked in anger at the two intruders, a cry so high-pitched it was almost beyond their hearing. All the nearby bats opened their eyes as well and hissed at the German soldiers.

"We should get out of…" Ralf began, but he never got the chance to finish his sentence. In that moment thousands of bats dropped from their perches and flew at the open doorway, the great mass of them forming a cloud like some massive black, silken shroud. Ralf and Gunther threw themselves down on the flagstones, wrapping their arms across the backs of their heads for protection. The flapping of so many wings and the bats' shrieking went on and on and on, as wave upon wave of bats swooped and thrashed at the intruders before escaping up the stairwell.

Moments later the sounds of gunfire and men screaming could be heard echoing down the stairwell from above as the bats flew up to the ground floor, startling the Panzergrenadiers as they entered the castle. Finally, after what seemed an eternity, the last of the bats had fled the dungeon, leaving Ralf and Gunther alone on the stone floor. Eventually the noises from the top of the stairwell died away too, to be replaced by an eerie silence. After checking there were no more bats lurking inside the dungeon, Ralf pulled himself upright. He helped Gunther to his feet and the two friends checked each other for bites or wounds from the colony of bats. They were surprised to find themselves unscathed, although their uniforms were badly soiled by bat droppings.

"Those can't have been vampyr," Gunther said. "They would have eaten us alive otherwise."

"Remember what happened at Ordzhonikidze?" Ralf asked. "The vampyr sent thousands of bats to attack us, so many they blotted the moon from the sky. This must be where Constanta kept them." He retrieved the burning torch from where he'd dropped it, using the flames to illuminate the dungeon interior. Now the bats had left, a few blackened, greasy windows could be seen in the far corners of the chamber close to the ceiling. Also visible was the outline of a hatch set high in a wall with footholds in the stone beneath it.

"That probably leads to a concealed tunnel of some sort," Ralf speculated. "It could be where they let the bats in and out."

But Gunther's attention was elsewhere. He pointed past Ralf to one of the torture victims hanging from the opposite wall. When the bats had been hanging from the ceiling, their presence stopped any light seeping into the chamber from the high windows. As a consequence, all the captives had been shrouded in shadow, their faces and features hard to make out in the murk. Now the bats were gone, there was a little more illumination. The half-naked figure chained to the wall opposite them was twitching, fingers flexing as if trying to get their attention.

"Ralf, that poor bastard over there... I think he's alive!" Gunther gasped.

"God in heaven, you're right," Ralf whispered.

The two friends scrambled over the uneven carpet of rotting corpses towards the survivor, trying to ignore the sound of their boots crunching the decomposing bones and organs underfoot. When they reached the bedraggled figure, they eased his hands out of the cold metal manacles, a task made easier by the prisoner's chronic emaciation. His wrists were red and raw from where he'd tried to escape his bindings, the skin worn away right down to the bone. A German soldier's uniform hung in shreds from his body, ribs protruding against skin, ankles bloody from where chains had bound his legs in place. Faeces and urine stained what was left of his trousers, while his hair was knotted into greasy cords and a wispy beard hung from his hollow-cheeked face. The prisoner coughed and gasped, trying to stammer out a few words, but his throat was too dry to speak.

Gunther pulled a drinking flask from his waist belt and tipped a few drops on the survivor's lips to moisten them. "Slowly… slowly… Not too much at once," he warned.

The prisoner nodded, letting the precious liquid trickle into his mouth. He swallowed and swallowed again, then licked his lips and smiled.

"Th-thank you…" His eyes rolled back into his head and he fell silent again. Ralf pressed an ear against the survivor's chest, listening intently.

"It's okay. He passed out, that's all."

"Poor bastard," Gunther muttered. He shook his head in amazement that anyone could have survived in such conditions. "Has he got any identification on him?"

Ralf felt inside the man's tattered tunic and discovered an oval-shaped metal ID disc. "Yes. His name's…" Ralf peered at the disc as if unable to believe its inscription. "Karl Richter."

Gunther shrugged. "Richter's not an uncommon name. Our last radio operator in the Panzer, Helmut, he was called Richter too, remember?"

"Of course I remember," Ralf snapped. "Don't you get it? This is Karl, Helmut's brother!"

\* \* \*

IT WAS ANOTHER three hours before Karl was able to speak again. By then he'd been moved up to the ground floor and the dungeon had been sealed shut once more. Ralf and Gunther looked after Karl while Hans and the other Panzergrenadiers secured their hold on Castle Constanta. Sentries were posted along the battlements while patrols went out to forage for food and fuel. A thorough search of the building found it had been stripped clean by the last occupiers with no ammunition, water or other supplies left behind. The castle was intact but utterly deserted, not a living soul within two miles of its stone towers and imposing presence.

Ralf and Gunther found Karl a fresh uniform by borrowing spare items of clothing from the other soldiers. Gunther smashed apart a set of six wooden chairs to provide fuel for a fire to warm enough water so the pitiful survivor could wash and cleanse himself. Once Karl was in the bath, the embers of the fire were used to cook a makeshift meal of cured sausage and tinned tomatoes augmented with some stale crusts of black bread. The Panzergrenadiers were sick to the stomach of this meagre fare, having eaten nothing else for days on end, but Karl fell on the food as if it were a feast fit for a king. He wolfed down the meal, drinking flask after flask of water to quench his thirst. Finally, when his hunger was sated, Karl asked Gunther for a haircut and a shave.

"I'd do it, but I doubt my arms have got the strength left in them," he said apologetically.

Gunther used the sharpened blade of his bayonet to slice away the mass of Karl's matted brown hair before shifting his attention to the wispy beard. As the last vestiges of his captivity were removed, Karl told his rescuers how he'd ended up in the dungeon of Castle Constanta.

"I always wanted to be in a Panzer crew like my brother Helmut, but when the time came I was only deemed good enough for the Panzergrenadiers. I was part of the initial assault upon Stalingrad back in August

1942. We stormed across the steppe from the Don River to the Volga in a day. I remember standing on a hillside looking down on Stalingrad in the late afternoon. Stukas and Heinkels had been carpet-bombing the city for hours. Fireballs and columns of smoke rose a mile into the sky and we could smell the burning from where we were. The river was on fire, oil slicks ablaze from where ships had been blown apart on the water. The Luftwaffe did victory rolls overhead and we all cheered them until we were hoarse. I thought victory could only be days away since we'd bombed the Bolsheviks into submission. But we didn't realise our bombs had turned the city into a killing ground for the Russians to use against us."

Ralf nodded, his face stricken by the memories of his own experiences in Stalingrad. Too many good men had been lost fighting for that damned city, Karl's brother among them. Did the survivor know what had happened to Helmut? Ralf wasn't sure but decided this wasn't the time to mention it.

"We were in Stalingrad too, fighting for the Mamaev Kurgan. That bloody hill must have changed hands dozens of times in the months we were there."

"My unit was further north trying to secure the Red October factory. Not that there was much left of the factory by the time we'd gotten a foothold inside the building – broken glass and twisted metal, all the machinery rusted beyond recognition. Half my comrades were slaughtered in a single Soviet counter-attack at the end of September. After that we were given a new commander, a Rumanian Hauptmann from this area..."

"Constanta?" Gunther asked.

"Yes," Karl replied, puzzlement evident in his face. "You know about him?"

Gunther and Ralf exchanged a look. "Our paths have crossed his," Ralf said.

"Well, he said he must become like the enemy to defeat the enemy; fight like them to have a hope of winning the city. We would only attack at night. In daytime we would use the sewers and tunnels to stay out of sight, travelling underground to infiltrate the Russian positions. We would take no prisoners, soldier or civilian. We had to fight without mercy, give no quarter."

"Sounds like Constanta," Ralf agreed. "When did you begin to suspect what he was?"

"To prove his resolve to us, the Hauptmann paraded a local girl in front of us. She couldn't have been more than thirteen or fourteen, but the Russians had used her to spy on our movements, or so Constanta said. Then he ripped her throat open with his teeth and sucked the blood from her neck. All the time he was draining her dry, he was looking at us and making sure we had no illusions about the sort of monster who was in command. I think he wanted us to be more afraid of him than of the Bolsheviks. It worked."

By this time Gunther had finished shaving him. Karl ran a weak, quivering hand across his smooth skin. With his dark hair trimmed close to the scalp and beard removed, he appeared decades younger than a few hours before. But the dark circles beneath his eyes and the haunted look within them spoke of the horrors he had witnessed.

Gunther had not seen a single vampyr during the cold, bitter months he'd spent in Stalingrad with Ralf and the other members of the former Panzer crew. He was perplexed by the revelation that the leader of the undead had been stationed within a few miles of him during that time. "Was Constanta with your unit the whole time?"

Karl shook his head. "No. He came and went. We wouldn't see him for days on end and then he'd reappear out of nowhere like a shadow suddenly thrown upon a wall. Always at night, always after dark, and always with some new, suicidal mission for us to perform. One time we had to fight a squad of Russian hunters who were armed with hammers, wooden stakes and silver-edged sickles. They butchered my comrades as if we were vampyr too. I was lucky to escape with my life. Constanta got away without a scratch, of course... His kind always do. He vanished when the Russians launched their major counter-attack. Within days we were encircled and trapped in the city."

"But you got out?" Ralf asked.

"I was injured, nearly blinded by a Russian incendiary that caught me across the eyes. One of my comrades got me on the last plane out of the encirclement. I still don't know how. I was flown back to Berlin and given a medal by the Führer for my bravery. But I never felt brave or courageous. I was terrified the whole time I was in Stalingrad, convinced I'd never get out of there alive." Karl laughed bitterly. "Looking back on it now, I realise I didn't know then what terror was."

Hans came in to see how the survivor was doing, interrupting Karl's reminisces. "Everything's in place," Hans told his brother. "The patrols are back but they didn't have much success finding food or fuel. Berkel's done his best arranging our men round the battlements, but we don't have nearly enough to defend this place from a concerted attack."

"That doesn't matter after tonight," Ralf said. "We'll pull out of here at dawn."

"You're not planning to stay in the castle after dark, are you?" Karl's voice was trembling with fear.

"Why shouldn't we? This place is deserted," Gunther observed.

"Constanta pulled out all his men when they heard about the Rumanians switching sides," Karl replied, "but that doesn't mean they won't come back."

"The castle is still on German-held territory. Now that Constanta's countrymen are fighting for the Bolsheviks, we should be safe here," Ralf said. He paused, biting his bottom lip. "Karl, how did you know the Rumanians were changing sides?"

"Constanta came down to the dungeon and told me personally. I don't know how long ago that was, but the sick bastard said he wanted to apologise for abandoning me down there."

"The Rumanians joined the Allies two or three days ago," Hans said.

"Is that all?" Karl shook his head in bewilderment. "It felt as though I'd been down there on my own for weeks. The only sounds I could hear were the bats talking to each other, and the maggots feasting on the corpses." He shuddered at the memory of what he'd endured.

Ralf folded his arms, studying the survivor's face. "Karl, I know this won't be easy, but can you tell us how you came to be in the dungeon?"

"I... I'm not sure that I... I can't go back there..."

Gunther rested a reassuring hand on the survivor's shoulder. "You don't ever have to go back there, but it might help us to know what happened here."

Karl smiled uncertainly, his brow furrowing. "I'll try. After I recovered from my injuries, I was given a position with the Führer's personal staff, travelling with him wherever he went. When news reached Berlin about the Russians invading Rumania, he decided to send a personal envoy to Sighisoara for a meeting with Constanta. There were rumours for months that representatives of King Michael had been in Cairo negotiating an armistice. The Führer wanted to ensure the people of Transylvania would fulfil their treaty with him, maintaining an aggressive resistance to the Soviet forces even if the rest of Rumania gave way in exchange for a sovereign state of their own once the war was over. I was chosen as escort to the envoy, not realising that the Führer's secret treaty had actually been made with the undead. He promised them a vampyr nation in return for their loyalty. But by the time we arrived at Sighisoara, the Rumanians had already ceased fire."

"What happened to the envoy?" Hans asked.

"On our first night Constanta took us to a POW camp nearby, ostensibly to review the procedures for dealing with Soviet prisoners. In fact he was more like a proud child, showing off his train set. Constanta strutted around the camp, making sure we got a good look at everything. He told us the facility had processed twenty thousand Russian POWs a week at its height. When we toured the camp there were fewer than a thousand left and most of those were at death's door: exhausted, emaciated and utterly anaemic."

"Processed? What did he mean by processed?"

"He put on a little demonstration for us, using a group of German deserters who'd been captured while trying to flee the Ostfront. They were herded into a long wooden hut and had their wrists bound to a crossbeam. Needles were shoved into both of their arms and they were systematically drained of blood. Orderlies in white coats marched up and down, examining the prisoners, checking to see every last possible drop was being removed. The blood was piped out to a holding tank before being transported away for what Constanta called 'purification'. I tried asking one of the German orderlies where this took place, but he stared straight through me, as if I wasn't there, as if he had no will of his own. I guess he was a thrall of the vampyr; all the staff must have been. I can't believe they would ever take part in such inhuman atrocities otherwise."

A warning cry from outside the room drew Hans away but Ralf was determined to hear about the rest of Karl's encounter with Constanta. "Did you discover where the blood was taken?"

Karl nodded. "There's a lake a few miles from here in a small valley between the hills. But what's in the valley isn't water, it's blood, a lake of blood."

"Did you see it?" Gunther asked, unable to believe what he was hearing.

"The prisoner next to me in the dungeon did, he told me about it. According to local legends, the lake is meant to be home to some vast monster, a creature so terrifying it makes Constanta tremble with fear..."

Hans burst back into the room. "Ralf, Gunther, we've got trouble!"

"In a minute!" Ralf snapped. "Karl, what happened to the Führer's envoy?"

"Constanta butchered him and had him served as a feast for other vampyr while I was made to watch. I was then taken down to the dungeons. I think Constanta was planning to keep me for later, like you keep a spare joint of meat in a larder, but then word came through about the Rumanians changing sides."

Karl turned to look at Hans. "It's them, isn't it? The vampyr have come back for me. I knew they would."

"You're wrong," Hans replied. "It's the Russians. They must have found a quicker way over the mountains than we did. They're outside, moving in to attack the castle!"

# Five

THE BATTLE FOR Castle Constanta was bloody and brutal, but at least it took place in daylight. All too frequently the deep knife squad had been fighting for its life in the darkness, urged on by our new commander, Sergeant Gorgo. Like all vampyr, daylight was anathema to him and he made no effort to conceal his true nature from us. In the few days since the five of us were brought together under Gorgo's leadership, we had been thrown into battle after battle against the retreating Wehrmacht, driving them up into the Transylvanian Alps before tearing them apart.

After our first night of fighting we were joined by a dozen thralls: Russian infantrymen whose will had been stolen away by Gorgo and his kind. When the sun rose each morning, Gorgo and his two bodyguards retreated to the safety of the shadows, leaving us to fend for ourselves. But the thralls kept watch over us, making sure we could neither escape nor attack our new master.

Inevitably, it was Eisenstein who questioned this servitude, demanding answers from Gorgo. The

Rumanian was only too pleased to oblige, smirking at our outrage, letting us all see the tips of his fangs as he explained the reasoning behind it. "The thralls are good fighters, eager to walk into death itself at my command, but they lack the intelligence and instinct that makes a truly great fighter on the battlefield."

"Because you've stolen away their will and turned them into mindless drones," Mariya growled.

"Precisely," Gorgo agreed. "The five of you were all skilled vampyr-hunters, each having claimed the lives of dozens of my kin in your time. You have the killer instinct needed to help us win this war, to succeed on missions for which my thralls are ill-suited. But your backgrounds also make you impossible to trust. Any of you five would murder me without a moment's hesitation, but for the presence of my bodyguards at night and my thralls during the day. Consider them an insurance policy, as well as useful cannon fodder for what lays ahead. We shall be fighting our way to Berlin together, so the sooner you learn to relax and make the best of this arrangement, the better. In the meantime, we have a particular target that needs to be secured immediately."

That target was Castle Constanta, on the outskirts of Sighisoara. Gorgo led us up and over a narrow mountain pass before racing down to his homeland of Transylvania below. At night he led from the front, picking out the path when our human eyes could see nothing in the darkness. By day he travelled beneath a shroud on a stretcher borne by four of his thralls. Gorgo's vampyr bodyguards were required to run alongside the stretcher, using cloaks, gloves and broad-brimmed hats to keep the sun's rays from incinerating their sensitive skin. We marched and climbed and ran all the way to Sighisoara, scarcely stopping for more than an hour at a spell.

When at last we reached the castle, Mariya and I were close to collapse from exhaustion. The Borjigin brothers

proved to have remarkable stamina, supporting Mariya
and me during the final stages of our journey. But it was
on Eisenstein that the trek had the most profound and
disturbing effect. The closer we got to Sighisoara, the
stronger my comrade became. He appeared to be
drawing sustenance from the land around him, as if he
was a traveller coming home. But as his body grew
stronger, so his resistance to sunlight grew weaker.
Eisenstein took to hiding his skin from daylight and
rarely opened his mouth to speak. When he did, I was
shocked to see a fully formed pair of fangs protruding
from his upper jaw. The closer we got to the birthplace
of the vampyr, the more Eisenstein became like one of
the undead, the very thing he had fought so valiantly to
avoid since first being attacked by Constanta two years
before.

If I still had any doubts about his precarious state, they
were swept away in the hour before dawn on the day we
attacked the castle. Gorgo had permitted us a brief
respite from our sprint across the lowlands of Transylvania, no doubt wanting us to be that little bit fresher for
the battle to come. I slumped to the ground, my lips
parched, my arms so leaden they lacked the strength to
open my drinking flask. Mariya had also collapsed amid
the gravel and grass, her head tipped forward, nodding
slightly in time with her breathing.

Eisenstein glowered at me before moving over to
Mariya and dropping into a crouch beside her. He whispered something into her ear but I couldn't hear the
words. Gorgo was barking orders at the thralls nearby,
distracting me for a moment. When I turned back, I
could see Eisenstein drawing back his lips and exposing
his fangs as he leaned nearer to Mariya's supple neck.

"Get away from her, Grigori!" I snarled, scrambling
across the stony surface towards them.

Eisenstein lurched backwards, his face tormented by
guilt and shame. Mariya opened her eyes, awakened by

the anger in my voice. She saw Eisenstein skulk away and instinctively grasped at her neck, checking she had no puncture wounds or bite marks.

"Bojemoi, did he...?"

I nodded, unable to look Mariya in the eyes. Grigori was my longest-surviving friend in this bloody war. That he should try to sate his hunger with Mariya's blood... It left me sickened. I strode after Eisenstein, who had scuttled away into the shelter provided by an outcrop of rocks. I was ready to accuse him of treachery but found him weeping in the shadows, his fingers clawing in frustration at the bandage round his neck.

"What the hell do you think you're doing?" I demanded.

"It burns, it burns," he mourned. His once proud voice was now a guttural sneer.

"I meant what you nearly did to Mariya. You would have ripped open her neck if I hadn't intervened. Is that what you want? To become like Gorgo and Constanta and the other vampyr?"

"I can't help it," Eisenstein whimpered pathetically. "The hunger, it gets stronger every day, more rabid with each step we get closer to the castle."

"We've noticed."

"I don't know how much longer I can fight it off."

"Try. You've held this infection back for two years, don't give in to it now!"

"You don't understand..."

"Back in Leningrad, you made me promise to kill you if I ever thought the vampyr taint was becoming too strong," I said, pressing my bayonet against his neck so its edge dug into the skin, drawing blood. "I think it's time I made good on that promise."

"No, Victor, don't." It was Mariya who stopped me, her hand closing around mine to remove the bayonet from Eisenstein's throat. "We need him."

"Not if he's going to feed on us," I protested.

But she laid a finger across my lips, silencing me. "Grigori is partway between us and them. He thirsts for blood like they do, but he also thinks and feels like a vampyr too. When the time comes for our war of blood with the vampyr, he can give us an edge against them."

"Are you sure about this?"

Mariya nodded, her face close to mine, her eyes pleading with me. "Yes. It's this place that's turning him, pushing him over the edge. If we can get through the next few days and move on from here, I believe he'll recover some of his humanity."

"But how much? Enough that we can trust him again?"

"Give me the chance to prove her right," Eisenstein muttered. "Please, I need your help."

I was still agonising over the decision when Gorgo called us back together. It would be dawn at any minute and he wanted to ensure we knew our orders for the rest of the day. We were to march on the castle, surround the perimeter, and then attack. Any Germans found inside were to be executed immediately since deep knife units did not have any way of looking after POWs. Gorgo wanted Castle Constanta reclaimed for its native people by nightfall. If we failed, he would make all of us suffer the consequences. His tone left little to the imagination.

As our commander retreated to the safety of his shroud, Eisenstein approached me hesitantly.

"Well?" he asked.

I could see Mariya nearby with the Borjigin brothers, watching us. Her skills as a translator were far superior to mine and she was already conducting rudimentary conversations with the two Mongolians. I had little doubt she was telling them what had taken place earlier, judging by their expressions. But the final decision about my friend's fate had been left to me.

I searched Eisenstein's eyes, grateful to see my comrade and not some blood-crazed creature looking back at me. He had been like a father to me during the Siege of

Leningrad, keeping me alive when others told him to abandon the hapless ex-kommisar. We had come a long way together since then, but I still thought of Eisenstein as a mentor. Now I found myself standing in judgement over him. Against the urging of my head, I let the feelings of my heart take charge.

"We'll give you another chance," I said finally. "But one lapse, one more attack upon any of us four and you'll be a cloud of dust and ash, understand?"

Eisenstein nodded gratefully before smiling at Mariya and the brothers.

"I only hope I've done the right thing," I muttered under my breath.

WE STORMED THE castle as afternoon slowly degraded towards dusk. The Germans defending the forbidding structure had put up a steadfast resistance for hours, keeping us back from its walls by the skill of their marksmen. Enemy snipers claimed more than half our thralls as we tried and failed to get inside.

Gorgo urged us forward from the shelter of his shroud. Eventually he allowed us to remain on the edge of the Germans' range, drawing their fire while minimising the risk to us. Slowly, gradually, the enemy marksmen ran out of ammunition, until their weapons clicked uselessly atop the battlements.

We crept closer to the castle, sending the thralls ahead of us to ensure the castle's defenders were not attempting to lure us into an ambush. It was Eisenstein who suggested using the thralls as a human shield for our advance.

"They're already under Gorgo's control, and we cannot save them from that fate," he reasoned. "But the fewer minions he has at his disposal, the greater our chances of assassinating him."

"We showed you mercy," Mariya said. "Don't the thralls deserve it too?"

"No, Grigori's right," I said. "They've already surrendered their souls to the vampyr."

"Not willingly," she replied.

"Probably not, but if they die capturing this castle, at least they're out of their misery."

Mariya turned away, repelled by the coldness of my reasoning. She joined the Borjigin brothers for the assault, preferring their company during the battle. Once the enemy's ammunition was exhausted, the remaining thralls burst into Castle Constanta via the main gates. At least a dozen German soldiers were waiting within, ready to fight for their lives. They retreated backwards into the castle's narrow corridors, taking advantage of the ancient architecture. The spaces inside were too congested for us to fire without wounding our own comrades, forcing us to engage in vicious, close-quarters combat.

I stayed close to Eisenstein, whose vampiric strength and savagery ripped through the defenders, scything past our thralls as they slowly advanced deeper into the castle. I used my bayonet as a dagger, stabbing and slicing at the Germans. When their numbers threatened to overwhelm us, a few shots from my pistol helped drive them back.

Eisenstein was stabbed and wounded repeatedly but kept going, his uniform spattered with blood and viscera. We got so far ahead of the thralls that the line of defenders closed in between us and Gorgo's slaves, leaving us surrounded by German soldiers. My pistol clicked empty and there was no time for reloading, so I tossed the weapon aside.

"We've come too far!" I shouted to Eisenstein.

He glanced over his shoulder at me, taking in our situation. "Stand back to back!" he urged. "Together we can hold them off until reinforcements get here!"

I did as he suggested, pressing my shoulder blades against his, both my hands clenched around my bayonet. Eisenstein hissed and spat at the enemy, flashing his fangs at them. I knew he would not use his teeth on the Germans but they didn't, giving us a psychological advantage. For a moment the enemy held back, unsure how to deal with us. They had been on the back foot since this battle began, and now they had the advantage but seemed uncertain how to use it.

"Come on, you bastards!" Eisenstein screamed at them, goading the Germans into action.

Seven of them lunged at us from all sides, stabbing and flailing with daggers, bayonets and rifle butts. I deflected two of the attackers' blows, but felt a wooden stock crash into the side of my skull, spots dancing in front of my eyes. Blinded and close to collapse, I stabbed sideways with my bayonet and the man who'd hit me went down screaming. Emboldened, I swiped my blade through the air and was rewarded with two more cries of pain. Then something sharp and cold invaded my right thigh and I was down on one knee. The Germans closed in around me, blocking out what little light there still was in the castle corridor.

"Urraaaiiii!" a Mongolian bellowed nearby, his cry echoed by another gruff voice with the same accent.

Fearful German faces twisted away from me in time to see the Borjigin brothers appear. A pair of curved swords sliced and severed and skewered. Within moments half the enemy were dead or dying, while the others were too busy fighting for their lives to worry about finishing me off. I saw my pistol trapped beneath the body of a German, the end of the barrel caught up in the chain of his identity disc. I ripped the weapon free, my eyes dimly registering the name on the metal oval: BERKEL, A. He was dead and that was all I cared to know about him.

I reached into a pouch on my waist belt and extracted a handful of bullets, quickly slotting them into my pistol. Behind me Eisenstein had dealt with most of the other Germans, putting the rest to flight. He ran after them, howling like an enraged animal, bellowing and screaming for more. The sound of men dying hung in the air like a fog, while my nostrils were filled with the stench of blood and cordite and fear.

Mariya crouched beside me, blood trickling from a scratch across her left cheek. "Are you all right?" she asked, concern in her voice. "I thought we'd lost you both for a second."

"I'm fine," I insisted. "My leg must have cramped."

Mariya looked at my thigh and gasped. "Not exactly." She reached into her knapsack and produced a roll of bandage.

I realised blood was running from a narrow slice in my trousers, soaking the material with a crimson stain. I had been stabbed in the melee and hardly noticed, so intense was the ferocity of the fighting. My hands started to shake, having been perfectly calm and steady until then.

"I don't understand," I mumbled, trying to stop my hands from trembling without success.

"It's delayed shock, from the wound," Mariya said. "Stand up and I'll bandage it."

Behind her the Borjigin brothers were counting on their fingers and muttering to each other in Mongolian, their brows furrowed by thought.

"What are they doing?" I asked Mariya.

"Keeping score," she said, smiling. "They've got some sort of contest to see who can kill the most enemy soldiers before the end of the war."

"I just want to get home alive."

"Where is home?"

"Moscow. At least, it was before the war."

I studied the corpses of the dead Germans around us, the sprays of blood on the peeling plaster walls, trying not to wince as Mariya pulled the bandage taut around my thigh.

"After this madness, who knows?" I said.

She straightened up and wiped her bloody hands clean on her tunic. "True. I was born and raised in Stalingrad, but there wasn't much left of the city last time I saw it. Nothing to call home."

Eisenstein reappeared, his uniform awash with blood, his eyes ablaze with excitement. "There's a handful of the enemy spread throughout the castle, but we've broken the back of their resistance. I'll go tell Gorgo his lordship's precious home is secured."

"I'll do it," Mariya volunteered. "You and Victor search the remaining areas down here, and make sure the Germans don't have any nasty surprises waiting for us. The Borjigin brothers can sweep the upper floors and search for any more survivors."

"Fine by me," he replied, shrugging. "Come on, Zunetov. Let's finish this."

"Thanks for the bandage," I whispered to Mariya before hurrying after Eisenstein. When I caught up with him he was smirking to himself.

"What's so amusing?" I asked him.

"I notice you and Charnosova are on first name terms now," he commented.

"She called me Victor, so what?"

"Nothing, nothing."

"Good."

Eisenstein paused outside a small, empty chamber, peering inside to make certain it was deserted. Once satisfied, he continued along the corridor with me at his heels.

"But you two do seem to be getting along well, especially considering you've just met."

"What are you, my mother?"

He stopped, his face suddenly serious. "A war is no place to fall in love, Zunetov. That's doubly true of this war. Trust me, I know."

"So do I." We glared at each other, neither one of us willing to mention Sofia, the woman who'd died at

Constanta's hand outside Leningrad, the woman Eisenstein had loved.

I was about to move on when somebody coughed nearby. Ahead of us in the corridor was a doorway leading into what looked like the largest room on the castle's ground floor. The sound had come from that direction, but it was muffled and faint, with a curious echo. I arched an eyebrow at Eisenstein, who nodded gently in response. We'd both heard the same thing and believed it came from the same place.

Slowly we crept along the corridor towards the open doorway, Eisenstein unslinging the submachine gun from across his back while I made certain my pistol was ready to fire. Our approach was masked by the sound of gunfire and men screaming on the upper levels as the Mongolians eagerly added to their tallies of dead Germans.

Eisenstein paused outside the doorway before stepping boldly inside and sweeping his weapon sideways round the room, a finger poised on the trigger. Satisfied there was nobody else inside, he nodded and I followed him inside. The chamber was massive but quite empty: no furniture behind which the enemy could wait, no other doors leading off the space. Tall windows on the far side of the room looked out at the barren fields beyond where the last rays of sunlight were dying on the stony ground. Where the hell had that sound come from?

Someone, somewhere, moved, quietly shifting their weight from one foot to the other. The sound was definitely not originating above us but its source remained elusive. I studied the walls of this vast chamber, trying to deduce what it was once used for. Long and broad, the wooden block flooring in the central area was all but unmarked, bound by a rectangle of indentations and scuffs. The outer edges of the floor were well-trodden, the patina of the wooden floor wore thin. There must have been a massive table in here once at least eight metres in length, protecting the central area from use.

Yes, this must have been the castle's main dining hall. I shuddered to think what sort of meals the likes of Constanta had feasted upon in here. Now that we had regained the castle for Gorgo, his kind would soon be using this as their headquarters once more. It sickened me to realise every victory we achieved was simply serving the will of the vampyr, the very creatures we had vowed to hunt down and destroy.

Eisenstein sniffed at the air, his sense of smell somehow made keener than mine by the undead taint coursing through his veins. I followed his example and became aware of rotting flesh, the rancorous odour of decomposition drifting into the chamber from nearby. Eisenstein followed the smell to one of the side walls, his nostrils flaring in search of the entry point. His hands caressed the wall, passing over an elaborate crest sculpted into the dark wooden panelling. A mechanism clicked within the crest and the panel slid aside, revealing a stone stairwell that curved down into darkness.

Someone beneath us caught their breath, startled by the sudden movement of the panel. They knew their hiding place had been discovered. A final confrontation was moments away. Eisenstein loosed a volley of bullets down the staircase before hurriedly stepping aside to escape any return fire.

A man cried out in pain, the urgency of his voice telling me the wound was probably fatal. After so long fighting on the front, I'd learnt to distinguish between the sound of death and less life-threatening pain. The man sobbed, begging his comrades for help. They tried to hush his voice but it was too late. In a few words he had given the others away.

"Hans, Ralf, help me!"

I held up three fingers to Eisenstein. He sniffed the air again, frowning before holding up four fingers and a

speckled with silver. A beard clung to his jawline, making him appear even more grizzled. I thought he must be in his late thirties, but wars like this one aged men before their time.

Next to him stood a younger man, fresh-faced and smooth of skin. His blond hair, blue eyes and chiselled jaw made him resemble every image of Aryan manhood I'd seen on Hitler Youth recruiting posters while I was in Berlin. What surprised me was the similarity of his features to the older man on his left. The two were so alike they could almost have been brothers.

On either side of them were two more Germans: a shorter, round-faced man who looked surprisingly cheerful in the circumstances, and a terrified figure with prominent ears and bulging eyes. By the time I'd surveyed them all, the match had burnt out. My grizzled accuser lit another, regarding me sourly. No doubt he and the others were studying me as I had looked over them. I couldn't help but wonder what they made of me, how I looked to their eyes. But there was no time for that now.

"I told you, my name is Victor," I persisted. "Which one of you is Hans Vollmer?"

"I am," the Aryan poster boy replied, smiling at me weakly. "We overheard what you were saying to your colleague at the top of the stairs. You believe the vampyr are planning another war after this one is over, yes? That's why you protected us from Gorgo?"

"Yes," I agreed. "Eisenstein can keep the vampyr busy for a while, but we need to get you out of here, one way or another."

"That's what we were trying to do," the veteran soldier snarled, glaring at his frightened colleague, "until Karl here almost got the lot of us killed."

"I didn't mean to," the terrified German protested. "God knows I don't want to go back through that dungeon but it's our only way out of here."

"What dungeon? Is that where these steps lead?" I asked.

"He's quick, I'll give him that," the cheerful man quipped. "I'm Stiefel, Gunther Stiefel. Ignore my sour friend, but Ralf's not one to trust strangers quickly."

Ralf pushed Karl aside, revealing a heavy wooden door behind them. A rusted metal bolt was holding the door shut. Ralf handed his matches to Gunther before bracing a foot against the wall and tugging hard on the bolt. Eventually it shifted, the metal crying out in protest at being moved. Another almighty pull and the bolt slid free. Ralf shoved his right shoulder hard against the door and it gave inwards, unleashing a vile stench of decay and a cloud of black flies. They swarmed into the stairwell, snuffing out the match and plunging us into darkness.

"Bojemoi!" I gasped, clamping a hand across my nose and mouth. "What is that smell?"

Gunther struck another match, the dancing flame throwing harsh light on his features. "As bad as that smells, where it comes from is worse."

Hans bent over to help the injured German to his feet, but the man slumped on the stairs did not move.

"He's gone. Beck's dead."

"Just as well," Ralf replied. "He'd have slowed us down too much. Come on." Ralf moved into the darkness of the dungeon, carefully working his way forward.

Gunther clapped an arm round Karl's shoulders. "You come with me, Richter. We can go in there together, okay?"

"O-Okay..." the frightened man muttered.

Gunther chattered happily as he ushered Karl into the dark, using words to distract his comrade. "Did Helmut ever tell you what Ralf and I did the day before Operation Barbarossa began? I was busy getting our Panzer ready for action, but Ralf? He was busy getting drunk."

Hans snapped off the bottom half of Beck's identity disc and stowed it away in a pocket. He caught me watching him and smiled bleakly. "No way of knowing if I'll ever make it back to Germany or get the chance to hand his disc in to the authorities, but I've got to try. Beck had a family, a wife and two young daughters. They deserve to know what happened to him. At least, to know that he died fighting for his country." Hans grimaced. "I won't tell them the rest." He marched into the dungeon, the darkness swallowing him within moments.

I followed Hans into the shadows, struggling to see where I was going. A few glimmers of twilight crept into the stinking chamber from small, greasy windows set high in the walls, but our main source of light came from the single lit match Gunther was carrying. I trod on something round and brittle. It collapsed beneath my boot and I nearly fell over, crying out in dismay at the thought of being trapped in this place. I reached down to steady myself and felt my fingers plunge into something moist and soft, the surface writhing beneath my palm. Gunther turned round to see what was wrong and suddenly I had a lot more light in front of me.

I was standing atop a pile of rotting human corpses, my hand inside the decomposing torso of a German soldier. Maggots crawled and wriggled around my fingers, several of them trying to climb up my wrist and inside my uniform. I snatched my hand away and beat it against my tunic, determined to shake off the insidious carrion-eaters.

Gunther chuckled at my panic and horror. "Careful, comrade! Trust me, you don't want to spend any longer in here than you have to. This is where the vampyr keep their larder. No doubt your friend upstairs will be looking for fresh supplies to restock it. Karl spent three days as a captive in this hole before we liberated him."

That explained his utter terror, I realised. Hans helped me get upright and we continued our uncertain journey across the corpse-strewn dungeon, Ralf leading us towards a far corner of the sinister chamber. I could see a glimmer of light seeping in from high on one wall, as if a rectangle was glowing on the stone surface. As we got closer I realised the shape was a small hatch, the rectangle formed by light creeping past the edges of the wooden door. There must be a tunnel or shaft behind it, leading out into the countryside.

Dusk was falling on the countryside around Sighisoara, but there was still enough light in the air to pick out the hatchway. Ralf clambered up several footholds in the wall and opened the small wooden door, letting more light into the dungeon. I knew better than to look around, not wanting to see any more of the horrors Constanta and his kind had kept in that subterranean hellhole. Instead I concentrated my attention on Ralf squeezing himself through the narrow hatchway in the wall. At one point his torso became jammed into the rectangle, but he fought his way onwards. His boots disappeared from view, but I could still hear his gasps for breath as he dragged himself along the tunnel.

After a few minutes even those sounds faded away. I stood in the fading light beneath the hatch with the three Germans, trying not to think what would happen if Gorgo found me helping four enemy soldiers escape the castle. After an agonising wait Ralf's voice echoed down the tunnel, calling the others after him.

"Come on, we can get out this way! The tunnel comes out behind the castle where it opens into a ditch. From there we can crawl away unseen. The tunnel's as narrow as the hatchway for the first section but it widens out after that. Come on!"

Gunther sent Karl through the hatch next, then followed him out of the dungeon. Hans paused to shake my hand, a smile visible on his face in the gathering twilight.

"Thank you, Victor Zunetov. I don't know how we'd have gotten out of here without your help. I never thought I'd hear myself saying that to one of Stalin's soldiers."

"We may be on different sides in this war, but we have a common foe."

"True. Perhaps, when this conflict is over, our two sides can unite to defeat that foe?"

"I hope so. It may be our only hope." I was going to add more, but the bellow of Gorgo's voice nearby froze the words in my mouth.

It sounded as if the vampyr was in the dining hall above us. I could hear him shouting my name, over and over, demanding to know where I was. I urged Hans into the tunnel, slamming the hatch shut after him. Now I had no choice but to turn round and face the dungeon. I could make out the shapes of the bodies sprawled across the cold stone floor, but little else. With the hatchway closed, the stench rising from the rotting flesh threatened to overwhelm. I scrambled across the carpet of corpses, breathing through my mouth instead of my nostrils, trying not to hear the sound of skulls grinding together beneath my boots.

A new light flooded into the dank chamber, spilling down the stairwell. Someone must have opened the secret entrance at the top of the stone steps. Please let it be Eisenstein, I prayed. But my pleadings went unanswered. The guttural voice of Gorgo bellowed down at me, demanding to know what I was doing in the dungeon. I ran across the remaining bodies to the door and scrambled up the steps to where Beck's corpse was crumpled, arriving at the German soldier moments before Gorgo came into view. He glared at me, one hand clutching a flaming torch, his other aiming a pistol at my head.

"What are you doing down here, Zunetov?"

I nudged Beck's body with my right boot. "I heard someone coughing while I was in the dining hall. I realised there must be a hidden entrance, leading to a concealed corridor or stairwell. This coward had hidden himself, hoping not to be found. I executed him."

"What else did you find down there?" Gorgo demanded.

"Some kind of dungeon filled with German corpses. Good riddance to them," I sneered.

The vampyr regarded me coldly, his eyes searching my expression, trying to find any hint of falsehood in my features. Eventually Gorgo turned away, seemingly satisfied by my explanation. He marched up the stairs, telling me to follow him. I did as I was told, hurrying to keep pace as the imposing vampyr took three steps at a time.

I emerged into the dining hall to find Eisenstein waiting outside, blood seeping from a vicious wound on his face where someone had struck him across the cheek with a weapon. No doubt Gorgo was responsible for the pistol-whipping, but Eisenstein did not flinch when the vampyr loomed over him. I closed the hidden panel, sealing off the secret stairwell and blocking out the stench of rotting corpses below.

"Nobody goes down there without the permission of myself or Lord Constanta, not unless they wish to share the fate of those already in the dungeon. Is that clear?" Gorgo demanded.

Eisenstein and I both saluted, acknowledging the order. I made a silent vow to myself. No matter what else happened in this war, I was determined never to visit that charnel house again. I was a good communist and did not believe in a deity, but I now knew what hell looked like.

# PART TWO: BERLIN

## One

IT WAS FRIDAY, April 20th – Adolf Hitler's birthday – when Gunther, Karl and the Vollmer brothers were reunited in Berlin. The quartet of Panzergrenadiers had escaped from Transylvania eight months earlier, retreating through the Rumanian territory on foot until they encountered a German motorised division. The four soldiers hitched a ride with their fellow countrymen, glad to escape the homeland of the vampyr.

None of them discussed what they had seen with members of the motorised division, and rarely with each other. To mention the vampyr during the hours of darkness felt to the likes of Hans and Ralf as if they were invoking a demon, while speaking the same word in daylight seemed strange. Once safely beyond the borders of Transylvania, it was hard to believe the horrors they had witnessed there were real.

At times one or another of the quartet tried to convince his comrades to speak out without success. A single voice among them always counselled against such a choice. Time and again Karl convinced the other three to

stay silent. His argument was a simple one: if they strug-
gled to cope with the truth themselves, how could they
hope to convince outsiders, fellow Germans who had
fought on the Ostfront but had never seen the vampyr?
Better to bide their time and wait for the right moment to
alert their countrymen.

The rest of 1944 and the early months of 1945 became
a long, slow, agonising retreat across the hills and valleys
that the Wehrmacht's Blitzkrieg tactics had once conquered in mere weeks. By April 1945, that same
Wehrmacht was a shadow of its former glory. The Luftwaffe was a broken, spent force, scarcely able to muster
enough planes to trouble the enemy squadrons control-
ling the sky over Germany. Far too much of its resources
and energies had been diverted to the wasteful and
largely ineffective V1 and V2 flying bomb campaigns.
There were even rumours that the Führer had authorised
a manned version of the V1, with a pilot steering the missile at his target before parachuting out at the last second.

Meanwhile, American and British bomber crews were
giving Berlin a pounding, knowing that the rapidly
advancing Allied ground forces would soon preclude further raids on the capital of the Reich. USAAF and RAF
planes marked the occasion of the Führer's fifty-sixth
birthday with a particularly heavy raid, pounding the city
with wave after wave of bombs in the morning. It was a
fine day, the fourth such day in succession.

While the battle for the sky above Berlin had been lost,
the ground war continued unabated. The four Panzergrenadiers had been split when they neared the capital a
few weeks earlier. In truth they were Panzergrenadiers in
name only now, the once mighty ranks of Panzer long
since destroyed by Soviet T-34s. Sightings of German
tanks were few and far between, and the men of the
Wehrmacht were just as depleted.

Ralf and the others found themselves fighting alongside boys and old men from the Volkssturm, Germany's

home guard. The People's Storm had been formed in October 1944 as a last line of defence should the worst come to the worst. That time was now upon the Fatherland's capital.

Hans had turned twenty-two since his short time within the walls of Castle Constanta. But he felt much older than his years when surrounded by teenage boys, all of them eager to die for the Führer. They were plucked from the ranks of the Hitler Youth, given little or no training, and sent forward to wherever the front was that day. There were often no military uniforms left with which to clothe them, so the Volkssturm was issued black and red armbands adorned with the words DEUTSCHE WEHRMACHT.

Guns and ammunition were at a premium, so youths were armed with Panzerfausts: a lightweight anti-tank weapon even an eleven year-old could fire. Hans had been horrified to see children cycling towards Russian T-34s, fearlessly riding to their deaths, believing they were achieving some kind of immortality for service to the Thousand-Year Reich.

Amazingly, some of the youths did succeed in destroying the Bolsheviks' battle armour, which was more than many Panzer had managed in the early months of Operation Barbarossa. But losses sustained by the Volkssturm were sickening, generals in Berlin using the brainwashed fervour of children to slow the Russian advance by a few hours at most. Hans knew, had he been born a few years later, that he would have been one of those teenagers cycling towards certain death. So he did his best to save as many of the boys as he could, training them to add stealth and cunning to their handful of Panzerfausts.

Even with help from Karl, Hans knew he could not save all the children. Perhaps he could not save any of them, but he could try. He took charge of several Volkssturm squads at the eastern edge of Berlin, giving the young warriors a leadership they had been sorely lacking. Most of the old men conscripted into the People's Storm had long since deserted, fleeing the battlefield for the comforts of home. It was shortly after dawn on Hitler's birthday that Karl had caught one of the elderly men sneaking back towards Berlin. Karl brought the aging deserter to Hans for interrogation.

The old man refused to give his unit, but did let slip his given name was Otto. Hans found part of an official document among the deserter's few possessions. It stated his age as fifty-eight, but Otto looked closer to eighty. He had fought in the previous war and counted himself lucky to have survived that conflict. He had no intention of perishing on the battlefield in this war.

"If I'm going to die in this madness, I want to die in my own bed with my wife Lotte at my side!" Otto said.

Hans couldn't help agreeing with the sentiment. He wished he could say the same, but the war had taken Hans far from home before he'd even thought about marriage. He shared a flask of vodka with the old man, the small quantity of alcohol looted while retreating through the southern regions of Poland. The coarse, acrid liquid helped loosen Otto's tongue.

"I was ready to fight until the finish," he explained. "We all were."

"All of you? There are others?"

"Not anymore," Otto said bleakly. "I was part of what our commander, Gefreiter Hartz, laughingly called an 'elite Volkssturm unit'. That meant we were all veterans of the last war so we knew one end of a rifle from the other. Not that many of us had rifles, let alone ammunition. When the Bolsheviks crossed the Oder on Monday, we were sent forward to help slow their advance. But the bastard Hartz never told us what was waiting out there in the darkness."

A familiar chill ran up Hans's spine. He had heard no official mention of the vampyr since returning to

Germany, nor of any mutterings about Rumanian monsters from other soldiers on the Ostfront. But he recognised the haunted look in Otto's eyes and the old man's quivering hands for what they were: not evidence of cowardice, but of someone who'd seen the undead and knew what those fiends were capable of.

"Vampyr?" Hans ventured. "You were sent to fight vampyr?"

"How did you...?" Otto began, but his words stopped as realisation hit home. "You know about them, don't you? You've fought them before."

"They were our allies when Operation Barbarossa began," Hans said quietly. "After Rumania switched sides, so did the undead. Now they hunt us as prey."

"But if our commanders know about these creatures, why didn't they warn us?"

"Would you have believed them if they had?"

Otto's eyes narrowed. "No, probably not," he conceded.

"I imagine our leaders don't want us to panic," Hans added.

"As if things weren't already bad enough."

"Indeed." Hans rasped a palm across the stubble on his chin. "When did you see them?"

"Last night," Otto whispered. Fuelling himself with mouthfuls of vodka, the old man told how his unit had been sent to fight a cluster of Russian commandoes operating behind German lines to the east of Berlin. Otto believed most of the enemy soldiers had been human, but the leader of the insurgents was not, nor his two bodyguards. The squad of elderly Volkssturm had the element of surprise for their initial attack on the Soviet commandoes, succeeding in killing half the invaders with a few well-timed and well-placed Panzerfausts. But the veterans were overrun by the survivors and torn apart where they stood. Otto saw his best friend's throat being ripped open, and then watched as the commander of the Russian squad supped on the dying man's blood.

"I already knew that monster wasn't human. It'd been caught in the blast of the first Panzerfaust. The Bolshevik soldiers nearby were shredded, but this fiend dissolved into the air before reappearing beside me, apparently unhurt. He smiled as he murdered Jürgen. I thought I was next but that thing decided to let me live. He said he wanted me to go back to Berlin and tell others what I'd seen and what was coming for them. I walked out of there, not a scratch on me, not knowing if I was cursed or blessed to have survived."

"Probably a bit of both," Hans replied. "What did you tell your commander?"

"I went back to HQ and I had murder in mind. Hartz had sent me and my friends out to die; used us like sacrificial lambs to test the strength of the enemy. I wanted to make him pay for that. But I was too late, the vampyr had beaten me to it. I walked into the communications tent as the sun came up this morning. Everyone one was dead: Hartz, the radio operator, everyone. The canvas of the tent was slowly turning crimson from the inside out. I'd never seen so much blood in my life. I was standing there, trying to decide what to do, when I heard Goebbels on the radio, making a speech for our glorious leader's birthday. He was calling on all Germans to trust blindly in Hitler, saying the Führer would lead us out of our difficulties."

Hans had heard the same broadcast himself. He still couldn't decide whether the Propaganda Minister Dr Paul Joseph Goebbels was mad or merely playing some cold-blooded trick on the people of Germany. The Red Army was racing towards Berlin, determined to capture it before the American and British forces did from the west. The Fatherland was being torn apart as vengeance for the war Hitler had waged upon Europe and the rest of the world. Was the Führer determined to see Berlin burn too, a monument to his folly and insanity? But that was a question for another time, another day.

Otto grimaced. "When I heard that madness Goebbels was spouting, I knew where my true duty lay. My wife and daughter are cowering in a basement beneath our apartment building, less than a mile from the Reich Chancellery. When the Bolsheviks conquer Berlin, they'll extract a terrible price from our women for this war. God help us all if they unleash the vampyr upon the city. I'm going home to try and save my family. Either I get them out of Berlin, or I'll put them out of their misery and then turn the gun on myself." He produced a revolver and showed Hans the three bullets loaded inside it. "One for each of us, if the time comes."

Otto stopped so he could listen to the nearby Stalin's Organs firing at our retreating armies. "When the time comes."

Hans let Otto leave, not bothering to dissuade the veteran from his murderous plan. The war was lost. It was comforting to hope the Americans might reach Berlin first, but Hans knew that that was a false hope. These final days of April were the Reich's twilight. When it did fall, Hans had little doubt the invaders' revenge would be as terrible as Otto feared. Already the Russian forces were notorious for raping and pillaging as they advanced, like some Twentieth century army of Vikings, savouring the spoils of war. Berlin and its civilian populace could hope for no better treatment. The longer the war dragged on, the worst would be the backlash against the city's people. That was bad enough, but it chilled Hans's blood to discover that the vampyr were abroad in the midst of this madness, undead participants in this Götterdämmerung.

Karl found Hans sitting quietly alone. "You let the deserter go. Why?"

"One man more or less will make little difference now," Hans replied. "You've heard the same rumours as me… The Russians will be on the streets of Berlin within a week. That's where we should be too. Better to fight our battles where the buildings can offer us some refuge, yes?"

"Yes," Karl agreed. He studied Hans's face curiously. "What did the old man tell you?"

"Deep knife units are operating behind German lines, outflanking our defences."

"That's not a surprise."

Hans smiled thinly. "Some of these units are commanded by vampyr. Judging by the description Otto gave, Constanta may be among them, leading one of the units."

"God in heaven," Karl gasped. "The leader of the vampyr, here? Why would he risk getting involved in such a dangerous, unstable environment?"

"The end is close. My guess? Constanta wants to be in Berlin for the kill."

Karl stroked a hand nervously across his throat as if to protect it from the mere mention of Constanta's name. "We have to warn the others. Ralf and Gunther will want to know this too."

"That's my other reason for pulling back to the city. The four of us are stronger together than apart. The knowledge we have about how best to combat the vampyr could be vital in the days ahead. The fate of Germany could rest in our hands soon. Gather the Volkssturm and get them ready to move out. I'll address them in a few minutes and tell them about our new posting. We'll take them into Berlin and find a safer posting for the boys. After that, we go to Ralf and Gunther."

"Last message I had from Gunther, he and your brother were being transferred to one of the Flaktürme, but they weren't sure which one," Karl said.

Hans smiled. "Weren't you part of Hitler's private staff once?"

"Yes, before I got sent to Rumania."

"Good. I think it's time we made use of your contacts inside the Wehrmacht hierarchy."

Karl nodded. "What do you think will happen once the war is over?"

"An orgy of blood and torment and horror," Hans replied. "Then, once the vampyr have finished gorging themselves on the ruins of Berlin, they'll sink their teeth into the rest of Europe. The coming war will make this one look like a friendly skirmish by comparison."

RALF AND GUNTHER had spent a week atop the Humboldthain Flaktürme, a massive building in the northern area of Berlin that formed a key part of the city's defences. Three of these mighty structures had been built during the war, each blessed with concrete walls two metres thick and ceilings that were even thicker. They served as radio towers, platforms for anti-aircraft guns, hospitals and bomb shelters for civilians, and were able to house nearly 20,000 people each. So solid was each Flaktürme that Soviet tanks would struggle to scratch the exterior, even if firing at point blank range. Close to each structure stood a similar but slightly smaller satellite tower where spotters gathered information for the guns atop the main buildings.

When they arrived in Berlin, Ralf and Gunther reported for duty at the nearest barracks. They were quickly despatched to the Humboldthain, their experience with Panzer crews on the Ostfront marking the pair out as courageous, skilled fighters. Berlin needed such men more than ever, Ralf and Gunther were told. They arrived at the Flaktürme and quickly discovered the truth of that statement. The building was in disarray, overwhelmed by terrified civilians seeking shelter and sorely lacking in military resources.

The battle-hardened veterans removed themselves to the anti-aircraft gun emplacement atop the Flaktürme where both felt they could do the most good. Sleep became an ever more precious commodity as the rumble of Russian bombardments grew closer. Aerial attacks on Berlin grew more frenzied, with the Americans and British determined to crush any resistance from the German capital.

The Führer's birthday went uncelebrated at the Flak-türme. Nobody there felt like praising the leader they'd once hailed as the Fatherland's saviour. Ralf and Gunther spent the morning exhausting their meagre supply of anti-aircraft ammunition, combating aerial attacks on the city. By mid-afternoon both men were also spent, their reserves of energy all but a memory. They watched as the last British dive-bomber peeled away into the sky, leaving behind a devastated city of blazing buildings choked by a black cloud of smoke.

Ralf watched the other members of the anti-aircraft crew descend into the Flaktürme until only Gunther remained with him atop the tower. Once the two men had been part of a crack Panzer crew, driving their metal behemoth deep into enemy territory, striking at the heart of Germany's enemies. Now they were little more than bystanders of a war in its dying days, reduced to trying to swat the enemy from the sky. The pair sat down on the southern edge of the platform, their legs hanging down over the edge of the concrete building, looking out over the remains of Berlin.

"Sometimes, I wonder who are the real monsters in this war," Gunther muttered, "those bloodsucking fiends under Constanta's command, or our masters here in Berlin, condemning an entire nation to death so a few fools can go down in history. At least with the vampyr you faced an enemy you knew was motivated solely by its lust for blood. "

Ralf smiled at his friend, a little surprised by the comment. "I thought I was the bitter, twisted one and you were the cheerful optimist."

"Not anymore," Gunther replied, gesturing at the rubble and ruins splayed out below them, all that remained of the German capital. Every building within sight was pitted and scarred by Allied aerial bombardments. Once the Soviet artillery got into range, the damage would only get worse. Berlin faced devastation within a matter of days, a devastation from which it might never recover. Soon it would be indistinguishable from the remains of Stalingrad or a hundred other cities that had been lain waste by the war.

"What's left to be cheerful or optimistic about?" Gunther said quietly.

The smile faded from Ralf's soot-stained features. "We're still alive, if nothing else."

"But for how much longer?" Gunther asked. "We both know what's coming when this war ends... Constanta and his vampyr horde. They've had four years to prepare, learning all about us from our triumphs and our mistakes, our tactics and our weaknesses. Once the Russians have done their worst, the vampyr will move in to finish the job." Gunther spat over the side of the Flaktürme. "If push comes to shove, I'd rather be dead than undead, Ralf."

"Jump, if that's the way you feel," another voice commented. The two men twisted round to see Karl standing nearby. Beyond him Hans was clambering up through a hatchway on to the platform. "Because this could be your last chance."

Ralf stood up. "What do you mean?"

Hans closed the hatch so their conversation could remain private. "Constanta's been spotted to the east of Berlin, less than ten kilometres from here. He was leading a Soviet deep knife unit on a convert mission."

"What mission?" Gunther asked, joining his friends in the centre of the platform.

"We're not certain," Karl admitted. "Constanta's men slaughtered a Volkssturm company of old men but made sure at least one survivor got away to tell others what they'd seen."

"Typical vampyr tactics: let fear win half the battles for you before the real fighting starts," Ralf observed. "When the real fiends appear, most people are too scared to do anything about it. Constanta's smart, I'll give him that."

"We can't win against the vampyr," Karl said quietly. "They'll tear this city apart and bleed every man, woman and child dry. Then the dead will become undead and Constanta will have an army of vampyr to fight his blood war. It's hopeless."

"Sounds like you should be the one contemplating jumping, if that's how you feel," Gunther replied sharply. "I've got no intention of giving in to these bloodsucking bastards, no matter how overwhelming the odds may be."

"But you said—"

"I'd rather be dead than undead," Gunther snapped. "That doesn't mean I'm willing to surrender Berlin to Constanta and his unholy kinsmen. We've all seen what they can do, what they're capable of. God in heaven, even dying isn't a final defence from these monsters! In Leningrad they resurrected the fallen – German and Russian – to attack us. I say we've waited long enough. It's time we fought back, one way or another."

Ralf nodded. "Gunther's right. We did as you suggested, Karl, to keep our own counsel while the war was stumbling to its conclusion. But those days are behind us now. We need to talk to those in charge of the German war machine, and alert them to the danger everyone faces."

"How?" Karl wailed, hopelessness in his voice.

Hans clapped a hand on his comrade's shoulder. "You were once part of Hitler's personal guard, remember? I think it's high time you reclaimed that job."

"Precisely," Ralf agreed. "With your contacts, you can get us close to the Führer. Then one of us has to convince that madman about the threat the vampyr pose to the Fatherland."

"It was Hitler's obsession with the supernatural that brought the undead into this war," Gunther added. "He can hardly deny they exist. He sent you with that envoy to Transylvania eight months ago, to try and convince Constanta to stay on our side against the Bolsheviks."

Hans shook his head. "I wouldn't be so sure about that. When Karl and I got assigned to shepherding the Volkssturm, we heard about a systematic purge of the Wehrmacht's official archives. They've destroyed anything in the files that even hints at Hitler's unholy alliance with the undead. The generals know the war is lost. All they care about now is protecting their reputation as noble soldiers. When the war is over, I doubt there'll be a single piece of evidence left to prove the Wehrmacht had anything to do with Constanta and his kind."

"That could work to our advantage," Ralf suggested. "If the purge is as ruthless as you say, it'll have wiped away any record of what we did at Ordzhonikidze in 1941. Should anyone ask questions about us, our files won't be there to betray us."

"Let's hope you're right," Gunther muttered.

"We have to try getting close to the Führer," Hans insisted. "He's the only one who can publicly declare war on the vampyr. Unless that happens, the German people will be like lambs to the slaughter, unaware that there are far worse enemies than the Red Army abroad in this conflict."

Karl bit his bottom lip nervously. "I don't know," he muttered. "I'm not sure I can get my old posting back. Even if I did, there's no guarantee I'll be able to get any of us close to Hitler."

Ralf rubbed a tired hand across the back of his neck. "You've got to try, Karl. You're our best hope of stopping this madness before it's too late."

# Two

I CAN STILL remember the night I first saw the blueprints for the Nazi's first nuclear weapon. It was the night of Hitler's last birthday, in April 1945. The Red Army had been surging towards Berlin in two distinct attacks, one from the east and another from the south-east. Our deep knife unit was active about twenty kilometres ahead of the latter attack, operating well behind the German defensive positions. Normally Gorgo kept the squad together as a single force, but that night he split the group into two. One of his vampyr bodyguards remained with the bulk of the commandos on the outskirts of a town called Luckenwalde. But the Rumanian sergeant chose a handful from among his troops for a special mission, travelling further north.

Inevitably, he picked his other bodyguard and the five who had been smert krofpeet before joining the deep knife unit: myself, Mariya, the Borjigin brothers and Eisenstein. In the eight months since we came under Gorgo's leadership, his thralls had been whittled away by the war. Every few weeks the sergeant would recruit a

119

fresh crop of recruits from the Red Army's ranks, but they never lasted long. Reducing them to almost mindless drones made them effective as slaves but far less effective as soldiers.

By the time we were within fifty kilometres of Berlin, I doubted there was a single one from the original thralls still alive. Whenever Gorgo needed fighters for a particular mission, he always turned to the few free minds he had at his command.

So it was I found myself helping a vampyr and his bloodsucking bodyguard break into a secret German scientific facility nestled in a small valley outside the settlement of Gottow on the night of April 20th. The research centre was basic in construction; simply a rectangular cluster of long wooden buildings, all grouped together behind two concentric barbed wire fences. The sole entrance was a broad set of barbed wire gates beneath which a set of railway tracks had been laid, disappearing into the largest of the buildings.

We had located the research centre by following a siding from a major train line that passed by a kilometre to the west of the facility. Raised lookout towers stood at the front corners of the encampment with guards inside sweeping the surrounding countryside with searchlights, cutting broad arcs across the pine forests and gently undulating hillocks. The seven of us observed the research centre for more than an hour from the shelter of a wooded copse, watching the guards go through a well-worn routine. The sentries were plainly not expecting an attack of any kind. They looked well fed and comfortable; nothing that would offer us any significant resistance. When I questioned Gorgo about the need for such caution, he sneered at me dismissively. "If those inside the facility realise they are under attack, they will destroy the secrets I seek. Stealth has its uses, mortal."

Once Gorgo was satisfied with his assessment of our target, he sent the two Mongolians to infiltrate the

perimeter fences, accompanied by one of his bodyguards
to make sure they obeyed orders. I had grown fond of
the Borjigin brothers over the preceding eight months,
even learning a few words and phrases of their native
tongue. The pair had been far more adept at picking up
a mixture of Russian, German and even some Rumanian,
enough for them to hold a halting conversation with any
of us. It transpired that the two brothers were identical
twins: Baatar and Saikhan. Roughly translated, their
names meant warrior and peace respectively. Since none
of us could tell them apart, I took to calling both of them
Baatar and left it at that. The others adopted the same
system which pleased the twins. They seemed to enjoy
the anonymity of being interchangeable, sharing many a
joke between them followed by their gruff but friendly
laughter.

The twins were adept thieves and burglars, able to penetrate almost any defence. They slipped beneath the lazy
sweep of the searchlights and cut a path through both
barbed wire fences, Gorgo's bodyguard close behind.
Within minutes the Rumanian gave us the "all-clear"
signal from atop the nearest watchtower, having dealt
with the sentry inside. The rest of us crept forward,
staying low to the ground, and not wishing to attract the
attention of any German soldiers outside of the perimeter
fence. We'd seen no evidence of external patrols, but that
didn't mean they weren't out there. By the time we were
all inside the fences, the twins had slit the throats of the
remaining watchtower sentries. Gorgo told the Mongolians to remain outside with his bodyguard and Mariya,
while the sergeant chose Eisenstein and I to go inside
with him.

"I want you two where I can see you," the Rumanian
hissed when I questioned his decision.

Eisenstein was a changed man since our departure
from Transylvania the previous autumn. All the time we
were within the boundaries of the vampyr heartland, I

was never sure I could trust him. But once we passed beyond that place of darkness and horror, he became much more like the Eisenstein I had grown to trust like a father during the Siege of Leningrad. He still carried the vampyr taint upon him, and it was plainly a heavy burden for any soul to sustain, no matter what their belief system. But he regained some of the dry humour and wit I had known before. The further we got from Castle Constanta, the more like his old self Eisenstein became. I realised Mariya had been right to argue for sparing our comrade's life. His soul might be damned or doomed, but he was still on our side in this war... And the next, when it came.

As midnight passed and Friday became Saturday, Gorgo led Eisenstein and me from one building to the next at the research facility. The first resembled a munitions factory, although I did not recognise much of the equipment stored inside the unlit structure. The second building held massive devices I'd heard much about but had never seen before: V1 flying bombs. Propaganda broadcasts from Moscow had told us about new weapons of terror being unleashed by the Nazis; unmanned rockets that dropped from the sky and exploded on impact with the ground. Fortunately for the Russian people these weapons of destruction had been predominantly directed at targets on the western front of the war in Europe.

To stand beside one of these powerful devices was a sobering experience, even after all I'd seen during the war. The fuselage resembled a long, metal cigar, with large wings attached one-third of the way back from its pointed nosecone and smaller wings near the tail. Fixed atop the fuselage was another cylinder that was slightly larger at its front end. I decided that it must be the pulse jet engine which generated the sputtering sound said to be so characteristic of the V1.

The bomb was deceptively simple in its outward appearance. It had been painted a dull grey-green, but there was no swastika adorning the seven-metre long fuselage. The bomb's wingspan was more than five metres. When seen from below while flying, it would resemble an unholy kind of crucifix. But the V1 brought death, not salvation or redemption.

Behind the V1 was a similar bomb, but that one had a glass canopy fitted over a small cockpit on the main fuselage, just in front of the intake ring for the pulse jet engine. That must be the piloted version of the V1, I realised, also known as the Reichenberg. Heaven help the poor bastard who has to fly that thing, I thought. Such a task was little more than suicide. The rear of the Reichenberg was sat atop a metal trolley, with gas canisters and hydraulic equipment linking the trolley to the V1. That must be some sort of launch mechanism, I reasoned, providing the rocket with sufficient power to launch it from the ground. No doubt the device would be stripped apart by our scientists once they reached this facility, for transportation back to Russia so the technology could be studied.

Gorgo hissed at me to pay attention. He had been briefing Eisenstein while my thoughts were elsewhere. "Our target should be in the next building. It contains his laboratory and his private quarters. The target's name is Kurt Rainer and he's a German physicist working on a special project for the Nazis."

"How will we know what he looks like?" I asked.

"My Lord Constanta and I were introduced to Rainer last summer when we visited Berlin. The Führer summoned the physicist to show us what he'd been developing. It was Hitler's way of showing us the Germans still had the upper hand in their war with your people."

"Why would a physicist be working at a rocket assembly facility?" Eisenstein asked. "What has Rainer developed for the Nazis?"

Gorgo's face darkened into a snarl, his lips drawing back to show his fangs. "You don't need to know that, human. Just do as I say or else…"

"Or else what?"

The Rumanian's eyes lit up. "If I do not succeed, my bodyguard waiting outside has orders to rip open your comrades' throats and bathe in their blood. I doubt either of you wish to see the Borjigin brothers murdered only to be resurrected as my thralls." Gorgo sneered at me. "And we all know how Zunetov feels about Charnosova. She will be violated in the most savage of ways before her life is taken. I'll make both of you watch unless you do as I say. Understand?"

Eisenstein grimaced. "We understand, you soulless parasite."

"That's better."

Gorgo turned and marched out of the rocket storage building, his bodyguard shoving a rifle into my back to get me moving. I stumbled after the Rumanian, my head still filled with the horrific images he'd planted there. Mariya and I had grown close in the months since we first met, but neither of us had acknowledged the strength of our feelings for each other. We thought we were being discreet. Plainly, that notion had been fool-hardy.

Eisenstein strode along beside me, moving close enough to whisper in my left ear. "I told you having a woman in any unit was a mistake, but you didn't listen, did you?"

I kept my own counsel, knowing it would gladden the vampyr to see me arguing with my mentor. Eisenstein and I had been through too much to let Gorgo turn us against each other. Ahead of us Gorgo thrust open the door to the next building and strode inside, paying no heed to the lack of lighting and making no attempt to conceal his arrival. The Rumanian's arrogance was almost our undoing as we followed him in, the vampyr bodyguard close at our heels.

Once all four of us were inside, the door slammed shut and the building's interior was flooded with light. Most of the space was filled with wooden benches, each one laden with scientific equipment. At the far end of the space I could see a frightened man in a white laboratory coat peering over the top of a bench. But most of my attention was focused on the twelve men in grey uniforms waiting in a loose semicircle and facing our position. A dozen German soldiers were standing between us and our target, all of them armed and ready to fire.

Eisenstein spat a curse at our commander. "You fool! You've lead us into an ambush!"

Gorgo glanced over his shoulder at us, gleeful malevolence in his black eyes. "Twelve of them against four of us? I call that a slaughter, not an ambush."

He threw both arms out sideways and screamed at the enemy soldiers, his cry a terrifying cacophony of sound and fury. The Germans staggered backwards, deafened by Gorgo's aural onslaught. The Rumanian faded into a mist, his face and form still visible amidst the cloud as it rose into the air. Behind us Gorgo's bodyguard threw aside his weapon, preferring to flash his fangs at the terrified sentries. One man among the guards stood his ground, the insignia on his uniform marking him out as a gefreiter.

"Stand your ground!" he bellowed at the others. "There are only four of them! Fire at will!"

Eisenstein and I were moving targets before the German soldiers had time to react, sprinting in opposite directions. As I ran I opened fire with my submachine gun, spraying the sentries with bullets and not bothering to aim carefully. There were so many of them huddled together beneath the spectral cloud of Gorgo that it was more like butchery than battle. Meanwhile Eisenstein was shooting out the massive lights suspended from the ceiling, each bulb exploding in a flash, showering the Germans below with shards of hot glass. By the time I'd reached the cover of a nearby laboratory bench, all but one of the lights were shattered and half the sentries were dead or dying on the concrete, blood seeping out into a pool beneath them.

The gefreiter was shooting up at the ceiling where Gorgo was hovering in the air while screaming at the other soldiers to join in. Some followed his example but their bullets passed uselessly through the insubstantial wraith. The remaining Germans were dividing their fire between the other vampyr, Eisenstein and me. Gorgo's bodyguard marched slowly and deliberately towards the enemy, grinning at them. The sentries fired round after round into his chest and head, wounds that would have killed an ordinary man a dozen times over, but their target was no ordinary man. The vampyr chose one of the soldiers at random and slashed a set of razor-sharp talons across the guard's neck, ripping through skin and bone and tendons, a spray of blood flying sideways from the fatal wound.

Eisenstein and I concentrated our fire on the rest of the sentries, not caring whether we hit Gorgo's bodyguard or not since he was all but immune to our weapons. Within a minute every one of the Germans bar the gefreiter were dead, shot to pieces by us or torn apart by the vampyr. The bodyguard had the sole survivor in his grasp, talons clasping the front of the gefreiter's bloodstained uniform. The vampyr was stretching forward, ready to plunge his fangs into the German's neck, but a snarl from Gorgo halted him.

The sergeant floated back down to the ground, his gaseous form solidifying once more. Once fully corporeal again, Gorgo strode towards his bodyguard, snapping at the underling in Rumanian. The Transylvanian dialect was beyond my understanding but the meaning was clear: Gorgo was claiming the right to slay the troublesome gefreiter for himself. The bodyguard acknowledged the will of his master, not noticing that the German soldier was retrieving a wooden stake from the concrete floor.

The gefreiter stabbed his crude weapon deep into the vampyr's body. The creature cried out in anguish, looking down in dismay at the stump protruding from its chest before exploding into a cloud of dust and ash. Gorgo stopped in his tracks, startled by the sudden demise of his bodyguard. The Rumanian faded into mist once more, disappearing before our eyes.

Moments later he reappeared behind the gefreiter, his fingers already closing round the enemy soldier's neck. One vicious, sideways twist and the last German sentry was dead, slaughtered like the rest of his men. Gorgo lifted the gefreiter's body into the air and threw it against a wall with a sickening thud, the impact so severe it must have shattered every bone inside the still-warm corpse. Gorgo moved to where his bodyguard had been killed, the dust and ash slowly settling on the floor. The Rumanian crouched on the cold concrete, letting his fingers touch the remains of his comrade as if he was caressing the dead vampyr.

Eisenstein and I emerged from where we'd taken cover, carefully approaching Gorgo. Neither of us had seen him act this way before, never seen him show any concern or affection for those under his charge. Had the bodyguard been someone important to him? A relative, perhaps a friend, or even something more? It was hard to imagine vampyr having families or friendships as we did. Their violence and bloodlust were so alien, so inhuman, that it defied belief to think of them as anything but supernatural monstrosities. But Gorgo was evidently hurt by what had happened to his bodyguard, so much so it was if he'd been on the end of that wooden stake.

A glass container shattered at the other end of the building. Gorgo, Eisenstein and I spun round, tensed and ready for another attack. There was a single living

soul left in that space with us: a quaking, terrified man
clasping the lapels of his white laboratory coat. He stood
beneath the remaining light, bathed in its illumination,
with fragments of glass strewn at his feet.

"Dr Rainer, I presume," Gorgo snarled in German.
"We've come a long way to find you, doctor, sent here
on orders of the Lord Constanta himself. Those orders
have cost me the life of one of my most trusted com-
panions. If I were you, I'd pray the effort was worth it,
otherwise your suffering and torment shall be long and
exquisite."

Rainer was a slight man with sallow skin and grey,
thinning hair scraped over a balding pate. He had small,
circular glasses perched on the tip of his prominent nose
and trembling afflicted his liver-spotted hands.

"What are you?" he asked meekly. "What do you
want?"

"You've already seen what I am," Gorgo replied imperiously. He moved towards the scientist, nonchalantly
stepping over the corpses of the German guards. The
vampyr paused by the last of them, removing three stick
grenades from his waist belts. His fearsome appearance
had so terrified the soldiers that they'd never thought to
use the explosive devices. Eisenstein and I followed
Gorgo, intrigued to discover what was so important that
Constanta himself had assigned Gorgo to come here
looking for it.

"As for what I want," the Rumanian continued, "well,
I think you already know the answer to that question,
don't you?"

Rainer gestured at the scientific equipment around
him. Much of it had been destroyed in the brief but
bloody battle, leaving little evidence of whatever
research was being done here. "My project? But it's still
years away from being complete. Besides, your men,
they've just destroyed much of what I've been working
on these past six months."

By now Gorgo was within reach of the doctor. He rested a hand gently on Rainer's left shoulder, as if he was a disappointed teacher quietly reprimanding a schoolboy who hadn't finished his homework.

"Please, Dr Rainer, let's not start with lies and deceptions, shall we? You and I both know the equipment in this laboratory has little to do with your true purpose here at Gottow. All of this," Gorgo gestured grandly at our surroundings, "is merely an illusion, a ruse constructed to hide the real work of this facility. Much like the V1 bombers in the adjoining building are there to fool the Allies when they reach this site in a few days. No, I'm talking about what is hidden underneath us." All trace of good humour vanished from the vampyr's face. "The Wunderwaffe, as you Germans rather grandly like to call it, the Wonder Weapon."

"I don't know what you're talking about," the scientist pleaded, his face all innocence and bewilderment.

Gorgo withdrew his hand from Rainer's shoulder, shifting it sideways to grasp the meek man's throat. Slowly, steadily, the Rumanian tightened his grip, threatening to squeeze the life from his captive while lifting him off the ground. Rainer's legs kicked and thrashed at Gorgo, while the scientist's hands tore at the talons crushing his neck, all to no avail.

"Stop it," Eisenstein said. "You're killing him!"

Gorgo twisted round to glare at my comrade. "Don't ever tell me what you do."

"Grigori's right," I interjected. "If you slay this scientist, you'll never learn his secrets. What would Constanta have to say about that?"

The Rumanian's face contorted with anger. For a moment I thought he might snap Rainer's neck out of spite, but instead he released the little German. Rainer fell to the floor, choking and gasping for breath, livid red marks evident on his throat. Gorgo waited until the scientist had regained some composure before crouching beside him.

"Well, Dr Rainer, what's it to be? Will you share what you've found out, or do I risk my master's wrath by slaughtering you?" The Rumanian smirked. "Perhaps I will make you my thrall, a worthless slave defiling yourself for my amusement, begging for table leavings, licking the blood from your countrymen's corpses?"

Rainer whimpered, a dark stain appearing round the crotch of his brown corduroy trousers as urine seeped through the fabric, dripping on to the concrete. "I'll show you," he conceded. "I'll tell you what you want to know."

"That's better." Gorgo straightened up, rubbing his hands together. "Well, lead on!"

The scientist scrambled to his feet, one hand feebly trying to hide the wet patch on his trousers. Rainer retreated to the far corner of the building and pulled down a lever on the wall. The laboratory bench he had been standing near slid aside, revealing a set of stairs leading down into a brightly lit basement. Gorgo sent Eisenstein down first to make certain there were no more soldiers waiting. After a minute my comrade reappeared at the foot of the stairs, calling up to us.

"There are five more scientists down here, but they're all dead. Looks like mass suicide, probably capsules of prussic acid. No more sentries in sight, and no other entrances or exits."

Satisfied, Gorgo sent Rainer down next before following me into the basement area. I was surprised to see how vast the underground chamber was, perhaps four times the size of the building above it. In fact the secret research laboratory was equivalent to the space covered by the entire facility. Constanta obviously had access to extremely accurate intelligence. Whatever the Germans had been developing here, it must be of great importance to merit such elaborate precautions. But what could this Wonder Weapon be, and why did the vampyr desire it?

Gorgo examined one of the dead scientists, checking Eisenstein's assessment of what killed them. An attractive blonde woman in her early thirties was sprawled on the cold floor, white foam seeping from her red lips, bright blue eyes staring accusingly at us.

The Rumanian grinned wolfishly up at Rainer. "You should have committed suicide down here with your comrades, doctor. That would have been an honourable death."

"You took us by surprise," the scientist replied weakly. "My assistant Inga was always saying I should keep one of the capsules with me at all times in case the worst happened." He turned away from the dead woman's gaze, not wanting to look at her corpse. "I never listened."

Gorgo stood up and folded his arms, glaring expectantly at the scientist. "I've come a long way to hear what you've discovered down here, Dr Rainer. Don't keep me waiting."

"No, of course not. I just need a few moments to gather my papers..." The small man bustled away, moving around the room, snatching papers, diagrams and blueprints from the various research areas. Finally he came back with armfuls of documentation, his head tilted back to stop the larger rolls of paper jabbing him in the nose. Rainer paused beside a large wooden table, two metres wide and twice as long. It was littered with plates, cups and cutlery. This must have been where the scientists ate their meals. A row of bunks against a nearby wall suggested they had slept down here. Now the men and women had died here too.

"Would you mind clearing a space for me?" the surviving scientist asked meekly.

Gorgo nodded to Eisenstein who lifted up one end of the long table and tipped its contents on to the floor.

Once the surface was cleared Rainer dumped everything he'd gathered on top of it, briskly sorting his documents into a rough order of importance. Finally satisfied with his arrangement, the little scientist pushed his glasses up his nose and began the remarkable, almost unbelievable tale of what the research team had discovered in this subterranean facility. I did my best to memorise his story in Russian so I could relay the details of it to Eisenstein later. My mentor had picked up a lot of German words and phrases in recent months, but needed me to fill in the blanks. I knew this would be such an occasion.

"FOR YEARS THERE have been wild theories and concepts circulating in the scientific community for a new kind of bomb," Rainer began. "What could be called nuclear bomb, I suppose. In 1938 Fritz Strassman and Otto Hahn published a paper proving an Italian physicist had witnessed a uranium nucleus being split, resulting in nuclear fission. Once news of this spread among my peers, the race was on to describe the theoretical mechanism of this fission. It soon became obvious that large amounts of energy could be released by this process if it was replicated on a larger scale.

"When the war began, the scientific community knew German physicists were leading the world in this bold new area of study. Many of my colleagues pressed for the establishment of a programme to develop nuclear weapons, so they became reality instead of theory. But those in charge of the purse strings did not believe such weapons would be ready for use during the war.

"The progress of the Wehrmacht was such that nobody in Berlin believed we would ever have a need for such devices." The scientist eased off his glasses and pinched the bridge of his nose between thumb and forefinger, gently massaging the area where his spectacles usually rested.

"That was our first mistake. By neglecting this new field, we allowed the British and Americans to catch up and overtake us. I've heard tell of a project in the United States that employs thousands of men and women, all racing to create a stable bomb using this new technology." He gestured at the handful of dead colleagues nearby. "As you can see, we've never had such resources."

"The weapon," Gorgo growled. "Tell me about the weapon!"

"Of course," Rainer replied, easing his glasses back on. His trembling hands smoothed up a coiled blueprint and then unrolled the indigo paper to display a complex schematic imprinted on it. "When the Ostfront ground to a halt in 1942, several separate groups of physicists pressed for the funding to pursue nuclear weaponry. At least three different research efforts were officially sanctioned: one led by Werner Heisenberg at the Kaiser Wilhelm Institute, a military team headed by Professor Kurt Diebner, and another cluster of scientists led by Dr Paul Harteck, operating under the auspices of the Kriegsmarine."

"Why would the German navy be interested in this weaponry?" I asked, intrigued.

Gorgo snarled at me and I fell silent, not wanting to antagonise our Rumanian commander further.

"Harteck's group was developing the gaseous uranium centrifuge invented by Dr Erich Bagge," Rainer explained. "It was hoped this could be utilised for a new U-boat propulsion system. My role was to move between the competing projects, using the progress of one team against the others in order to apply pressure. In fact, I had a secondary and far more significant job. I was responsible for collating the results of all three teams and bringing them here where an independent group of physicists and rocket scientists could identify the best elements from each group.

"By the end of 1944, it became obvious that the Wehrmacht was losing the war and everything that happened afterwards would merely delay the inevitable. I was summoned to Berlin and brought before the Führer. He gave me a new mission: to create a single weapon that could reverse the course of the war and guarantee that Germany's borders remained sacrosanct. It was Hitler who coined the name Wunderwaffe: the Wonder Weapon."

The physicist pointed at the diagrams beneath his hands. Gorgo moved closer for a better view, allowing me a glimpse of the designs. The Wonder Weapon looked no different from any other bomb to my eyes, and certainly less advanced than the V1 we had passed earlier. But Rainer's words made it obvious that the impact of this weapon could be catastrophic.

"As I understand it, the Americans have spent millions creating an atomic bomb, a primitive nuclear fission device. We abandoned such a course since we lacked the time and resources. Instead I had my colleagues concentrate on constructing a bomb made of conventional high explosives, but packed around a nuclear core. It would be a tactical battlefield weapon we could deploy against the Bolsheviks. If it worked, the bomb would detonate in midair, spraying deadly radioactive particles over a wide area. Everything caught in the blast radius would die in an instant. Everything within a hundred kilometres' radius of the explosion would perish from radioactive poisoning within a few days: crops, animals, humans, everything. The explosion would also create a massive cloud of particles in the air, blocking out the sun, almost turning day into night."

"How long would this cloud block out the sun?" Gorgo asked eagerly.

"Days, even weeks," the scientist said, frowning a little at the specific nature of the question. "It would depend upon local weather conditions. Rather than immediately disperse as a normal cloud would, this one would slowly shift sideways, transported by the natural movement of the planet. I suppose you could call it a kind of shroud, turning a summer's day into a wintry night. Crops would fail, temperatures would fall, and people would not see the sun for long spells."

"And how far did you get with this bomb of yours?"

"We have been detonating small test devices for months. The first explosion was at a small island off the coast of northern Germany last October. We had no idea whether it would work or not, nor the effects of the explosion. I had a massive concrete bunker built as a safety precaution, with glass windows half a metre thick through which to watch the detonation.

"When it came, the ground shook beneath our feet and there was a sudden, blinding flash of light. I was wearing tinted goggles, but for several hours afterwards I kept seeing the blast whenever I closed my eyes. Bear in mind, this device was a fraction of the size of the bomb we planned to build, yet its effects were utterly devastating. Once the initial flash of light had passed, I saw a thick cloud of smoke rising upwards in a column before it blossomed out into the shape of a flower."

The scientist fell silent, staring into the distance, his thoughts elsewhere. Gorgo closed a hand on Rainer's shoulder, bringing him back to the present.

"We stayed in the bunker for several hours to avoid any problems from exposure to the bomb's aftermath. I made everyone put on clothes and masks lined with asbestos as added protection before we visited the site of the explosion on the other side of the island. The effects were startling, to say the least. Trees had been reduced to carbon in a matter of moments: no leaves, no life, nothing. We had penned a dozen sheep in the blast area to test how the weapon affected animal tissue. They were all burnt to cinders. I had never seen anything like it before in my life.

"The scientists among us were sickened by the spectacle but it seemed to excite our military masters. They wanted more bombs, larger examples and more testing. I did as I was told, followed my orders, helped my colleagues here construct a device twice the size and scale of the first one. We were not permitted to know where that would be tested. I only found out about the results by chance after the base commander here left me waiting in his office with the report open on his desk. He thought me a meek, terrified creature, too scared of my own shadow to cause trouble, and he was right. But my own curiosity got the better of me, so I glanced through the contents of that report. If seeing the first blast for myself had been disturbing, the notes and photographs contained in that folder were far worse."

Rainer shuffled his papers and produced a pair of monochrome images; stark portrayals of what had happened near the town of Ohrdruf seven weeks earlier, in March 1945. The pictures showed malnourished prisoners loading shapes on to massive wooden platforms. I caught a glimpse of the photographs and flinched.

We'd heard of Nazi resettlement camps where Jews and others considered undesirable by the German hierarchy were sent to work and to suffer, gassed to death in clinically efficient chambers, their corpses burned in gigantic incinerators. The men in the pictures were mere skin and bones, gaunt-faced ghosts, no doubt survivors of the camps. But it was the shapes they were moving that shocked me: bodies covered in horrific burns, skin and flesh scorched away, bones protruding whitely from seared and blackened surroundings. Human bodies, burnt alive by some apocalyptic blast or fire. Rainer stared dully at the images, his own eyes now inured to the atrocities depicted by them.

"I managed to sneak those out of the commander's office to show the others what was being done with our work. The generals in Berlin had taken our second device and detonated it over a concentration camp to test how effective the weapon was against live human subjects. Afterwards they had prisoners from the nearby camp at Buchenwald pile the scorched remains on to cremation platforms and the evidence was destroyed. Even the report sent to my commander had been marked for burning once he'd read its contents. It wouldn't surprise me if those in power have done everything possible to conceal this project from history. They know a reckoning is coming and they fear what those who shall sit in judgement upon them will say."

"You showed these pictures to your colleagues?" Gorgo asked, gesturing towards the bodies of those who'd committed suicide rather than be taken prisoner alive.

"I felt they deserved to know the truth. After that, we agreed to do everything in our power to sabotage the project. If the Führer or some other madman had gotten hold of the full-sized Wunderwaffe we'd been constructing, the fallout from its devastation might have plunged all of Europe into a wintry midnight that could have lasted for months, even years. We were determined to make sure that that didn't happen.

"Little by little, piece by piece, we've been destroying the plans and paperwork for the doomsday device Hitler wanted us to construct. I had hoped to complete that task sooner but the military contingent at this facility became suspicious of our actions. I was upstairs trying to explain to the gefreiter and enlist his aid, when you arrived." Rainer fell silent, his story at an end, his hands resting listlessly atop the blueprints and photographs.

Gorgo studied the collection of documents and schematics, one hand thoughtfully stroking his chin. "My Lord Constanta was right to send me here," the Rumanian finally said to Rainer. "You will accompany me back to Transylvania where you will be given every resource, every asset, every assistance you need to make one of these Wunderwaffen – a full-sized device. When the time is right, we shall detonate it over the centre of Europe, creating this everlasting winter you speak of. Our kind will be able to feed whenever they wish, and will not have to skulk in the shadows or hide from the sunlight anymore. We shall be free to carry out our every whim, every desire. The people of Europe shall be our prey, our cattle, our carrion. We shall gorge ourselves on the blood of nations, savouring every last drop. This continent shall be our dominion!"

"No." Eisenstein stepped forward, aiming his submachine gun at Gorgo. "I can't allow that to happen. You and your kind are an abomination that deserves to be wiped from the face of the earth. I won't allow you to make science the tool for your triumph."

"And how do you intend to stop me?" Gorgo asked, chuckling at him.

"Any way I can."

"But you forget yourself, Jew," the Rumanian sneered, his good humour fading away. "You are one of us; you carry the vampyr urge inside your body."

"I bear your taint, your infection," Eisenstein whispered, "but you do not control me! I may share your thirst for blood but I can resist that thirst and I can resist you."

"Perhaps, but not forever. One day it will get the better of you, and when that day comes, you shall live in the night ever afterwards."

Gorgo took a step closer to Eisenstein, his hand reaching out towards the PPSh, his eyes boring into those of my comrade.

"Give me the weapon. It cannot harm me. You cannot harm me. I am all but immortal, sired by my Lord Constanta, who was made immortal by the Sire himself. I am but two steps from godhood, Jew. You should bow down and pray before me."

"You're right," Eisenstein said, his face a tumult of emotion. "I can't hurt you, can't stop you... Not with this weapon. But I can stop your sick, evil plans for humanity."

Gorgo shook his head, lips curling with disdain. "It is over for you."

Eisenstein turned to look at Rainer, his eyes full of compassion. "I'm sorry."

Before Gorgo had time to react, Eisenstein opened fire at the German scientist, putting an entire magazine into Rainer's body. The physicist collapsed to the floor, his torso punctured more than a dozen times, a spray of blood and bone spattering the area behind him as he fell. Gorgo screamed in anger, his fangs revealed as his lips drew back, his face flushed crimson with rage.

"What have you done?" he demanded.

"Saved the people of Europe from what you'd have done to them," Eisenstein replied. He smiled wistfully at me, mouthing the word "goodbye" as he let the PPSh fall from his grasp.

Gorgo ripped my mentor to shreds, flailing at his body with razor-sharp talons long after all life must have departed from the tattered, torn corpse. The Rumanian raged and roared, pounding his fists upon Eisenstein's chest, each blow accompanied by a hollow popping sound as another rib was snapped into pieces. Still not satisfied, Gorgo snatched up the discarded submachine gun and used it as a club to beat the body until it was a bloody pulp, all but unrecognisable.

Finally, his anger spent, Gorgo turned on me. I backed away, expecting at any moment to suffer the same grisly fate as my friend.

"As for you..." he snarled, his breath hitting my face as hot puffs of air stinking of rotten blood and decay. "You can gather all these papers together and bring them with you. The Jew may have denied me possession of Rainer himself, but we still have all the notes and blueprints for the Wunderwaffe. The vampyr may not be able to deploy the weapon this year, but with these it could still become a reality in the future."

He watched as I did his bidding, carefully folding and rolling the papers before sealing them into a knapsack. Once I'd finished, Gorgo ripped the pack from my grasp and pointed at the nearby steps.

"Get out."

I did as he commanded but paused long enough to see him activate the stick grenades he'd taken upstairs. The vampyr tossed the three devices into the centre of the chamber before striding briskly towards the stairs.

"I told you to move," he snarled at me. I rushed up into the building above the concealed laboratory, Gorgo hard at my heels. Once at ground level, he activated the lever that returned the bench to its usual position over the staircase concealing the secret laboratory underneath. Within moments three dull thuds sounded beneath our feet and the floor trembled. I could smell burning and smoke began to seep out from under the bench. The Rumanian gave a grim smile of satisfaction.

"That place will become your comrade's tomb."

He shoved me back the way we'd come, and we hurried past the cooling corpses of slaughtered German soldiers and the dusty remains of the vampyr bodyguard. We marched outside, ignoring the nearby building with its cargo of V1 rockets. They were not important to Gorgo.

I had lost my best friend, someone who meant more to me than my own father. Grigori had been more of a father than my real one ever had. But the sad, horrible truth of Eisenstein's death didn't hit me until we were reunited with Mariya, the Borjigin brothers and Gorgo's surviving bodyguard. The four of them saw us coming and looked puzzled, expecting to see two more in our group. Mariya waited until I'd reached her before asking what had happened to Eisenstein.

"He's dead," I said. "Gorgo murdered him."

"I executed him for insubordination," the Rumanian interjected. "He disobeyed my direct orders and killed a scientist with information valuable to the vampyr war effort."

"You enjoyed every second of it," I spat at him.

"Yes," he replied, grinning broadly. "It's too long since I killed a worthy adversary. The Jew was many things – a thorn in my Lord Constanta's side, an irritant to our crusade – but he was also a brave man. That's why I made sure his funeral pyre would be a suitable memorial."

Behind us, the building where Eisenstein's body lay exploded. A massive fireball curled up into the sky, followed by a mushroom cloud of black smoke. I didn't want to think about what had caused the blast or what was being thrown into the atmosphere. If Rainer and his team had been experimenting with such hazardous materials, the chemicals spilling from that laboratory could be a toxic time bomb for this region of Germany.

Mariya took one of my hands in her own, giving it a squeeze. "Maybe it's for the best."

"I know. He's at peace now; his suffering is at an end. Grigori doesn't have to carry his burden any longer… I'm almost happy for him."

Deep down inside, I wanted to weep for my dead friend, but I'd lost the ability to cry during the Siege of Leningrad. Somehow the torments of those long months had stolen away all the tears from my eyes. Most of the time I was grateful for this, but that night I wanted to weep and couldn't. I hoped Grigori could understand, wherever he was. I wasn't sure I understood anything about this bloody war anymore. I had long suspected the war would be the death of us all, but I had never expected Eisenstein to perish before me.

# Three

It took Karl four days to talk his way back into the Führer's personal bodyguard, with Hans, Ralf and Gunther joining him at the new posting. The rumours Hans had heard about Wehrmacht files being purged was proven correct. Nobody questioned the four Panzergrenadiers about their backgrounds since there were far more pressing matters to worry about.

The Russians had advanced through the outskirts of Berlin, and then into the suburbs. By April 25th the city was encircled, with little hope of relief from the remaining German forces still fighting nearby. The capital's civilian population of women, children and the elderly were trapped, hiding in basements and tunnels, praying for a miracle they knew would not come.

The presence of Red Army troops on the streets meant dive-bombers could no longer target the city. Instead the capital was being pounded into submission by near-constant artillery barrages, with Stalin's Organs singing day and night as they bombarded the broken buildings and boulevards of Berlin.

The four Panzergrenadiers received official notification of their new postings as they were evacuating the final few wounded from the Humboldthain Flaktürme. The quartet were directed to make their way into central Berlin and wait outside the Reich Chancellery on the Wilhelmstrasse at dusk. None of them had been near the centre of the city since the Red Army entered Germany. For Hans, Ralf and Gunther, it was their first visit into the capital. All of them had seen its stunning architecture in newsreels shown to civilians before the war. But what they found on the Wilhelmstrasse was almost unrecognisable as the place designed to stand as a National Socialist monument for a millennium and beyond. The buildings were bombed out wrecks, the windows long since destroyed. Once proud banners were mere scraps of cloth, hanging limply from broken flagpoles.

The streets were piled high with rubble and abandoned vehicles. No surface had been left untouched by the Allies' merciless onslaught. Every wall was damaged, every surface pitted and scarred, every corner revealed another crumbling ruin where grandeur had once stood.

Amazingly, in the midst of all this chaos, a few civilians tried to continue with their lives by standing in line for rations of meat and bread and butter, or collecting water from one of the few out-pipes still flowing freely in the benighted city. Berlin was close to collapse, its only sign of resistance coming from gangs of teenage boys with black and red armbands running between the ruins, clutching a Panzerfaust in each hand. This was what the defence of the Reich had fallen to: young boys who saw the war as an adventure, not a slaughterhouse. In a few days even they would be made to recognise the harsh reality, if they lived that long.

A strapping guard in an immaculate uniform emerged from the Reich Chancellery at dusk, crouching low as a bombardment exploded a building down the street. Tall and broad-shouldered, he had a square jaw and brown hair slicked back close to his scalp. He introduced himself as Otto Günsche and thanked the foursome for volunteering to be in the bunker.

"Most of the senior officers are finding any excuse to abandon the Führer now, when he needs them most." He asked to see their orders and identity discs to make certain all was well.

Karl stepped forward and shook Günsche's hand. "Otto, don't you recognise me? It's Karl, Karl Richter. I was with you as part of the Führer's personal guard last summer."

Günsche stared at Karl, his brow furrowing. "My God... Karl? Is that you?"

The two men embraced, old friends reunited.

"What happened? I remember you being called away to meet the Führer, but you never came back. I thought you'd been... Well, I wasn't sure what to think."

"He sent me to Transylvania in August, as bodyguard for a personal envoy to the leader of a local contingent. The Führer suspected the Rumanians were about to betray us but he wanted to make sure the Transylvanians did not go with them."

Günsche stepped back to take another look at Karl. "Judging by the state of you, the trip wasn't a success. You look like you've been through hell these past few months."

The four Panzergrenadiers were covered in blood, dust and dirt, their uniforms as tattered and war-torn as the surrounding buildings. Unfed and unkempt, they resembled scarecrows next to Günsche.

Karl nodded. "These three got me out of Rumania alive. We've been fighting a rearguard action ever since, all the way back here to Berlin."

After checking their documents, Günsche shook each of the three by the hand, thanking them repeatedly for their efforts. As he finished, a shell exploded on a building north of them on the Wilhelmstrasse, and smoke billowed outwards from the wreckage.

"Come, let's get you down into the bunker. You'll need to get yourselves cleaned up and a good meal wouldn't go amiss either."

The proud soldier led them through a maze of corridors and then down into a tunnel, descending into the bowels of Berlin. Eventually they reached the entrance to the Vorbunker where tired sentries waved Günsche and the others past.

"Things have probably changed considerably since you were here last," Günsche said to Karl.

"Have they finished building the Führerbunker then?" Karl asked.

"Not quite, but parts of it are already being used."

After leading them through a guardroom, Günsche stopped in a dining room with long wooden tables and benches lining either side of the concrete chamber. He yelled out and orderlies appeared with platefuls of hot, steaming stew and cutlery for the newcomers. The Panzergrenadiers stared in amazement at the meals. For the likes of Ralf and Gunther, it was years since they had sat down to eat from a plate, let alone with a real knife and fork. The food was a revelation too: a large portion of stew with real meat and chunks of vegetables protruding from the gravy.

Günsche laughed at the expressions on the new arrivals' faces. "Eat, all of you! It's basic fare but you won't starve down here, that much I can promise you. Go on, eat."

Within moments the four men were hungrily shovelling the hot food into their mouths. Günsche watched them, a wry smile on his face. "You're now in the Vorbunker, the front bunker beneath the Diplomat's Hall in the Reich Chancellery. Two years ago it became obvious this space wasn't sufficient for the needs of the Führer and his personal staff, so the Führerbunker was constructed behind it during 1943 and 1944. The entrance to that is through here so this section is sometimes referred to as the Entrance Bunker. You've already seen the guardroom, and there's another of those in this section. Goebbels's wife and six children are also housed in here."

Günsche pointed over his shoulder. "Go through there and you'll eventually come to the Führerbunker. There's a large guardroom at the front, and that leads into a waiting area. We've got a telephone exchange, sick bay, toilets, offices and workrooms for the Führer and his secretaries; conference rooms and private quarters for the Führer and Miss Braun, pretty much everything we need. The bunkers have their own generators to maintain the lighting and power supply, but you'll find matches and candles in every room as a precaution."

Having finished his meal, Ralf pulled out his pipe and began filling it with the last of his tobacco. Günsche urged him to put both items away.

"No smoking in the bunker by orders of the Führer, and count yourself lucky to have had some meat in the stew."

"When do we meet him?" Hans asked. "The Führer gave me a medal during the early months of Operation Barbarossa. I wanted to tell him how much that meant to me."

"There's no guarantee you will meet him," Günsche replied gravely. "The strain of the past few months... They have not been kind to his health. Sometimes, it's as if he had the burden of all Germany upon his shoulders, bearing down upon him. He suffers greatly for us."

When the newcomers had finished eating, Günsche took them away to wash and get into fresh uniforms. As midnight approached, he escorted the four into the Führerbunker, leaving them in a waiting area while he went in search of an official to acknowledge their presence. The quartet remained standing at attention, all too aware of the fact that their supreme commander was perhaps only one or two doors away. The waiting area was a rectangular chamber, but the interior felt narrower than it was due to a block of metal lockers lining one of the longer walls. A set of wooden cabinets stood opposite the lockers, further constricting the space in the centre of the room.

Hans let his eyes rove around the space, taking in the home of the Führer. The walls, floor and ceiling were all grey with lines running horizontally along the surface of the concrete, marking the joins between the wooden boxing that was used to hold the cement in place when the bunker was being constructed. These horizontal ridges made Hans all the more aware of how close the walls and ceiling were, heightening the underground facility's oppressive atmosphere. Stark illumination was provided by bulbs that hung nakedly from the ceiling and by utilitarian fixtures set into the walls. Looking at the lights, Hans was perturbed by how low the ceilings were in the bunker. After so long fighting out in the open, it felt strange to be encased in a concrete cell like this without windows or natural light. He fought back the panic rising in his gut, telling himself not to think about what would happen if the bunker's entrance was blocked by an explosion from outside. They would be entombed down here, buried alive, with no hope of escape or rescue...

Stop it, Hans told himself. Concentrate on what you came here to do. That's all that matters now. The fate of all Germany rests with us in the next few days.

It was Reichsminister Joseph Goebbels who came out of a side door to welcome the new sentries. He limped into the waiting area, his uniform crisp and clean. The gaunt-faced Nazi propaganda master acknowledged the salutes of the Panzergrenadiers before shaking each of them by the hand, his gimlet eyes staring intensely at the newcomers while Günsche introduced them by name. Satisfied by whatever he'd seen within them, Goebbels stepped back and regarded the quartet as a whole.

"These are difficult times for the Fatherland. No matter what happens in the days to come, I will expect utter loyalty from all of you. You must obey without question, fulfilling your oath of honour as soldiers of the glorious Fatherland. Your Führer expects nothing less of you, and neither would the people of Germany. Is that understood?"

The four men saluted, shouting back their response. Moments later a proud, haughty woman walked past them, leading six fresh-faced children deeper into the bunker. A look passed between her and the Reichsminister, a coolness that Hans recognised from when his parents had argued about something. The woman must be Goebbels's wife and those are their children, he realised. God in heaven, who would bring their young into such a place?

Hans felt goose pimples forming on his flesh as Goebbels turned away from him and the other three. If was as if somebody had just walked over Hans's grave. In that moment he knew not all four of them would get out of the bunker alive. Hans suddenly felt it deep within his bones that coming here had been a terrible mistake, but it was too late to change that. Death was waiting in this place, curled like a serpent in the corner, biding its time before emerging to strike. The four of them had delivered themselves to madmen believing they could change history, and now they were going to pay for that folly. It was monstrous arrogance to believe four Panzergrenadiers could change the course of the war. They were merely pawns in a greater game fate was playing with all humanity.

DAY AND NIGHT quickly ceased to have much meaning inside the bunker. The Panzergrenadiers were split into two pairs, with Hans and Ralf allocated to one shift of sentries while Karl and Gunther joined another. The bunker guards were on permanent rotation, one third of them sleeping while the others remained awake and active, ready to repel the imminent, surely inevitable, attack by the Bolsheviks. Generals came and went from the battlefields around Berlin, their uniforms coated in dust, their faces haunted by the news they brought for the Führer's ears. Personal visitors for Hitler also appeared at the bunker, arriving against all odds in a city under siege. Most left swiftly after private audiences with the Führer or his associates, their eyes downcast and refusing to meet the gaze of those charged with guarding the entranceway.

When not on duty, Hans and Ralf made it their habit to linger around the telephone exchange. This small cell-block was now the communications centre for the Third Reich, with field reports being channelled through the machinery in that cold room. By staying close to the operator the Vollmer brothers were able to hear how the battle for Berlin was progressing. Both men were hungry for news of the Red Army's progress into the city centre, knowing all too well that the end of this fight was the prelude to another, far more terrifying conflict.

The telephone exchange had other merits to recommend it. To one side was the machine room, a deep, noisy chamber holding all the mechanisms that kept the bunker habitable. The underground rooms were well ventilated, but Hans always woke with the stench of despair in his nostrils, as palpable and noxious as fumes from a factory. Besides an engineer, the only people to use the machine room were other guards and the secretarial staff. They snuck inside to smoke furtive cigarettes, staying as far from the door as possible. Bitter gallows humour was the order of the day in the machine room, as the smokers exchanged bleak jokes about what they planned to do after the war. But any laughter was always short-lived, crushed by the noise of the machinery and the knowledge of how little time was left before the war reached its tragic conclusion.

Adjoining the telephone exchange was Traudl Junge's workroom. The Führer's youngest secretary was surprisingly fresh-faced, but she knew as much about what was happening within the bunker as anybody else. Traudl had direct access to Hitler and his lover, Eva Braun. The secretary's time was divided between tasks of great national importance for the Führer and far more mundane duties, such as helping to look after the Goebbels's children.

Junge would not hear anything said against Hitler himself, but she had little time for those in his government who'd fled Berlin to save their own skins. Hans frequently shared a cigarette in the machine room with her and another secretary, Gerda. He was not a smoker by habit, but had survived enough hopeless battles to appreciate the feeling of acrid fumes invading his lungs. Somehow, the pain reminded him that he was still alive. Besides, it enabled him to have the ear of the secretaries. They might not have the official power of the generals who strutted about the bunker, arguing and cursing, but the secretaries were the gatekeepers for anyone wanting access to the Führer.

It was Traudl who got Hans a meeting with Hitler, succumbing to his charms after two days of pestering and gentle persuasion. She finally agreed to mention the possibility to Hitler when next summoned for dictation, but promised nothing more.

"He will see you or he won't," Traudl said. "Even now, he knows his own mind better than any other man I've ever met." She paused, biting her bottom lip. "Perhaps now more than ever…"

Hans waited for her to elaborate, but the young woman turned away, her shoulders slumping beneath some personal burden only she knew about. After she'd disappeared into the Führer's quarters, Hans went in search of Ralf, eager to tell his brother what was happening. He found the former Panzer commander slumped on a wooden chair in the telephone exchange room.

"What is it? What's wrong?" Hans asked, worried by the resignation in Ralf's eyes.

"I was in the toilet, sat in one of the cubicles when some of the generals came in. They'd been drinking, judging by the way their voices were slurring. Those bastards, they couldn't care less what happens to the civilians outside. Apparently the Russian troops are raping their way into the city, and the generals were laughing about it! One of them said anyone stupid enough to stay in Berlin deserved whatever happened to them, as if what's going on outside was the fault of the German people!"

Ralf spat on floor, shaking his head in disgust. "Women and children are being defiled less than a mile from here, and all the generals care about is their legacy… of how history will see them. They're too busy deciding how they'll sneak out of here after the Führer kills himself. I heard one of them say that should be any day now."

Hans mentioned Traudl trying to arrange a meeting for him with Hitler. "Perhaps I can still persuade the Führer to warn those outside about the vampyr. It might not be too late yet…"

Ralf snorted derisively. "You'd do better to put a bullet through that bastard's brain. The sooner he's dead, the sooner the atrocities outside will come to an end. Tens of thousands are dying every day because of that madman. The quicker he dies, the better."

"I have to try," Hans insisted.

"You're wasting your time." Ralf produced a scrap of paper he'd been holding crumpled in hand. He folded the page flat on his left thigh before handing it to Hans.

The younger brother glanced at the words on the paper, frowning at what they said.

"Where did you get this?"

"Found it in the corner," Ralf replied, jerking a thumb towards a wire basket on the floor. "Our glorious leader must have dictated it earlier today."

Hans shook his head, unable to believe what he'd read. "This can't be accurate."

"Can't it?"

Hans read the words again, neatly typed with a tired, erratic signature underneath them: "If the war is lost, then it is of no concern to me if the people perish in it. I still would not shed a single tear for them; because they did not deserve any better. Adolf Hitler."

Traudl appeared in the doorway behind Hans. "I've spoken with him. He's very tired, but hearing about your previous encounter seemed to cheer him up a little. The Führer would like to meet you." Her eyes drifted to the crumpled piece of paper in Hans's grasp. A look of utter despair passed between the two of them before she forced a smile.

"If you'd like to follow me, the Führer will see you in his living room…"

HANS WAS USHERED into a small room no larger than the cramped telephone exchange he'd left a few moments before. A sofa was pressed against one wall, a coffee table in front of it. Facing these was a padded armchair and an upright, wooden chair. A pair of black-framed photographs hung on the wall above the sofa, while a wooden bookcase stood to one side with a lamp atop it.

Hans wasn't sure whether he should sit down to wait and Traudl withdrew before he thought to ask her. After a few seconds, a door to his right opened and a small, stooping figure shuffled in. Hans got a glimpse of the adjoining room. Inside was a single bed, a small table beside it with a black telephone on top, and an oxygen cylinder and mask nearby.

"I understand we've met before," the stooped figure said, slowly straightening up.

Hans was shocked to realise the identity of the old man addressing him, to realise that this crumpled figure was the Führer. Adolf Hitler was all but unrecognisable as the towering giant so familiar in newsreels, the legendary leader with the ramrod posture and the aristocratic tilt of the head. Hans had twice been in the Führer's presence: the first time at a Hitler Youth rally in 1935, and six years later at a medal-giving ceremony on foreign soil. A decade ago the Führer had been a godlike figure to twelve year-old Hans, appearing before more than fifty thousand children gathered from across the Fatherland to willingly scream his praise at Nuremberg stadium.

In 1941 Hitler had given Hans a medal for single-handedly wiping out a Russian patrol during the early days of Operation Barbarossa. In fact it had been a company of Constanta's vampyr who'd dealt with the Bolsheviks, but the Rumanians were all too happy for Hans to receive the credit. The young soldier recalled the moment when he came face to face with the Führer then, and how surprised he'd been to discover that he was slightly taller than the Wehrmacht's Supreme Commander. Hans had looked Hitler in the eye and asked how far they should be willing to go to defeat the Red Army, and what means should they be ready to employ for victory?

The Führer had smiled at him, but with cold eyes. "We must win by any means necessary," was the reply.

Constanta had also been present at the ceremony, receiving the Iron Cross. Hitler's eyes had shifted sideways to look at the vampyr leader while answering Hans's question that day, confirming what Hans already suspected: that it was the Führer who sealed a pact with the vampyr for their help in fighting the Soviets. It had been a salutary lesson for the young soldier, setting him on a path that led to the mutiny at Ordzhonikidze. Now, nearly four years later, he was face to face with the Führer once more. So much had happened since then that Hans felt he'd lived a hundred lives in that time. But Hitler looked as if he had lived a hundred lifetimes more, with every moment reflected on his face.

The hair was still slicked across the head but it seemed thinner now. The face below was exhausted, wrinkled and sallow, with bloodshot eyes and slack lips. The clipped moustache was speckled by grey, and flecks of saliva moistened the thin, cruel lips. Hitler was gaunt, bent over, a quivering mass of tics and vibrations. His left hand shook as if he was suffering from palsy and Hans detected a weakness round the muscles on that same side of the Führer's face. Though Hitler's uniform was crisp and clean, it hung from his bent, twisted body like a blanket. Hans realised this pathetic figure was still waiting for an answer from him.

"Yes, my Führer. We met on August 4th, 1941, on the outskirts of Uman. Our forces had captured the airfield a few days before. You flew in to review troops and tour the captured city. I was fortunate enough to be among those chosen for the honour of receiving a medal from you."

Hitler smiled, not without some difficulty. "I can't say that I remember you, but I gave out so many medals during the early months of Operation Barbarossa. Ahh, those were glorious days, were they not? I would have given anything to be among those advancing against the Bolshevik scum, fighting alongside the vanguard of our mighty Blitzkrieg!"

He lowered himself slowly on to the sofa, his joints creaking audibly in the small room. "So, my secretary told me you had something to say to me, a personal request of some sort?"

Hans swallowed hard, thinking about the note Ralf had shown him. His brother was right: the sooner Hitler was dead, the sooner the madness of this war would be over. But Hans could not shake off a lifetime of indoctrination and propaganda in a few minutes. He had believed in this man for so long... To execute him, here and now, it was unthinkable. Hans knew Ralf would have no such hesitations, but that was only one of the ways in which they differed.

"When Operation Barbarossa began, we took the Rumanians as our allies in the war against Russia."

"Yes, for all the good it did us! No sooner had the tide turned than those cowardly curs swapped sides like rats leaving a sinking ship," Hitler raged. He curled his right hand into a fist and smashed it on the coffee table, upsetting a cup and saucer. "We should have crushed them when we had the chance. Their alliance was nothing but an anchor round the neck of our fine warriors!"

"Among the Rumanians was a particular group of soldiers; a mountain troop under the command of a Hauptmann Constanta," Hans ventured, watching carefully for a reaction. But the Führer remained blank-faced, showing no recognition of the name. "He and his men came from a particular region within Rumania, from the area known as Transylvania."

Hitler frowned. "I have no recollection of this Constanta, nor his troops, but many thousands of foreigners fought alongside our own brave men."

"These mountain troops were not like ordinary soldiers. They fought only at night, abhorring the daylight. There were," Hans paused, choosing his next words carefully, "rumours about them. Some believed the Transylvanians were not truly human."

"I know exactly what you mean," the old man snarled.

"You do?" Hans was heartened. Perhaps the Führer was not the broken man he looked.

Hitler nodded vigorously, his eyes widening. "The Rumanians, the Italians – subhuman, the lot of them. Little better than the Asiatic scum Moscow sent against my brave warriors!"

Hans fought the urge to scream in frustration. Was the Führer merely being obtuse, or did he genuinely not recall striking a deal to use vampyr as weapons of terror on the Ostfront? I have to keep trying, Hans told himself, for the sake of the German people.

"No, that's not the kind of creature I meant. On the battlefield, I heard tales that these Transylvanians drank human blood."

But Hitler was not listening. Instead he launched into a long tirade about the purity of the Aryan race and how its strength had been corrupted, polluted by association with other peoples, by races without the willpower to see the war through to its rightful conclusion. After a few minutes of this polemic, the Führer was shouting and banging his fist on the table, spittle flying from his mouth as he ranted and raved. Hans was almost relieved when Traudl returned, hurrying into the room to see what was upsetting her master.

"You must leave," she whispered to Hans, "now!"

But he refused to go, waiting until Hitler paused for breath before briskly saluting the Führer. "Thank you for seeing me again. It's been the greatest honour of my life to fight for the ideals of our Fatherland."

Hans marched from the room, suddenly aware that his hands were shaking and damp patches of perspiration had formed beneath his armpits. Hans kept going until he saw Ralf lurking outside the machine room. The younger man pushed his brother inside, hurriedly closing the door behind them. After ensuring they would not be overheard, Hans quickly related what had happened during his audience with the Führer.

"You were right. I'm sorry I couldn't see it before, but you were right. The man's insane, frothing at the mouth like some rabid dog. I tried to talk to him about Constanta and the vampyr, but he wouldn't listen, wouldn't hear what I had to say. It was as if he'd purged the pact with the Transylvanians from his memory, just like when the generals had any mention of the vampyr removed from official files."

Ralf listened silently, his face set in a grimace, his arms folded. He waited until Hans had run out of words before speaking. "You did what you could, little brother, but it's too late for talking." Ralf drew his pistol and checked that it was fully loaded. "Now's the time for action."

Hans gripped Ralf by the arm, stopping him from leaving the machine room.

"What are you going to do?"

"Put an end to this war. One bullet in that bastard's brain and the generals will surrender to the Russians within hours. If our glorious Führer won't see sense, maybe his underlings will."

"But if you kill him, you'll be tried and executed for treason," Hans protested.

"Every hour Hitler stays alive, thousands of German civilians are being murdered, raped and robbed. Do you want that on your conscience, knowing you could have saved them from that fate? The sooner the Führer dies, the better for everyone."

"I know, but–"

"Hans, I don't care if history remembers me as a murderer or as a hero. I don't care if history remembers me at all. God knows I've done nothing to be proud of. But this is something I *can* do, something that can only be for the good of everyone: German and Russian, soldier and civilian, men, women and children." Ralf smiled briefly at his brother. "You know I'm right."

"What about the vampyr? As soon as this conflict is finished, Constanta will launch his own war, and pit his army of the undead and all his thralls against mankind. And he won't be satisfied until all of humanity is at his feet."

"That's no reason to leave Hitler alive any longer. We can only fight one battle at a time. Let's finish this madness first, then we can figure out what to do about the vampyr." Ralf glared at his brother. "Now, are you going to let me go, or do I have to shoot you too?"

Hans couldn't believe what he was hearing. "You wouldn't… Not your own brother."

"Wouldn't I?" Ralf asked. "Look into my face and decide what I'm capable of doing."

The younger Vollmer stared into his brother's eyes and saw nothing there but ruthless determination. Reluctantly, Hans released his grip on Ralf's arm and stepped aside. As Ralf moved towards the machine room door, Hans called for him to slow down.

"Why?" Ralf demanded, a finger lingering on the trigger of his pistol, ready to put an end to any further argument.

Hans produced his own pistol and grimaced. "Because I'm coming to help you."

THE VOLLMER BROTHERS emerged from the machine room and strode purposefully across to the workroom that led to Hitler's private quarters. But the outer door was firmly locked and nobody answered when Hans knocked on it.

"Traudl? It's Hans, Hans Vollmer. I think I left something in the Führer's living room. Could you let me in, I need to get it back…"

After a few moments the two brothers heard a key turning in the lock and quickly holstered their weapons. But when the door opened, they found Günsche and Goebbels standing on the other side of it, not Traudl Junge. The Reichsminister glared at the two Panzergrenadiers suspiciously while Günsche appeared exasperated.

"She's in with the Führer at the moment," the flustered sentry explained, gesturing over his shoulder at the closed living room door. "He's had a… The Führer's not feeling at all well. Something seems to have upset him."

"Something, or someone," Goebbels snapped.

"I'm sorry to hear that," Ralf replied smoothly. "I certainly hope he feels better soon. Come, Hans, we should go." He stepped back from the door, gently tugging on Hans's left arm.

"What precisely did you leave in the Führer's living room?" Goebbels demanded.

"M-my, err, my…" the younger soldier stammered.

Ralf pointed at the sleeve of his brother's tunic. "A button. It's been hanging by a thread for days, threatening to fall off. I kept telling my brother to borrow a needle and thread off one of the secretaries or get it darned, but he never listens to me."

Goebbels grabbed Hans's arm and peered at the sleeve Ralf had indicated. There was a button missing, but this still didn't appear to satisfy the Reichsminister. "I was just in the Führer's living room," he whispered angrily. "I didn't see any buttons on the floor."

"It must have rolled under one of the chairs," Ralf replied quickly. "Hans, we should get back to the guardroom. Our next shift is due to start soon and you don't want to be late. You've caused enough trouble for one day, don't you think?"

"Y-Yes, y-you're right," Hans stammered, backing away from Goebbels. "If you'll excuse us, Reichsminister, we don't wish to waste any more of your time." The two brothers snapped to attention and saluted, turned on their heels and marched away towards the guardroom.

"Wait where you are!" Goebbels ordered after them. "I haven't dismissed you yet."

Ralf and Hans stopped, both of them facing away from their inquisitor. Goebbels whispered something to Günsche, engaging him in a hushed conversation the brothers could not hear.

"What should we do?" Hans quietly said out the side of his mouth. "He suspects us."

"Goebbels suspects everybody," Ralf replied in a mutter. "It's his job. He can't know what we were planning to do. Act natural and we'll be fine."

"But what about–"

"You two. Come here!" Günsche called out before Hans could finish his sentence.

The brothers returned to the doorway where Günsche stood with his arms folded, Goebbels lurking behind him. "The Reichsminister has decided that you should be reassigned. In these unstable times, it's best for the Führer to be guarded by more familiar faces. From now on you two will be located in the Vorbunker and shall remain there at all times. Is that clear?"

Ralf and Hans acknowledged their new assignment.

"Very well. You have your orders – carry them out. Dismissed!"

The Vollmers marched out through the Führerbunker's waiting area into the guardroom that linked the front and rear bunkers. Gunther and Karl were sat playing cards, whiling away the hours until their next stint on duty. Gunther saw the look on Ralf's face and hurried after the brothers as they continued their brief journey to the front bunker.

"What's wrong? What happened?" he demanded.

Ralf waited until he and Hans were in the Vorbunker before replying. He ushered Gunther to an empty side room and Hans followed them in, closing the door. Ralf quickly detailed Hans's attempt to reason with the Führer and their close encounter with Goebbels.

"We've failed, Gunther. You've got to assassinate Adolf Hitler before it's too late. Every hour, every minute he lives pushes Germany closer to the abyss. It's up to you and Karl now. We had our chance and failed." Ralf rested his hands on Gunther's shoulders. "Can you do it, old friend?"

"I can try."

Ralf nodded, sadness in his eyes. "Even if you and Karl don't succeed, I do not doubt that one of the other sentries will immediately gun you down for trying. You've seen what it's like inside the Führerbunker: a collection of bloody fanatics, all gathered around their lord and master, waiting for his next insane proclamation, every one of them cowering before his impotent wrath."

Gunther shrugged. "I always thought this war was a one-way ticket for me. I'm still surprised to have lasted this long." He put out a hand for Ralf to shake. "Goodbye, old friend. Hopefully I can finish what you and Hans started."

Ralf pushed the hand aside and embraced his friend, clapping Gunther on the back. "You were the best damned Panzer driver in the Wehrmacht, you know. Nobody else even got close."

"Shame I got stuck with such a useless commander, eh?" Gunther quipped. He released Ralf and gave Hans a hug. "You look after your big brother, okay? If he hasn't got me to keep him out of the scheisse, God only knows what kind of trouble he'll get into."

"I'll do my best," Hans promised, blinking back tears. He'd grown close to Gunther over the past eight months, enjoying the veteran's capacity to find humour in the bleakest of situations.

"Well, I'd better get back and share the good news to Karl," Gunther said cheerfully.

He opened the door and strode out, not looking back at the two brothers. Hans and Ralf listened to their friend's footsteps fading away, quickly getting swallowed up by the hubbub of chatter inside the Vorbunker and the distant pounding of explosions overhead. Both men knew they would never see Gunther alive again. Sadly for them, they were proved correct.

GUNTHER AND KARL had to wait another nineteen hours before they got a chance to assassinate the Führer. The two men found themselves cleaning up after Blondi, Hitler's German shepherd bitch. For days the dog had been kept tied up in the toilets, barking at anyone who came in and pawing at its collar. Gunther took pity on the dog and sought permission to take it for a walk outside but was refused.

By now the Russians were penetrating the centre of Berlin. Officers came and went from the bunker, several of them bringing reports about Soviet commando units scouring the streets for an entrance to the bunker. The sound of artillery barrages was no longer distant or rare; it had become a constant background noise, like a permanent thunderstorm overhead.

At first Karl had been reluctant to join Gunther's conspiracy to murder the Führer. Like Hans before him, he argued in favour of trying to persuade Hitler about the impending threat of the vampyr. But Gunther rejected Karl's urgings.

"The other two tried that and failed. There's only one course of action left open to us. You have to help me, or at least promise not to tell the others what I'm planning. Will you do that much?" Gunther pleaded.

Karl nodded. "Of course. I'm with you, but..."

"I know," the former Panzer driver agreed. "You wish this poisoned chalice had passed to someone else. But fate or chance or some other force has put us in this position, here and now."

Karl rubbed a hand across his tired face. "Everyone believes the Führer will commit suicide rather than be captured by the Russians. They say it's only a matter of time."

"We can't wait that long. It's up to us. We have to stop this madness, or at least try."

On April 28th, the two sentries were summoned to the outer conference room, along with eight of their colleagues. It was one of the better-furnished places in the Führerbunker, with a long ochre rug on the floor, black leather armchairs lining the walls, and a selection of black-framed, monochrome photographs on the walls.

But the ten guards remained at attention, knowing better than to sit in any of the plush, well-upholstered seats; such luxury was reserved for the generals and senior officers. Mere sentries were restricted to hard wooden benches and chairs, the better to keep them awake and alert through the long days and nights of guard duty.

After more than five minutes, a side door opened and three figures emerged into the outer conference room, one after another. Günsche was the first, walking back and forth along the line, ensuring each of the men was immaculately turned out. Goebbels came next, his gaunt features betraying no emotion or any hint of what was happening. Finally the Führer shuffled out, almost stumbling on the edge of the rug. He steadied himself by grabbing at Goebbels's arm before straightening a little to regard the ten sentries facing him.

"I wanted to thank you, before the end," Hitler said, his words little more than a whisper. He cleared his throat and repeated himself, louder this time and with greater authority.

"We are facing our twilight, the Götterdämmerung as Wagner called it. No doubt you've heard rumours and speculation about what will happen in the coming days. I say to all of you, don't listen to idle gossip. I gave the order earlier today for our armies waiting outside Berlin to launch the counter-attack. The godless Bolsheviks believe us beaten, but the Wehrmacht is not vanquished yet! Our forces shall encircle those that would destroy the capital of the Fatherland and crush them mercilessly. When they have reclaimed this city for its citizens, we shall emerge stronger than ever before! Our enemies shall recognise their folly and flee before our might!"

The words sounded powerful, a hint of the Führer's once great oratorical skills still lingering within his withered body. But he crumpled into a coughing, feeble old man once more, his last reserves of energy spent.

Goebbels and Günsche stepped between Hitler and the sentries, shielding him from the guards' gaze until he could recover.

Eventually the Führer was strong enough to approach the line of guards. Starting at the opposite end from Karl and Gunther, Hitler thanked each man individually, touching a hand lightly on their shoulder or gesturing at them appreciatively. Goebbels and Günsche followed Hitler along the line, reinforcing and affirming what their leader had said. At the other end of the line, Gunther undid the clasp holding his pistol in its holster. Karl noticed the tiny movement.

"God in heaven. You're planning to do it now?" he whispered out the corner of his mouth.

"When are we going to get another chance like this?" Gunther replied quietly.

"Don't. Please, don't! You'll get us both killed. I was the one who got you a posting to this bunker. They'll realise I must have known what you were planning to do."

"We don't have a choice anymore," Gunther said, his voice surprisingly calm.

Karl undid the clasp on his own holster. "Do this and I'll shoot you myself," he promised.

"That's your choice."

"I mean it!"

Gunther's eyes slid sideways to look at Karl, then past him to the Führer. Hitler had paused to talk with one of the other sentries, but he would be level with the conspirators in thirty seconds' time, perhaps less.

"Do what you feel you must. That's what I'm doing," Gunther said.

Hitler moved straight past the next three guards, including Karl, and stopped opposite Gunther. The Führer smiled at him. "Stiefel, isn't it?"

"Y-Yes, my Führer," Gunther replied, visibly startled that Hitler knew him by name. The assassin's hand lingered beside his pistol, its purpose forgotten for the moment.

"Don't look so surprised. I had my secretary bring me the files of all the sentries so I could select the best of them. You were a Panzer driver, yes?"

Gunther nodded uncertainly.

"You became a Panzergrenadier near the end of 1941, but your file is missing the pages that explain why you made that change."

"I..." By now Goebbels was standing behind the Führer, his piercing black eyes fixed on the trembling sentry. "Our Panzer was disabled in a battle, but the crew survived. All five of us joined the Panzergrenadiers as a way of keeping ourselves at the front."

"You hear that?" Hitler asked Goebbels, twisting round to look at the Reichsminister. "If only we'd had more brave warriors like them!" He turned back to face Gunther, a glint in his eye. "And what happened to your comrades? Are they still fighting the good fight?"

"We lost two of them at Stalingrad, and another at Kursk, but my commander is on sentry duty out in the Vorbunker." Günsche whispered in Goebbels's ear and the Reichsminister stepped forward, clearing his throat to get Hitler's attention.

"Forgive me for interrupting you, my Führer, but there are pressing matters that require your presence elsewhere," Goebbels said, his voice an oily, sibilant hiss.

Hitler frowned but nodded nevertheless. "Very well. Good to meet you, Stiefel."

Gunther saluted the Führer, using the movement to mask his hand sliding the pistol from its holster. As Goebbels and Hitler turned away, Gunther took a step after them, raising his weapon to fire at the Führer's back.

"This is for Helmut, Martin and Will!" he exclaimed.

A single shot split the air, the sound magnified over and over again by the concrete walls, floor and ceiling.

The body slumped down onto the rug, a pool of blood rapidly spreading outwards from beneath the collapsed victim.

For a second nobody spoke, a stunned silence replacing the dying echoes of the gunshot. Then everyone in the outer conference room was shouting and screaming, a cacophony of voices battling to be heard above each other. Orders were bellowed and countermanded just as loudly, while several of the sentries ran for help. Within seconds they were replaced by new arrivals as doors were flung open and people spilled into the already chaotic space. It took another gunshot, this time fired point blank at the dying man, to bring silence to the anarchy. The crowd of sentries, generals and secretarial staff drew back, opening a space around the body on the floor.

Gunther was sprawled awkwardly on the diamond-patterned rug, his pistol lying unfired nearby, just beyond his grasp. Karl stood over the mortally wounded man, a curl of smoke escaping from the barrel of his pistol. The smell of cordite was strong in the air, giving an acrid taste to each and every breath. Hitler was stood opposite Karl, with Gunther's twitching body between them.

"Why?" the Führer asked, befuddlement in his voice.

"He was trying to assassinate you," Karl replied in a blank monotone.

"That much was obvious," Goebbels snapped. "The Führer asked why."

"I think he blamed you for the loss of comrades; the deaths of his friends," Karl said. "He seemed perfectly rational when I first met him in Rumania last October. But after his former commander was reassigned to the Vorbunker, Stiefel started mumbling dark threats under his breath. I was about to report his behaviour when we were summoned here."

Gunther tried to say something, but all that came from his mouth was a weak, wet gurgle. Karl reacted by kicking Gunther in the head, his heavy boot knocking him senseless.

The Führer arched an eyebrow at the prostrate figure staining the rug with blood. "Get this carcass out of here. No more newcomers are to be allowed into the bunker, under any circumstances. We must keep our ranks pure and safe from the infiltration of madmen." He pointed at Karl while glaring at the other sentries.

"I, your leader, would be dead now but for the quick thinking of your comrade. Remember that, and re-examine your own actions! You, too, may be called to account, sooner than you think."

Hitler stomped out of the conference room, leaving his underlings to clean up the mess. Goebbels hurried after his master while Günsche did his best to restore order. The shocked secretaries were sent back to work and the guards that had flooded into the conference room were ordered to return to their duties elsewhere. The remaining men were given a dressing down for their failure to stop Gunther in time.

Only Karl was immune from this chastisement. He crouched down on one knee, leaning forward to whisper into the dying man's right ear. "I'm sorry, but you left me no choice."

Gunther stirred, a bloodshot eye swivelling in its socket to stare at Karl. Lips moved soundlessly for several seconds, until slowly, painfully, a single word slipped from them.

"Why?"

Karl glanced about, but nobody was paying him any attention for the moment. "My master wants this war to continue for as long as humanly possible. The greater the chaos and carnage here in Europe, the easier his ultimate, inevitable triumph shall be. Even a few extra hours of fighting makes a world of difference as it gives him time to put his pawns into place."

"Who?"

"The Lord Constanta, of course," Karl replied, scolding Gunther as if the dying man was a simple-minded child who was unable to grasp the obvious. "I'm one of his thralls. I have been ever since I first met him in Stalingrad, two and a half years ago. I pledged my allegiance to him then and nothing I've seen or experienced in this war has made me regret that decision. He left me in his dungeon at Sighisoara, knowing your squad of German soldiers would find me and take me in. You didn't honestly believe finding Helmut Richter's brother could be a coincidence, did you?"

Gunther tried to spit a curse at Karl but the words died in his mouth.

"There, there... Don't fight it. Let death claim you, as it will claim most of mankind soon. The vampyr will feast on the souls of this city. Then, when the Allies are proclaiming victory in Europe, the undead shall rise up and unleash their blood war upon the continent."

Gunther was not listening. His eyelids fluttered closed as a last, rasping breath escaped from his lungs. Then he moved no more, the last of his lifeblood ebbing away into the rug. Günsche came and stood over the dead man, folding his arms.

"Is he...?"

"Dead. Yes, quite dead," Karl said, standing upright.

"Did he say anything?"

"He asked for forgiveness."

Günsche snorted derisively. "Not much chance of that. Goebbels has forbidden any mention or official record of what happened here. All those who witnessed the incident have been sworn to silence. That includes you, I'm afraid."

"Why be afraid? I was only doing my duty."

"You deserve a medal for what you did."

Karl smiled. "It was all in the service of my commander."

"You entered the bunker with this man and two other Panzergrenadiers; two brothers. They're still in the Vor-bunker. Did they know of what Stiefel was planning?" Günsche asked.

"I doubt it. As I told the Reichsminister, Gunther only began making threats after Ralf and Hans were reassigned yesterday." Karl frowned. "Perhaps it would be best if I told them what happened to their comrade? I could deter-mine whether or not they're a danger to the Führer..."

Günsche nodded. "They can help you dispose of the traitor's body; that should be a good test of their loyalty. If they show any signs of sympathising with this scum, shoot them."

Karl saluted crisply before making his way out to the front bunker. He found Hans and Ralf dozing fitfully beneath the tables in the dining room, along with several other sentries. Karl woke the pair and led them back towards the Führerbunker, talking in a low, calm voice.

"Whatever you do, don't react in any way to what I'm about to tell you," he began. "We're being watched; you two especially. Your actions in the next few minutes will determine whether or not we get out of here alive. Do you understand?"

Ralf simply nodded, but Hans wanted more informa-tion. "This is about Gunther, isn't it? What happened to him, Karl?"

"Keep walking and I'll tell you. He tried to assassinate the Führer but another one of the sentries intervened, shooting Gunther."

"How is he?" Hans persisted. "Is he–"

"He's dead," Ralf interjected, his voice a dull monotone. "Do they suspect us too?"

"They're not sure," Karl admitted. "You're to help me get rid of Gunther's body outside. That'll be our chance to get away from here." By now the trio had entered the Führerbunker and were pushing their way through the crowded guardroom.

"How is the Führer?" Ralf asked quietly. "Will we see him?"

Karl shook his head. "He's surrounded by generals. He's too well guarded now."

"Then we've failed," Hans mumbled. "We had our chance and Gunther paid the price."

"Keep it together," Ralf said coldly. "Otherwise we'll end up the same way as him."

The three men marched into the conference room where a coarse grey blanket had been thrown carelessly across the body on the floor. Günsche was waiting for them, his eyes watching the trio intently, his fingers lingering on the handle of his pistol. Beyond him a door stood ajar, allowing Goebbels to observe what was happening.

Günsche pointed at the body. "Your comrade, Stiefel, has been executed for treason. You three are to take his body outside and get rid of it. Dig him an unmarked grave; he deserves no recognition for his disloyalty. Understand?"

The Panzergrenadiers saluted crisply, barking their response in unison. Günsche stood aside, giving access to Gunther's body. They rolled his corpse inside the blanket, Hans taking charge of the head while Ralf grabbed his dead friend's feet. The brothers lifted Gunther up and took him back out through the Führerbunker into the Vorbunker. Karl went ahead of them, clearing a path. The trio continued onwards, going from the Vorbunker up the winding staircase that rose to ground level. The three men emerged into the open air to find it was late afternoon, the setting sun blearily visible beyond the clouds of smoke and fumes from the battered city around them.

It was only four days since Ralf, Hans and Karl had gone down into the bunker, but the devastation brought upon Berlin in that short time was remarkable. The centre of the city was now clearly within range of Stalin's Organs, as a barrage of nearby explosions amply testified. The trio crouched low as they ran for cover, the Vollmer brothers still carrying the body of their dead comrade. No sooner had the threesome reached the nearest shelter than an artillery shell exploded behind them, gouging a mighty hole in the ground behind the Reich Chancellery while throwing masses of earth and concrete into the air. This debris rained down hard on the area, showering the guards by the bunker entrance and forcing them back inside.

Ralf saw the sentries retreating and dropped Gunther's legs. "Now's our chance!"

Hans hung on to the corpse's shoulders. "We can't just leave him here!"

"We don't have a choice," Karl argued. "If we don't go now, Goebbels will send men out to bring us back or hunt us down."

"But what about Gunther?"

Ralf went to his brother, slipping an arm round his shoulders. "He's gone. That's not him anymore; it's what is left of him. He wouldn't want us dying to bury him, would he?"

Hans clung on to the dead man a moment longer before letting the body slip from his grasp. "No. No, he wouldn't."

Karl had already run to the far end of the building they were sheltering against and was peering round the corner. "It's all clear! Come on!"

Ralf and Hans sprinted after him, leaving the remains of their comrade on the ground, swaddled in a bloodstained blanket. As the brothers reached the corner, the whistle of another incoming shell cut through the air. Moments later it exploded on the spot where they'd been standing, blowing a hole in the side of the building. When the dust and debris cleared, there was nothing left of Gunther's body.

Hans was first up on his feet, urging the others to quickly follow him. "Come on! Let's go!"

# Four

IT WAS MAY Day when I first heard of Adolf Hitler's death. The battle for Berlin was still raging at the time, the fighting nowhere fiercer than inside the Reichstag. Capturing that mighty building was the perfect symbol for a Red Army victory over the Axis forces. All possible efforts were concentrated upon raising the red banner atop the Reichstag by the 1st of May, a key day in the history of communism.

So important was this goal that SMERSH ordered Gorgo to disband our deep knife unit on April 29th, freeing Mariya, the Borjigin brothers and I to join the assault on the Reichstag planned for the next day. The surly Rumanian was irritated by having to surrender our command but he pretended otherwise, sneering at us as we prepared to leave.

"Don't worry," he taunted, "we'll meet again soon enough. Once victory is declared my thralls will hunt you down, no matter where you try to hide in the ruins of this accursed city. They have your scent in their nostrils now; you can never hope to escape them." Gorgo

173

had his thralls confiscate our submachine guns, leaving us with only pistols and daggers. "Scum like you don't deserve such weapons," he said.

"How are we supposed to defend ourselves, let alone fight in a battle?" I demanded.

"Use your imagination," the Rumanian replied. "There are plenty of dead German soldiers rotting in the streets of Berlin. Steal what you need from them."

Both the Mongolians spat on the ground in front of Gorgo, while Mariya shouted obscenities at him as he stalked away. I kept my own counsel, preferring not to have the vampyr know my thoughts. He had murdered my best friend, slaughtering Eisenstein in front of me, and rejoiced in his triumph. There would be a reckoning between Gorgo and me before either of us departed the German capital. But if I had my way, it was the Rumanian who would die that day.

Gorgo and his company of thralls vanished into the fog of war that constantly choked the air in central Berlin. Once the Rumanian and his charges were gone, the four of us made our own way towards the Reichstag. Each of us accumulated fresh weapons as we moved through the city, ripping MP38 machine pistols from the lifeless hands of corpses, breaking fingers stiffened by rigor mortis when necessary. Finding ammunition for the weapons was much harder. Most of the enemy soldiers had fought to their last bullet before dying. But the four of us had all accumulated full clips by the time we reached what was left of the Reichstag.

Finding the grey, shell-shocked building was not difficult; all we had to do was walk to where the battle for Berlin was loudest and deadliest. The closer we got, the worse visibility became. Soon we were stumbling forward, clambering over burnt-out, bullet-riddled cars and piles of shattered masonry. When we reached the Red Army's forward positions, I could see our comrades were within a few hundred metres of their target. But crossing that short distance was costing hundreds of lives, and conquering the interior would mean days of brutal combat.

Heavy artillery and tank fire bombarded the Reichstag, driving its defenders back from the windows on upper floors. But still the Germans clung on, supported by their own artillery fire from the nearest Flaktürme. Back and forth raged fire from each side's heavy guns, leaving our ground troops waiting impotently outside the Reichstag, unable to advance.

By late afternoon on April 30th the smoke and dust created by the bombardment was so thick that dusk fell early in that part of the city. When our riflemen finally tried to storm the building, they discovered all the ground floor windows and doors had been bricked up or barricaded. Heavy guns were brought forward to blast a way in, and at last we were able to pour inside the main hall.

Then the fighting began in earnest, a devastating melee of brutal, close-quarters combat. The Germans threw Panzerfausts and grenades down at us from stone balconies, while other enemy soldiers retreated to the basement, threatening to sandwich us between them and the forces massed overhead.

Fires were soon raging through the interior of the building and smoke from these blazes choked the great hall, providing our troops with some camouflage from the enemy. The four of us were part of a dozen riflemen and women that fought their way up to the Reichstag's second floor, only to be pinned down by a German machine gun emplacement. For more than an hour we clung together, those at the edges getting picked off by the enemy, one by one.

When our dozen had shrunk to five, I asked the grizzled veteran leading us what we should do. Levshin scowled at me, his back pressed firmly against a tall stone pillar which sheltered him from the machine gun fire peppering our position.

"We need somebody brave enough – or stupid enough – to charge that machine gun. Unless it's taken out soon, we'll be dead before help arrives."

I nodded, satisfied that his grim assessment matched my own. I pulled two stick grenades from my waist belt, both of them taken from the corpses of fallen German soldiers in the main hall. I rose to a crouch, looking for the best way forward from our exposed position. The area around us was a flat, empty expanse of marble, offering no protection from the merciless aim of the machine gunner. They were beyond throwing distance from where we'd been forced to take shelter. Somebody needed to cover seven or eight metres, running directly towards the enemy emplacement, before throwing the stick grenades at the Germans with precision and accuracy.

I swallowed hard, searching inside myself for the will to run out into the open. As I began to stand up a firm hand on my shoulder pressed me back down again. The Mongolian twins were already on their feet with determined looks set on both their faces.

"We go," Saikhan said. As a joke he'd shaved his beard into a goatee when we entered Berlin, saying it would make his body easier to identify if the two brothers died together. I had a sinking feeling his prophecy was about to come true. Saikhan took the stick grenades from my grasp and gave one to his sibling.

"You stay," Baatar said, gesturing at Mariya while winking to me. "Look after her."

"Are you sure?" I asked, still ready to go myself despite the gnawing fear in my gut.

"Da," Saikhan replied. "May 1st is good day to die." He nodded to Levshin, who had watched our exchange impassively. The veteran rifleman had seen too many deaths, too many senseless sacrifices, to care about anyone's fate except his own.

"Give them some covering fire!" he snarled, leaning round the pillar to empty his PPSh at the German machine gunners.

Mariya and I followed his example, firing our confiscated MP38s at the enemy, driving them back behind a stone balcony. The Borjigin brothers raced out into the open and sprinted towards the Germans' position, activating their stick grenades as they tore across the marble tiles. But the covering fire died as we emptied our weapons. Within moments the enemy soldiers were back behind their machine guns, taking aim at the Mongolians. Baatar threw his stick grenade at the Germans, but his brother never got that chance. Both of them were cut down by the enemy's bullets, stumbling forward in a heap on the cold, pitiless floor.

Baatar's stick grenade landed in the middle of the Germans. I heard them cry out in dismay, one appealing to God in heaven for mercy before the device exploded. The second grenade spilled from Saikhan's grasp on to the marble beneath him and detonated moments later, blowing apart the bodies of both brothers. Levshin, Mariya and I stayed behind our pillar, not certain the suicidal attack had been a success. But as the smoke ahead of us cleared, Levshin peered round the column for a quick look.

"Yes!" he said triumphantly. "They got those bastards!" He was up and running before Mariya or I had a chance to react. The veteran campaigner had been among those defending the outskirts of Moscow in December 1941, when the Germans came within twenty kilometres of Red Square. He'd fought in dozens of battles, lost count of the comrades he'd seen riddled with bullets or blown apart by enemy shells and bombs. He'd battled his way halfway across the continent and was within a few floors of achieving the ultimate glory, being among those who planted the Red Flag atop the Reichstag.

Maybe it was the thought of achieving that immortality that sent him racing forward, or maybe he'd
simply had enough of death and destruction. Whatever
the reason, he hadn't advanced more than a few metres
when a single gunshot cut through the air. Levshin staggered on a few more steps before tumbling down the
staircase on which we'd lost dozens of good men and
women earlier.

I began to rise, determined to succeed where Levshin
had failed, but Mariya pulled me back behind the pillar,
saving me from being the German sniper's next target.

"We're staying here until we know it's safe to come
out, okay?" she said.

Bullets sprayed the other side of the pillar, thudding
into the stone column. I nodded my agreement. Better to
stay silent and not let her hear the fear in my voice, I
decided. We settled down to wait, clinging to each other
for comfort while the battle for the Reichstag raged on
the floors below. There were just the two of us left now,
from all those who had mattered in this bloody conflict.
I slipped an arm round Mariya's shoulders and pulled
her closer as she silently wept for Baatar and Saikhan,
the latest casualties of war.

"DAS FÜHRER IST kaput!" I wasn't sure which surprised
me most when I first heard those words: the news that
Hitler might be dead or that I'd somehow fallen asleep
amidst the sound and fury of the battle still raging for
the Reichstag. I was woken by triumphant shouting from
below us, drifting up to Mariya and I between explosions
and volleys of gunfire. The voices calling out were
Russian, but they were speaking in the enemy's language, using some of the few German words every
soldier in the Red Army knew.

I shook Mariya awake while listening intently to the
shouts flying back and forth between my comrades
below and the Reichstag's defenders. The Germans

refused to believe the news about Hitler, but the Russians seemed certain. They claimed to have heard of the Führer's demise from a captured German general who'd been in the bunker where Hitler committed suicide. This inflamed the defenders, who showered those below with a rain of grenades and Panzerfausts, creating a thunderstorm of explosions in the main hall.

Mariya pointed past me to the staircase. A squad of Russian riflemen were creeping up the steps, using the smoke clouds from the fires below as cover for their advance. There were dozens of men, all well-armed and grimly determined. Reinforcements must have been brought in while we slumbered against the pillar. Perhaps the claims about Hitler were mere propaganda, but they served their purpose, diverting the Germans' attention.

The advancing squad swept past us and continued onwards, climbing up to the next level. Once that was secured, I knew it wouldn't be long before the primary objective was achieved: raising the Red Flag. Mariya and I were preparing to follow the reinforcements upwards when a chilling, nerve-jangling shriek sliced through the air. It echoed around the Reichstag, becoming louder and louder until all inside were forced to clamp their hands over their ears.

The high-pitched cry continued for at least a minute before ceasing as abruptly as it had started. Silence lingered afterwards, as if everyone was afraid to break the spell of that inhuman howling. Then the rattle of machine guns firing echoed inside the building once more and the onslaught resumed.

"I know that sound," Mariya whispered to me. "When Gorgo was interrogating me in that Rumanian farmhouse and your unit attacked, he used that shriek to summon his followers."

I nodded. "It's a rallying cry; a call to arms. But that voice we just heard, it wasn't Gorgo."

Mariya stared at me, wide-eyed with fear. "Constanta?"

"Yes. He must be here in Berlin, close by, gathering his vampyr together. But why now?"

"Perhaps they're forming into a single unit, to be used against a specific target."

"Perhaps. Or else what the men below were shouting was accurate: Hitler is dead. If that's true, his generals will be forced to surrender in the next day or two. They can't hope to hold out any longer than that."

"And once they surrender…" Mariya whispered, her words trailing away.

"The next war can begin: vampyr versus mankind."

The shriek rose up once more, calling out to the undead, summoning them away from whatever battles they were fighting. This time it was ignored by those near us in the Reichstag; dismissed as merely one more noise in the cacophony of conflict and carnage. But Mariya and I knew better. The sound was a warning. One war was ending but another waited in the wings, a battle that would determine the future of all humanity, and nobody on our side was ready for it. Constanta's scheme for supremacy was proceeding exactly to plan.

I searched our surroundings, looking for a window that might tell us whether it was day or night outside. Eventually I spotted a grey rectangle in the distance, the last glimmers of twilight visible through the smoke and dust that hung like a shroud inside the Reichstag. It had taken us long hours to penetrate the building, and longer still to get up to this level. I had little idea of how long we'd been dozing, but the darkening dusk outside suggested it was late afternoon or early evening on the 1st of May. The battle for the Reichstag was tipping in favour of the Red Army, and our comrades had little need now for Mariya and me to bolster their numbers. Besides, the precious knowledge we had about the vampyr and their few weaknesses would be needed elsewhere.

"Let's get out of here," Mariya said, pulling her weapon closer.

"You must have read my mind," I replied, smiling at how similar our thinking had become.

Waking up with Mariya in my arms, even in the middle of a murderous battle, was the best I'd felt in a long, long time. The warmth in her eyes, the way she bit her bottom lip when afraid, the way her breasts pushed against the fabric of her tunic: all of these stirred feelings in me that had lain dormant since the war began. There was little time for love on the battlefield, when death could claim you at any moment. Forbidding such feelings from your heart was emotional armour, a sound defence to stop yourself being destroyed.

At that moment, looking at Mariya while others fought and died for a devastated building in the middle of a blistered and battered Berlin, I knew my defences had been swept away. I felt a fear chill my heart unlike any other I'd experienced. I wasn't scared for myself or about what might happen to me. Now I was scared for Mariya.

I did my best to push these futile thoughts aside and peered round the pillar at the staircase beyond it. "That's the most direct route out of here, but also the most dangerous."

"It'll do," she replied, already on her feet and running towards the stairs in a low crouch. I scurried after her, my eyes sweeping the balconies and doorways around us for enemy soldiers. I had been raised a good communist, denying the existence of God and religion, but I prayed to God to keep Mariya safe as we descended into the flaming hell of the Reichstag's main hall.

We emerged from the building to find the Red Army celebrating. Nothing had been officially announced, but the rumours about Hitler's suicide were spreading rapidly through the centre of Berlin, passed from one excited soldier to another; whispered in the gathering dusk like a benediction. For most of our comrades, being alive in the German capital on this day was an honour. To Mariya and I, it felt more like a death sentence. I stopped an officer who was on his way into the Reichstag, pressing him for more details about the Führer.

"The fascists sent emissaries to meet with Chuikov before dawn this morning, hoping to negotiate a ceasefire. They told Chuikov that Hitler committed suicide yesterday in his bunker, a kilometre south of here. The war's as good as over, comrade!"

"So why are we still fighting?" Mariya asked. "Good men and women are dying in there."

"Orders came back from Moscow that Stalin wants an unconditional surrender."

The officer embraced both of us before leading his men into the Reichstag. It was the first time in weeks I'd seen so many soldiers all smiling at once. As they were swallowed up by the murky interior, the vampyr summoning rent the air again, the noise clawing at our minds like so many fingernails being dragged across countless blackboards.

Mariya and I both wrapped our arms over our ears, trying to block out the inhuman shrieking. It died away after a minute, the pitch of the sound changing as it faded away once more.

"That's a recording," I realised. "Constanta's voice is being broadcast across the city."

"How?" Mariya wondered. "Electricity supplies were cut off days ago."

I searched our darkening surroundings for the source of the vampyr's howling. Flashes of light from nearby explosions gave me the answer. I pointed at a loudspeaker mounted on a nearby lamppost, the wooden beam tilting listlessly amid the rubble.

"He's using the city's air raid sirens. They must have somehow altered the noise, replacing it with his summoning cry. That'll be heard all across Berlin, gathering every vampyr in the city to their master."

"This could be our chance to hurt them," Mariya said. "If they're assembling in one place, that makes them vulnerable to attack. But how can we find out where they are gathering?"

I heard a familiar voice in the distance and heard the crunch of boots on nearby rubble. I clamped a hand over Mariya's mouth and dragged her into the shadows of the Reichstag, ignoring her mute protests.

"Quiet," I whispered, pulling us both down beside the rotting corpse of a German soldier. The stench of his decomposing flesh assaulted my nostrils, but I was hoping it might also save us. Mariya stopped fighting against me, her senses becoming alert to the danger getting nearer by the moment. We breathed shallow, trying to melt into the darkness.

The footfalls got closer and louder, more and more of them becoming audible as they grew nearer to our position. There was another sound mingling with them, a curious sniffing noise. My fingers crept for the trigger of my MP38 and I could feel Mariya doing the same. She had quickly realised what I feared was approaching and shared my apprehension. Human shapes shuffled past us, their heads twisting and turning in the air, visible against the black and blue sky. One silhouette stood out, strutting arrogantly among the others.

"Keep searching!" Gorgo bellowed, his voice like gravel and thunder combined. "If the last two are not inside the Reichstag, they must be out here!"

As one of the shapes moved closer, I caught a glimpse of his face, lit from above by an aerial explosion. It was Gorgo's vampyr bodyguard, his nostrils flared, his red eyes scanning the ground urgently. I caught my breath, not wanting the slightest movement or sound to give us away. Gorgo and his thralls would tear us apart if we were discovered.

The Rumanian stopped abruptly, something halting his movement. He was opening his mouth to speak when the inhuman wailing sounded again from the nearby loudspeaker, drowning out all other noise. The shapes in the darkness turned as one to stare at the siren, slowly shuffling closer to the source of the beckoning sound. When its cry died a minute later, Gorgo called his thralls to attention.

"The hunt will have to wait: our Lord Constanta summons us. Follow me and I shall take you to him. Come!"

The vampyr marched away, quickly vanishing into the darkness. His thralls trailed along after him, their feet shuffling carelessly through the debris. They were gone before the next siren sounded, leaving a glinting cloud of dust behind them.

Only when they'd gone did Mariya and I relax. She staggered away from the rotting corpse whose stench had saved us before bending over to vomit. I waited for her retching spasms to subside and for my own hands to cease their shaking. Once Mariya had recovered, I moved over to be beside her.

"We can't wait much longer, otherwise they'll get too far ahead," I said.

"Bojemoi, Victor, the vampyr nearly had us then... And now you want to follow them?"

"Not really," I admitted. Given the chance, I'd much rather go home with you, I thought. Back to Russia, back to somewhere we could be together, somewhere we could be safe. But I knew there would be no such place once the vampyr instigated their blood war. It was selfish to want Mariya by my side, but I'd rather we died together than apart, if that was what the future held. For better or for worse, we had to follow this bloody destiny to its conclusion. I could only hope it was for the better - for both our sakes. "But we need to know what Constanta is planning. Gorgo will lead us right to him."

"I know, but…" She rubbed a hand across her temples. "I wish there was somebody else to do this. If the war is over, I want to go home, go back to Stalingrad."

"If we don't do this, there won't be homes for anyone to go back to. Don't forget, Gorgo's got the plans for Rainer's winter bomb. Imagine what life would be like if the vampyr succeeded in building and using such a weapon? Permanent night, day after day, no relief, no hiding place from the undead. That's what the future holds unless we stop them."

Mariya shook her head. "Two of us against an army of vampyr. It's hopeless."

"But we've still got to try."

"I know." She slung her machine pistol over one shoulder and set off in the same direction Gorgo had taken. "Come on, then. We haven't got all night."

WE STALKED THE vampyr and their thralls as they moved south from the remnants of the Reichstag, passing the Brandenburg Gate. Mariya and I were careful to stay at least a hundred metres back, not wanting to risk our scent being detected on the night air. Having spent time in Berlin before the war, I kept scouring my memories, trying to anticipate where the vampyr might be gathering. But my student days were a beer-soaked haze of sunshine in a city blessed with magnificent architecture. What remained was a brutalised, beaten ruin; the corpses of German soldiers littering the streets and Russian tanks sat like behemoths in the dark. It was only when we passed the Reich Chancellery on our left that I realised we were still on Hermann Göringstrasse.

"Potsdamer Station," I whispered to Mariya. "I think they're headed for Potsdamer Station."

"Is that good?"

"Perhaps. I visited it before the war so I might be able to find us a vantage point."

As we got closer to the station, more vampyr and thralls emerged from side streets, swelling the numbers around Gorgo. By the time they reached what was left of the battered station, there must have been a hundred undead and their servants clustered outside. A full moon was rising over the remains of Berlin, casting an eerie blue light across the throng.

Mariya and I slipped into the shadows, keeping watch on the gathering. As we waited, Constanta's piercing cry filled the air once more. But this time it was not being channelled through any loudspeaker. I heard his voice so clearly it was as if he was standing next to me. The effect was mesmerising, calling me from the darkness and urging me to join his crusade.

I was already stepping from the shadows when Mariya grabbed my arm, snapping me out of my trance. "Victor, look! More vampyr but they're German!"

I followed her gaze across the barren road to see many more thralls creeping forward into the moonlight, all of them clad in enemy uniforms. They joined the others, mingling freely with them.

"Of course," I realised. "Constanta spent three years as part of the Axis forces. He must have converted hundreds, even thousands of Germans into his servants. When the Rumanians switched sides, the thralls were left in place: a fifth column to use against the Wehrmacht from within. These must be the survivors, the ones who made it back to Berlin alive."

Mariya gasped as the last of the thralls passed close to our hiding place. After they had gone by, she put her lips to my left ear and whispered to me.

"I've met one of them before, in Stalingrad. When the Germans surrendered, the NKVD seconded me from signals to help interrogate an enemy prisoner of war. Berlin was arranging a POW exchange with Moscow, trading the son of a senior Politburo member for this prisoner and the NKVD wanted to know why.

Bojemoi, what was his name?" She shook her head, frustrated at not being able to remember.

"Anyway, I talked with this prisoner. He seemed to be terrified of being sent back to Germany and said he was a dead man if we went through with the exchange. He told me about his experiences with a Panzergrenadier unit assigned to capture the Red October factory zone in the autumn of 1941. Constanta was given command of the unit and led them on several suicidal raids behind the Soviet lines. The Rumanian made no effort to hide the fact he was a vampyr. Instead he used it as a weapon to terrify the Germans into following his orders. They slaughtered a smert krofpeet squad I later discovered included my brother Josef. Constanta was training the men for a particular mission. He'd heard reports of Jewish soldiers within the Red Army at Stalingrad raising a golem to fight the vampyr."

I had kept up with Mariya's recollection until then, but now I was lost. "A golem?"

"It's a kind of bodyguard, a man-made creature created from clay and brought to life by words from a holy book. According to legend, Jews have created golems to protect them from rumours they were committing ritual murder. Anyway, this prisoner claimed to see Constanta fight a golem in the tunnels beneath Stalingrad."

"Did the exchange go ahead?" I asked.

Mariya nodded. "Yes. When the prisoner was leaving, he pulled aside his collar so I could see two puncture wounds on the side of his neck. There were two puncture wounds. He wasn't terrified of the vampyr – he'd been Constanta's thrall. The only true statement the prisoner said was the one that hurt me most, about the killing of my brother, Josef. That was why I volunteered for a smert krofpeet unit. Like you and Grigori, I've been hunting Constanta ever since, but I've also been searching for that German prisoner."

A piece of concrete shifted in the rubble behind us. We swung round, bringing our weapons up to fire, fingers reaching for the triggers. Two German soldiers were crouched in the ruined building we'd been using as cover. Both had their machine pistols ready to shoot but neither man was firing. I put my hand out to stop Mariya from pulling her trigger.

"Don't shoot!"

"Why the hell not?" she demanded, not moving her gaze from the Germans.

"They could have shot us before but they didn't. I think they're…" My words ran dry as I peered at the enemy soldiers' faces. "I know these men. I've seen them before."

"Where?"

"Castle Constanta. I helped them escape from Gorgo." I lowered my weapon and addressed the two men in German. "I'm sorry but I don't remember your names. It's been a while since Sighisoara."

The younger German smiled and nodded. "I thought it was you," he replied. "Ralf didn't believe me, but he's always been the suspicious one in our family. I'm Hans, Hans Vollmer."

"Being suspicious has kept me alive," Hans's brother said quietly. He gestured at Mariya. "Does your girlfriend speak any German?"

"I speak plenty of German," Mariya replied tartly, "but I'm not his girlfriend."

"You seem closer than most of the comrades I've met," Ralf growled.

I could feel myself starting to blush and was grateful for a cloud passing in front of the moon. "How long have you been watching us?"

"Several minutes," Hans said. "We've picked up enough Russian over the years to understand enemy transmissions and conversations." He pointed at Mariya. "She was telling you about Constanta and a German prisoner in Stalingrad, yes?"

"One of the vampyr thralls, yes," Mariya agreed. "I've just seen him with dozens of others, all in German uniforms. They went into Potsdamer Station. We think Constanta is inside."

"That shrieking on the air raid sirens, it drew them here," Hans said. "We were fighting a battle west of here when half our men simply walked away. In the confusion we got separated from our comrade, Karl. We followed the thralls here and saw you watching from the shadows."

"That was his name. Karl, Karl Richter!" Mariya said.

"You know Karl?" Ralf glared at us, fingers shifting uneasily on his weapon.

"He was the reason Constanta flew back into Stalingrad after the Germans surrendered," she said. "He must be important to the Rumanians, for the vampyr lord to make such an effort."

"Y-You're wrong," Hans said, turning to his brother. "Karl can't be a vampyr, can he? It's impossible. I mean, he's fought alongside us in daylight. The sun burns the undead."

"He could be a daywalker," I said, remembering how Eisenstein carried the vampyr taint but was still able to function like other humans. "One of my comrades was bitten by Constanta but managed to fight off the infection, the hunger for blood. He gained the strength and resilience of the vampyr but could still walk in daylight."

"He sounds like a good man to have on your side," Ralf muttered. "Where is he now?"

"Dead. Murdered by Gorgo," Mariya replied, sparing me from having to say the words.

"Maybe Karl is a daywalker," Ralf muttered. "Or maybe he's one of Constanta's personal thralls, assigned to infiltrate our ranks after the Rumanians switched sides. That'd explain why Gunther died in the Führerbunker and Karl got out of there alive, unscathed." The German spat on the ground, his features souring as a fresh thought occurred to him.

"God, for all we know it was Karl who murdered Gunther. That's why he made us leave the bunker with him after Gunther died, so we wouldn't find out who pulled the trigger."

Dismay crept across Hans's young face. "Karl was the only person left alive at Castle Constanta when we got there last August." His face darkened. "The vampyr must have known we were coming. They pulled out but left him there in the dungeon for us to find…"

"That means he's been watching us ever since," Ralf snarled. "Manipulating us."

I didn't understand then much of what Ralf was saying, but I got the gist of his words. "Why? Why would Constanta have one of his thralls pick you two out for such special treatment?"

"Revenge for what we did to the vampyr at Ordzhonikidze," Hans said.

"You're the mutineers, the men who ambushed the vampyr?" Mariya asked. I'd told her about what the Vollmer brothers had done, never thinking we would meet them again.

"For all the good it did us," Ralf replied. "If Karl did betray us, if he did murder Gunther, then that godless bastard is mine, understand? I want him to die by my hand… slowly." He started towards the nearby station where the undead were gathered, but Hans pulled him back.

"Constanta has more than a hundred Rumanians and even more of their thralls in there," he said. "You go in there, all guns blazing, and you'll be throwing your life away and ours!"

"He's right," I said. "We've got to find out what the vampyr have planned so we can prepare."

"How?" Ralf asked, frustration in his voice.

"There used to be an external staircase on the western side of the station," I recalled. "It led up to a cafe

overlooking the platforms. I went in for coffee once when
I was a student. If the steps are still intact, we could climb
up to a vantage point above the vampyr and maybe listen
to them without being seen."

I could see Ralf wasn't convinced.

"Have you got any better ideas?"

IT TOOK US a quarter of an hour to locate a safe path to
the bomb-blasted staircase and climb the twisted, tortured metalwork to where the cafe had been. Like the
station's roof, most of it was missing, devastated by
artillery fire, but enough remained for all four of us to
get a clear view of the spectacle below. Amid the rubble
and carnage of ruptured train tracks and fallen masonry,
close to two hundred figures stood in the moonlight, listening as a lone figure addressed them from atop a heap
of debris. The aristocratic posture of the speaker and his
flowing black cape with its raised collar suggested it was
Constanta, but it was the sound of his haughty voice that
confirmed my suspicion. The vampyr lord was congrat-
ulating his warriors, praising their efforts to infiltrate
both sides of the battle for Berlin, using their presence to
undermine each army's efforts.

"You have fought a campaign of insurgency and terror,
turning the weapons of these foolish mortals against
them. Earlier tonight my second-in-command, Sergeant
Gorgo, presented me with the blueprints for a bomb that
can transform day into night. With such a device in our
arsenal, we could feed whenever we choose, no longer
forced to cower in the darkness while searching for sustenance.

"Soon our true purpose in this war will be revealed;
our real crusade will be unleashed upon German and
Russian alike. We shall storm forth and show them how
to run a Blitzkrieg, and let them bear witness to the true
meaning of terror. They shall soil themselves with shame
before our fury and flee before our might! We shall

ascend to our rightful status as the new master race and bring a new order to all of Europe. Already our allies in other lands are preparing their own revolutions, moving into positions of power and influence. The vampyr nation, so long a dream for many of us, shall become reality – a reality that will stand for a thousand years!"

The crowd roared back its approval, their adulation rising and falling and rising again, like waves crashing upon a beach. Constanta appeared to be savouring the moment, proudly surveying the dozens of vampyr and thralls gathered around him.

Finally, after more than a minute of cheering and roaring from the throng, he silenced all of them with a single gesture. "Tomorrow, all vampyr will return with me to Transylvania, where we shall prepare ourselves for the coming blood war. The thralls shall remain in Berlin, continuing their efforts to destabilise both sides of the humans' petty conflict. The longer each side keeps fighting, the easier our ultimate conquest becomes. It will not be long before we are reunited, bound together for all eternity under one flag, one nation: the vampyr nation!"

Again, the crowd of blood drinkers and slaves roared its approval for their master's voice. I could see Constanta laughing, his head thrown back as he soaked up the noise, letting it wash over him. When the chanting and shouting finally died down again, the vampyr lord stretched out his arms sideways in a messianic gesture.

"All that is tomorrow. Until then, I give you your freedom. Let us have one night of pure, unadulterated bloodlust. Go out on to the streets of Berlin and sate yourselves. Feed on the humans until you are bloated by this victory. Sup until you can sup no more. Drain the lifeblood from their veins as we shall soon drain the sunlight from the sky. Go, my brethren! Drink blood and be merry. The twilight of humanity is at hand. Go!"

# Five

THAT NIGHT WAS the most gruesome seen in the lifespan of Berlin. You will find no record of it in the official history books; no mention of it among the military despatches issued by German and Russian forces in the capital. That long night of blood has been stricken from the record of the past, lost among a thousand other atrocities.

Across the city many Red Army soldiers were busy celebrating their victory by raping and looting the civilians left to die by Hitler and his generals. For years afterwards, the horrific reality of what happened in the days after the Führer committed suicide was rarely discussed or even mentioned. Even now, decades later, the truth is being suppressed.

Is it no wonder people are unwilling to acknowledge the truth? Who would believe such a thing possible if they had not witnessed it? I survived that long, dark night of terror, else I would not be writing these words, and the carnage I saw then still haunts my nightmares and torments my waking hours. Perhaps the truth is best buried in the past, for it does no good now to talk about it. There are enough monsters in our modern world, happily going about their crusades and wars, claiming everything they do is for the best. We have little need to revive monsters from the past, certainly not ones with the ferocity and savagery of Constanta's vampyr. But I have promised myself that I will tell the whole truth in this volume, so I must continue.

The four of us stayed in our vantage point overlooking the ruined station for close to an hour after Constanta dismissed his undead warriors. The vampyr went searching for easy prey, ready victims for slaughtering. Berlin had plenty of them, cowering in basements and tunnels, pleading for their lives when doors were kicked open and creatures lurched in from the darkness outside. Most of the marauders were Red Army soldiers, I'm sorry to say, drunk on vodka and victory, searching for somewhere to sate their lust, someone on whom to revenge the Soviet people. The elderly and the children were safe, but teenage girls and women suffered terribly from the attentions of my comrades. What happened in Berlin as the Wehrmacht staggered towards capitulation was a disgrace, but it's a disgrace that's been repeated in many wars, before and since.

But the other marauders abroad that night lusted after something else: blood. They tore into homes and hovels, shelters and basements, throwing themselves upon all those within: women, children, the old and infirm alike. None were safe from the attentions of the vampyr.

The thralls assisted in this carnage, sniffing out fresh victims in the darkness for their bloodsucking masters, shooting those who tried to flee, and holding down those who tried to fight back. The centre of Berlin was a killing ground where whole buildings were emptied of human souls in a few minutes of brutality. Throats were ripped open, veins gouged and gorged upon. By the time a team of vampyr had finished in a basement, not one person was left alive and the floor was awash with blood, still draining from corpses carelessly tossed aside.

We waited until the sound of screaming was no longer audible before making our way down the broken staircase. All of us were still absorbing what Constanta had told his followers. I quickly explained to Hans and Ralf about the bomb Rainer and his team of scientists had been developing in the underground laboratory near Gottow, some fifty kilometres south of Berlin.

"God in heaven, if the vampyr can make such a weapon..." Hans whispered, his words trailing away as the full implications of this horror hit home. "What hope is there for any of us?"

"Forget about that for now," Ralf said. "We have a duty to the people still alive in Berlin. We can't leave them to be slaughtered by the vampyr like cattle."

"Ralf's right," Mariya agreed. "We all heard the screams from nearby as the undead set off on their killing spree. We have to do something."

"But these aren't your people," Hans replied. "The Red Army has spent the past four years fighting against Germany, and now you want to save my country from the vampyr?"

"We fought soldiers of the Wehrmacht, not civilians. We were at war with Germany, but not with its civilians," she snapped. "For better or for worse, that war's over now. We have a common enemy. If we want to defeat Constanta and his kind, we need to work together."

"Workers of the world unite?" Ralf asked, sarcasm evident in his tone.

"No, warriors of the world unite," I said. "We're offering to fight alongside you against the vampyr, to save some of your people from these monsters. Do you want our help, or are you too proud to admit you need it?"

Ralf glared at me, the muscles in his jawline rippling, one of his fists clenching and unclenching. I felt certain he was about to take a swing at me, and tensed myself to sway away from the blow when it came. Instead he opened his right hand and extended it to me. I pressed my palm against his and we shook hands.

"Congratulations, comrade," Ralf growled at me. "You just joined the defenders of Berlin."

"What about weapons?" Mariya asked. "Bullets are useless against these fiends."

Hans pulled out magazines of ammunition from his knapsack. "Silver-tipped rounds. Use these well; we haven't got many to spare. Aim for the heart or the brain."

"We know," I said, exchanging the new clip with the one in my borrowed MP38.

I couldn't help smiling at the irony of the situation. If Gorgo hadn't confiscated our Russian submachine guns, Mariya and I wouldn't have been able to use Hans's special ammunition. The vampyr had thought he was hurting us, delivering one last blow to our dignity before we parted. I hoped for the chance to use my machine pistol on the Rumanian, to show him what a mistake he'd made.

FINDING VAMPYR WAS not difficult that night. We walked slowly north, heading back towards the Brandenburg Gate, listening for the sound of screaming from the buildings nearby. The first victim we saw was a child; a girl no older than seven. She ran out of the shadows, her nightdress stained red with blood, both hands clasped over the wound on her neck. Two vampyr came after her, howling at the air as they pursued her across the rubble-strewn street, taunting and toying with her. They didn't notice us until we were standing only a few metres away, our weapons ready to fire.

"Fools! Your weapons are for no match for our kind," the nearest vampyr growled.

"Are you sure about that?" Ralf asked.

He fired three shots into the creature and it exploded into dust and ashes. The other vampyr staggered away from the child, the monster's face clouded by disbelief. Two more silver-tipped bullets spat from Ralf's MP38 and the second blood-drinker was destroyed, the faintest of breezes scattering the remains across nearby rubble.

Mariya crouched beside the girl, softly whispering to her in German, and persuading the child to take her hands away from the seeping bite marks.

"She'll live, if more vampyr don't find her."

Ralf pulled his pistol from its holster and fired a single shot through the girl's skull. Blood from the wound spattered Mariya's face, forcing her to drop the child's body on the ground.

"Bojemoi. I thought Constanta and his kind were the monsters!" Mariya snarled at Ralf. "Why did you kill her?"

"You said she'd live. We all know what happens to survivors of vampyr attacks, those who've already been bitten. They become thralls or gradually turn into vampyr." Ralf shoved his pistol back into its holster. "The Rumanians have enough soldiers in their army already. I don't intend to add any more to their ranks, not if I can help it."

"So that's what we're reduced to? Executing children to make life easier for ourselves?"

"Ralf's right," I interjected. "You know he's right. We all do."

Mariya glared at me, her mouth set in a grimace. "Grigori Eisenstein: he got bitten by Constanta but he didn't become one of them."

"He would have. Sooner or later, he would have turned. Remember how close he was when we were still in Transylvania?" I stepped closer to Mariya, reaching out a hand to wipe the child's blood from her face, but she pulled away.

"We should get moving," Hans said quietly. "There's another six hours before dawn, and the vampyr could kill hundreds, even thousands in that time."

As if to prove his point, fresh screams echoed into the night air from nearby, a woman howling for mercy. We hurried towards her voice, searching for the source. When another woman started crying out to the heavens for help, we quickly realised their pleas were emanating from beneath our feet.

Mariya twisted round, searching for a doorway or a stairwell that led into the concealed space below us.

"There must be a way down close by!" she said.

I hurried past her, determined to find the entrance. But passing clouds hid the moon and we were plunged into near darkness. I stumbled on a chunk of broken masonry and was pitched into the black. But instead of hitting the ground I tumbled forward, head over heels down a flight of concrete steps, and fell into a vision of hell.

Half a dozen women, all of them aged over fifty, were trapped in the basement of a building that no longer existed above ground. Twelve vampyr were feasting on the civilians, one each suckling on either side of their victims' throats. As many thralls were gathered in the basement, holding down the women to make it easy for the undead to gorge themselves. The ground was coated with a slick of blood, crimson and sticky to the touch. A few candles burned in hollows round the walls, throwing cruel shadows across the bleak tableau.

I'd been winded when I tumbled down the staircase and fell on top of my MP38, the machine pistol wedging itself beneath my torso. I tried to pull myself up into a crouch, but the floor was so wet with blood my hands slid out from under me. My chin crashed back down on the cold concrete floor and I saw stars, everything around me blurring in and out of focus.

The thralls laughed at me but the vampyr were too busy draining their victims to bother. One of the fiends pulled his mouth away from a bloodstained neck long enough to mutter a few words at his slaves.

"Deal with this intruder. Now."

The thralls let go of their captives and moved towards me, forming a crowded semicircle in the claustrophobically small space. I threw myself backwards, fingers scrambling for the trigger of my weapon, boots digging into the pool of blood, searching for traction. The thralls moved closer, fingers reaching for me, eager to paw my flesh.

I pulled the MP38 out of the crimson slick and opened fire, sweeping the barrel from one side to the other and back again, emptying my clip of ammunition into the playthings of the vampyr. The thralls fell backwards, crying out to their masters, my bullets stealing away their vile, pitiable lives. I kept pulling the trigger until the machine pistol clicked uselessly in my hands.

Most of the thralls I'd killed outright, but a few survived, wounded but alive. Urged on by the hissing of the undead, the thralls crawled towards me, clambering over the bodies of their comrades. I tried not to think what would happen if these creatures got hold of me, preferring to concentrate on removing the spent clip from my weapon. Once I'd ripped it free, I reached into my knapsack and extracted the only other ammunition I was carrying: a half empty clip of conventional rounds.

I rammed it into place as the first thrall got hold of my left boot. I blew his face off before turning my weapon on the others. Three short bursts sent them all to hell where they belonged. I fired the last of my bullets at the far corner of the basement, not at the vampyr but at their victims. Nobody deserved to live through that horror, I thought.

One by one the undead rose from their feast, hissing and spitting at me. My MP38 clicked empty once more, not that it would have done any good by then.

"Foolish creature," the closest vampyr snarled at me. "Did you think to stop us with that puny weapon? We are the undead, blood-drinkers, nightwalkers! We cannot be hurt by your bullets!"

"I wouldn't be so sure about that," Mariya said from the doorway behind me.

She fired a series of short, controlled bursts at the monsters, her ammunition more than enough to deal with these bloated creatures. One by one they exploded, howling with tormented rage. The last of them cried out before it died, the same sort of cry we'd heard earlier when Constanta was summoning his soldiers to the railway station.

Mariya's silver-tipped ammunition caught short the call for reinforcements, but the sound of the vampyr's voice seemed to echo around us for several seconds afterwards, mingling with the dust and ashes choking the air down there.

"What took you so long?" I asked as Mariya helped me up from the blood-soaked floor.

"Eight more of them were close by. They came running when you opened fire."

She pulled a pistol from her holster and handed it to me, jerking her head towards the women in the corner. "You'd better finish them off. I know it's necessary, but I can't bring myself to do it."

I nodded and took the pistol from her. She went back up the concrete steps while I dispensed a merciful death to the two women still breathing in that basement. I forced myself to look in their eyes as I pulled the trigger, imprinting their faces into my mind. They deserved to be remembered by somebody after this was over, to be mourned by someone. I activated a stick grenade as I walked out of the basement, tossing it over my shoulder on to the bloody floor. The explosion sealed the doorway, entombing the remains of the women and their murderers.

\*\*\*

THE VAMPYR SUMMONING cry may have been brief but it was still effective. Within a minute of my emergence from the basement, all four of us were fighting a running battle against a growing crowd of undead and their thralls. In the darkness, it was difficult to know which of our enemies was which, so we fired conventional bullets at all the shadows pursuing us through the moonlit streets of Berlin.

Wounded and dying thralls went down screaming, but the vampyr simply cursed us. It didn't take long for our standard issue ammunition to become all but useless. It was clear to the four of us that most of the creatures now stalking us were vampyr. They seemed content to keep us on the run, always moving, never allowing us any time to pause for breath or thought. The fiends would make a feint from one side before striking at us from the opposite direction, their numbers growing larger all the time while our supply of silver-tipped ammunition was steadily dwindling. It was Ralf who realised what was happening.

"We're being herded!" he shouted between staccato bursts of gunfire. "They're driving us towards the Brandenburg Gate. These undead bastards must have something special waiting for us!"

"Probably Gorgo or Constanta," I yelled back. "What should we do?"

"We've got to make a stand," Mariya called out. "We need to get ourselves barricaded into somewhere we can successfully defend and try and hold them off until sunrise!"

"That's hours away," Hans shouted. "Our ammunition won't last that long."

Ralf paused to throw a stick grenade at our pursuers. It exploded among the vampyr, scattering them temporarily and providing us with a brief respite. We sprinted round the next corner where Ralf gathered the rest of us close to him.

"Hans is right," Ralf said, panting. "We haven't enough bullets to keep fighting like this. We need somewhere the vampyr won't find quickly. While they're busy searching for us, they won't have the time to attack any more civilians."

"Where can we hide?" Hans asked, watching warily for the vampyr.

A wry smile split Ralf's face as he pointed to a nearby sign: Kaffee Keller. A doorway to the underground cafe was standing ajar, beckoning us to come inside.

"Quickly, you three go in there. I'll run on ahead and lead these godless monsters away from here before circling back."

"No, it's too dangerous," Hans protested. "You'll never–"

Ralf aimed a pistol at his brother's face. "Go. Now!"

Mariya ran towards the cafe's entrance while I dragged Hans after her. He tried to fight me off but the sound of approaching vampyr was clearly audible. Finally, Hans turned away from his brother and ran in through the door Mariya was holding open. I glanced back to see Ralf already sprinting away from us, cursing the vampyr at the top of his voice and firing wildly into the air, drawing as much attention to himself as possible.

Mariya pulled me inside and hurriedly closed the door, ramming home both bolts. The three of us held our breath as the vampyr surged past, their feet making little sound as they ran lightly along the street. We waited until we'd heard no sounds outside for more than a minute before venturing down a rickety wooden staircase into the cafe. Weak shafts of moonlight filtered into the basement from street-level windows high in the walls. It was enough to assess our surroundings while we got accustomed to the darkness.

The Kaffee Keller was aptly named, its air thick with the aroma of stale coffee. Broken tables and chairs were scattered round the cramped cellar, evidence of other illicit visitors before us. There was little doubt the cafe had been ransacked, probably by half-starved citizens of Berlin, and most recently by Soviet soldiers. A hammer and sickle insignia had been crudely carved into the stained wood floor, no doubt by someone using a bayonet tip, while a Russian joke about Hitler's testicles was etched into the cafe's broad oak counter. Mariya translated the words for Hans, who shrugged in response.

"That's nothing. You should hear the songs our troops sang about him during the long retreat from Russia."

"We've heard a rumour the Führer has committed suicide," I said.

Hans grimaced. "I wouldn't be surprised. Ralf and I were in Hitler's bunker a few days ago. The generals spent most of them arguing about who would take charge once our glorious leader was dead." He snorted in disgust. "As if it matters who surrenders for Germany! I hope the Allies hang the lot of them. If those spineless cowards had stood up to Hitler during the war, we might have won, or at least been able to negotiate a cease-fire with Stalin. Instead the country's being torn apart by the Bolsheviks and now vampyr have been let loose on the people of Berlin."

He stopped abruptly, realising to whom he was talking.

"Sorry, I didn't mean any of this was your... I mean... With both of you speaking in German all the time, I forgot–"

"Don't worry about it," Mariya said. "Our generals are no better than yours. I used to believe in them, have faith in their decisions. But they forged a pact with Constanta and his kind the first chance they got." She set a chair upright and sank on to it wearily. "Both sides are just as much to blame for this bloody war. Bojemoi, the things it's made us do..."

I felt an emptiness inside me and realised I couldn't remember the last time we'd had something to eat.

Searching in the kitchen, I discovered two dented tins that had evaded previous visitors to the Kaffee Keller. Neither can had a label, so it was impossible to know what they contained. To my surprise the cafe's water supply was still running, so I filled a jug and carried it through to the others, along with bowls, glasses, cutlery and the mystery tins.

Hans opened one of the cans with his bayonet while I investigated the other. His contained ham, mine was filled with peaches in syrup. I emptied the peaches into one bowl and Hans sliced the ham into another. We shared the food between us, a rare treat in the midst of such madness.

Halfway through the meal my brain suddenly made a connection to something Mariya had said earlier. "How did you know about the golem? Are you Jewish?"

She nodded. "Once a Jew, always a Jew; that's what my mother used to say. Why?"

I pointed at the remains of the ham. "But doesn't that mean…?"

Mariya laughed. "You eat what you can find. I'll atone for it later, if I get the chance." She raised an eyebrow at Hans. "There don't seem to be many synagogues in Berlin."

He glared at her. "As soon as you said you were Jewish, I knew this would come up. I had nothing to do with the transit camps, and neither did my brother."

"Don't you mean concentration camps?" Mariya snarled back. "We've heard about what your comrades in the SS have been doing at places like Auschwtiz!"

Hans stood up, abandoning the remains of his food. "What about the Russian soldiers raping innocent German women and children? Aren't they your comrades?"

"Nobody is innocent in a war!" she replied, rising from her chair. "But that doesn't give you an excuse for mass murder in the name of the Fatherland!"

"I've spent the past four years fighting for my country, just like you. That doesn't make me guilty of every war crime and atrocity committed in the name of the Führer!"

"Are you sure about that?" Mariya demanded.

I stepped between the two of them. "Keep your voices down!" I said. "There could still be vampyr outside. Fighting amongst ourselves is not going to do anybody any good. The war is all but over, remember? We've got a common enemy now: the undead."

Hans and Mariya glared at each other for several seconds before Hans turned away, walking towards the stairs up to ground level.

"Ralf should've been back by now."

TWO MORE HOURS passed without any sign or signal from Hans's brother. We heard screaming a few times and fleet-footed figures running past the entrance to the Kaffee Keller, but our refuge remained safe and undiscovered. Hans positioned himself at the top of the staircase, resting his head against the door to the street, listening for Ralf's return. Eventually he drifted into a fitful sleep, his breathing even and regular, his hands twitching sometimes.

Mariya cleared a space behind the counter as her resting place. I tried not to watch when she went into the kitchen to bathe, making use of rare access to running water. But my eyes wandered to her as she stripped off her tunic, my gaze lingering over the curve of her breasts, the small of her back, the arch of her neck. I'd fought the urge to notice her gender, and tried to treat Mariya as simply another soldier. Eisenstein was right. Having a woman in the unit complicated matters and brought to the surface feelings I'd rather have k buried until this madness was over. But that wa said than done when a beautiful woman w day and night.

She emerged from the kitchen and smiled at me. "Did you like what you saw, Victor?"

I blushed, embarrassed to have been caught. "Sorry, I didn't... I wasn't..."

Mariya arched an eyebrow at me playfully. "Now it's your turn."

"Sorry?"

"You need to wash even more than I did. Now's your chance."

"Right. Of course." I hurried past her into the kitchen, peeling off my tunic and quickly dousing myself with cold water. A coarse bar of soap helped clean some of the grime from my face and hands, but there was nothing with which to dry myself. I pulled my tunic back on and went back into the main area of the cafe. Mariya was waiting for me, her arms folded.

"Not bad," she said appreciatively. "Not bad at all."

"You were watching me?"

"It was my turn to enjoy the view." Mariya moved close enough to whisper in my ear. "If we get out of this alive, you and I need to do more than watch."

I swallowed, trying to stop myself from blushing again. She stepped back, plainly enjoying the look on my face.

"You can take first watch. Wake me in an hour if nothing's happened."

No sooner had she spoken the words than there was a hammering on the cafe door. "Hans, let me in! It's Ralf! Let me in, for God's sake!"

Hans had jerked awake immediately, scrambling to his feet. Mariya and I hurried up the stairs to join him. We leaned closer to the door, listening intently.

"Hans, are you still in there? If you are, let me in before the vampyr find me!"

The voice was definitely that of Ralf. He sounded tired and breathless but still like himself. Hans reached for the bolts on the door but Mariya stopped him.

"How can we be sure your brother hasn't been captured and turned by the vampyr?" she whispered.

"We can't," Hans replied. "But I can't leave him out there, either."

I remembered the small, engraved silver flask I'd carried with me for months. Gorgo had let me keep it when I joined his deep knife unit on the condition that I emptied it of holy water. I'd obeyed his order but refilled the container a few days later when I got the chance. The liquid inside was not enough to kill a vampyr, but it would hurt them. I showed my flask to the others.

"I could flick holy water in his face. If Ralf is one of the undead, we will know instantly."

Mariya relented, letting Hans get to the bolts. But she took several steps back from the door, aiming her MP38 at the entrance. Hans slid the bolts sideways and opened the door a crack. Through the gap I could see Ralf waiting outside, three livid scratches down the left side of his face. As he hurried inside I sprayed holy water on his face. He was startled at the dousing, but his skin did not burn at the liquid's touch. Hans shut the door and fastened the bolts once more.

"You won't need that," Ralf told Mariya, who still kept her weapon trained on him. "It took forever, but I finally shook off the vampyr." He touched a hand to the gouges on his face, wincing in pain. "Had a few close scrapes along the way."

Hans pointed at our abandoned meal. "There's food if you want it."

"Good, I'm starving," Ralf replied, pushing past Mariya and taking the stairs two at a time.

"Did you see Constanta or Gorgo?" she asked, following him.

Ralf shook his head. "Plenty of vampyr, but none of the upper echelon. The monsters are gorging themselves on Berlin's civilians; it's a bloodbath outsi

Hans hurried down the stairs to talk with his brother. "How long until sunrise? Now the moon's set, it's impossible to tell down here."

"Less than an hour," Ralf muttered between mouthfuls of tinned ham. "The vampyr were complaining about how short the nights are getting."

Hans took a step back. "Since when have you spoken Rumanian?"

"I can't," his brother said, still chewing.

Mariya moved to stand beside Hans. "Then how could you understand them? The undead only speak in other languages when they're talking to their thralls or their captives..."

Ralf stopped chewing, his mouth still open as he turned to face them.

"Now!" he shouted.

Suddenly the exterior door behind me burst inwards, wood splintering apart beneath a massive blow, the metal bolts turning somersaults in the air as they flew past me. I spun round to find our only escape route bulked by the fearsome shape of Sergeant Gorgo. He roared at us, the savage cry of a predator when its prey is cornered and the kill is moments away. Mariya swivelled her weapon round to fire but Ralf lashed out with a foot, kicking it from her grasp.

Acting on pure instinct, I showered Gorgo with the rest of the holy water in my flask. The liquid spattered his features, burning into his skin and flesh like acid, eating its way down to the bones. He staggered backwards into the street, screaming in agony. As he gave way, other vampyr poured inside. The first few burst in so quickly they knocked me backwards down the staircase. I tumbled over and over, finally sprawling out on the wooden floor below, Mariya's MP38 lying directly in front on me. I grabbed hold of it and fired off a few silver-tipped rounds over my shoulder, knowing that the invading vampyr must be almost on top of me. Inhuman screams rent the air as five of the creatures exploded into dust and ashes.

As I rolled over on to my back to face the stairs, I caught a glimpse of Ralf and Mariya grappling while Hans lashed at his brother with the butt of a machine pistol. It took several blows before Ralf crumpled, knocked senseless by the brutal assault. In the meantime another half dozen vampyr had streamed into the cafe, some bounding down the stairs while others jumped over the banister to the floor below.

I loosed off several short bursts, exterminating those racing down the steps and two of those already among the tables and chairs. Hans must have turned his weapon on the undead then as another volley of shots peppered them, puncturing the Transylvanians' torsos before they turned to ashen dust. Mariya retrieved my MP38 and added its firepower to ours, decimating more vampyr as they stormed into the cafe, a relentless wave of undead that kept coming and coming and coming.

"God in heaven, there must be dozens of them," Hans cried out. "Hundreds!"

"Gorgo must have captured Ralf; used mesmerism to turn your brother. He knew we'd suspect Ralf was one of the undead, so Gorgo turned him into a thrall instead!" I shouted back.

"Poor bastard led them right to us," Mariya snarled, shaking her head.

Still we kept firing, tearing through our meagre supply of silver-tipped ammunition, but still the vampyr kept coming. Finally, as the invading throng began to slow down, I ran out of bullets. Moments later Mariya's weapon also clicked empty. The two of us scrambled to safety behind Hans, who reloaded his MP38 with one last clip. In front of him Ralf stirred on the floor, slowly drifting back to consciousness. Mariya lashed out with a foot, booting him in the head.

When Hans glared at her, she didn't bother to apologise. "The last thing we need is him helping them any more than he already has."

I looked round the cafe for anything else we could use as weapons to help Hans. There was nothing obvious amid the chairs and tables, broken legs and struts littering the...

"Mariya, grab one of those chair legs!" I shouted. "We can use them to impale the vampyr!"

She nodded, smiling. We both grabbed improvised stakes from the floor, brandishing them as the vampyr grew closer. Hans was firing single shots now, not wanting to waste any of the precious silver-tipped bullets he had left. But choosing his targets meant he couldn't cope with the numbers coming down the stairs. There were not so many as before, but still they were too many. Several slipped past Hans's line of fire, circling round either wall of the café towards us.

I waited until the one nearest me got close before lunging the chair leg I was clutching with all my might. The broken wood punctured the creature's chest, stabbing it through the heart. The vampyr exploded as its kind always did, and I felt myself breathing in the vile ashes since I was so close. I spat them back out, not wanting the acrid, sickening taste in my mouth.

Mariya had a chair leg in each hand. She lashed one of her weapons sideways through the air, sending the nearest vampyr sprawling. Another closed in on her but she thrust the other stake into its chest. As that monster was still dissipating, Mariya stamped a foot on the first vampyr, pinning it facedown on the floor. She rammed a stake down into the creature's back. It detonated, dust and ash spraying out sideways across the floor. Mariya looked over her shoulder at me and grinned before her expression changed to one of horror.

"Victor! Behind you!"

I didn't even look round, simply stabbing my stake blindly through the air. It plunged through the chest of another vampyr, exploding the blood-drinker into atoms. Beside me Hans fired his last three shots, the MP38 stuttering to a halt in his hands. He swore copiously, tossing the useless weapon at the advancing vampyr before crouching to grab a pair of improvised wooden stakes for himself.

Another of the undead charged at Hans while he was still down on one knee. He ducked beneath the attack, stabbing a chair leg up into the air as the creature passed over him, ending its evil existence. We were keeping the monsters at bay for the moment, but how much longer could we hope to hold out?

"You'll never last until sunrise," a sinister, sibilant voice said from the café's doorway. Gorgo had returned, his face a mass of smoking scar tissue, his expression alive with hatred. "You may have slaughtered dozens of my brethren, but your time is over, humans!"

"Our kind will always triumph over yours, parasite!" Hans spat back at Gorgo.

"Even if your bloodsucking scum kill us, there are millions more who will stand against you," Mariya added. "The vampyr belong to history, myths and legends. Your kind are the stuff of nightmares; you have no place in the modern world."

Gorgo laughed at us, roaring his hilarity to the heavens. "I will take the greatest of pleasure in delivering you to my Lord Constanta. He will tear your souls apart."

"You want us?" I asked, trying to keep my fear hidden. "Come and get us!"

A dozen or more vampyr had gathered in a semicircle on the café floor, slowly driving the three of us back towards the counter. Mariya jumped atop the broad wooden surface while Hans and I stood shoulder to shoulder in front of her, our wooden stakes flailing the air, keeping the fiends back.

"Very well," Gorgo agreed. He took one stride towards the staircase, about to come down to our level for the final confrontation, but stopped abruptly. Something was distracting him, taking his attention away from us. The other vampyr also paused, twisting round to discover what was wrong with their master. I squinted, trying to see what was happening. Gorgo brought both hands up to his chest, where the sharpened tips of three wooden bolts protruded from his uniform.

"No..." the Rumanian whispered hoarsely. "Impossible!"

Another trio of bolts appeared through Gorgo's chest, impaling him from behind. He clawed at them with his black, ragged talons. Something flashed through the air, silver and almost too quick for the human eye to see.

I watched, mesmerised, as Gorgo's head bounced down the stairs before coming to rest on the café floor. His lips screamed soundlessly, but he had been decapitated above the voice box and could not cry out. When the elite vampyr perished, it was in two balls of blue and white fire, a smaller one round his head, and a raging inferno where the rest of him was still standing. The café was bathed in blinding light from the twin fires, forcing humans and vampyr alike to cover their eyes before the blaze evaporated.

Gorgo was gone, destroyed.

The other vampyr screamed in anguish, bereft without their leader to guide them.

"Now's our chance!" Hans shouted. "Get them!"

He had killed two of the creatures before Mariya or I had a chance to react. But we quickly followed his lead, swiftly changing the balance of power within the café, turning our predators into our prey. The three of us devastated the ranks of vampyr in a few minutes, running them down and then running them through. The last one was pinned in a corner, below the café door. Hans pulled back his right hand, ready to administer the killing blow. But a low, gravelly voice stopped him.

"No, let me do it." Ralf took the stake from his brother's hand and thrust it clean through the final vampyr's chest. It blew apart, leaving glinting particles of ash floating in the air.

Mariya pushed Ralf into the corner where the vampyr had been, a wooden stake ready to impale him. "You betrayed us!" she snarled. "How can we ever trust you again? Give me one good reason why we shouldn't put you out of your misery, here and now!"

"Because the vampyr that enslaved him is dead," a familiar voice interjected from above us. We looked up at the doorway to see who had spoken.

"Your comrade is no longer in thrall to the undead," the newcomer continued. "He's completely free of their taint." The first glimmerings of dawn made it impossible to see a face, the rising sun casting the new arrival in silhouette. But I did not need my eyes to recognise the voice, to know its identity even if it seemed impossible.

"Bojemoi! Is that you?" I gasped.

Grigori Eisenstein smiled down at us. "Hello, Victor. It seems I got here just in time."

# PART THREE: BLOODSHED

## One

EISENSTEIN CAME DOWN the stairs into the café, a wooden crossbow slung over his shoulder and a silver-edged sword clutched in his grasp. He ran a black-gloved hand along the wall as he descended, three fingers making parallel lines in the dust left by the vampyr we'd destroyed.

"You've done well, even without my intervention. How many did you kill, dozens?"

"Probably. You lose count after a while," I said, striding over to embrace him. But when he turned to face me, I was taken aback by his ghoulish appearance.

Much of the skin and flesh had been burnt from his face, replaced by scar tissue. His hair had been burnt away and so had his eyebrows, the scalp and forehead a mess of seared skin stretched taut across the bones in Eisenstein's skull. He was missing the thumb and forefinger from his left hand, while another finger was absent from his right. I didn't like to think what the rest of his body must look like beneath his dusty, dirt-stained Russian uniform.

"What happened to you?" I asked. "How'd you survive that inferno at Gottow?"

"I didn't," Eisenstein replied quietly. "The man you knew is dead, Victor. I'm what's left of him: a walking husk, kept alive by my hunger for vengeance. It's all that matters to me now."

"But you found us; you saved us," I said, gesturing towards Mariya and the others.

"I've been stalking Sergeant Gorgo, hoping he would lead me to Constanta. But I discovered the vampyr lord has already left Berlin for his home in Transylvania. Gorgo was the last of ten elite vampyr who first entered the war as Constanta's personal cadre, so I decided he had to die. I watched Gorgo overpowering the mind of a German soldier, ordering him to find a trio of troublesome vampyr-killers nearby. It never occurred to me you and Mariya might be part of that trio." Eisenstein glanced at Hans and Ralf. "Nor that you'd be fighting alongside the enemy."

Ralf joined us by the staircase. "We have a common enemy: the undead. We joined forces to fight these fiends. We've all lost friends and allies to the vampyr. And we all know what's at stake now Berlin has fallen."

Eisenstein studied Ralf and Hans. "You two... You were at Castle Constanta, weren't you? I recognise your faces..."

"Yes," Hans said. "Zunetov helped us escape. There was a hidden tunnel that got us away from the castle."

"Could you find this tunnel again if you had to?"

"I suppose so, if it was still there," Ralf replied. "Why?"

Eisenstein studied the four of us, his eyes narrowing. "How far is each of you prepared to go in your fight against the vampyr? How far will you carry your personal crusades?"

"To the ends of the earth, if we have to," Ralf said. "Gorgo stole my will, made me his plaything. I want to make these monsters pay for what they've done to my people, my country, my comrades... And my family."

"Gorgo is dust now, he cannot mesmerise you again."

"So you said. But I'd still walk into hell itself if I could rid the world of these fiends."

Eisenstein nodded, apparently satisfied by this response. He looked inquiringly at Hans. The younger Vollmer did not flinch before Eisenstein's gaze.

"Where Ralf goes, I go too. I lost one brother to Constanta and his kind. I'm not losing another."

Mariya moved closer. "Whatever you're planning, I want to be part of it," she said. "Unless we strike first, the vampyr will launch a blood war to enslave everyone, everywhere: German or Russian, man or woman, Christian or Jew, fascist or communist. Nobody will be safe."

Finally, the horrifically scarred face turned to me. "And you, Victor? How far will you go to protect the ones you love? How much are you willing to sacrifice for the future of mankind?"

I glanced at Mariya, taking in her beauty, her courage, her resolution. I knew I had to be with her, no matter what. There was no other choice.

"Whatever it takes, Grigori."

I noticed a shadow pass over his face. Was it doubt? Pride? Resignation? To this day, I do not know the answers to those questions, because I never thought to ask him. There were so many other questions to which I wanted answers, but that moment has stayed with me ever since. Strange, how the slightest of looks and glances linger in the mind.

"Good," Eisenstein said, nodding to all of us. "Dawn's breaking. The vampyr are returning to their hiding places and refuges, waiting for the thralls to transport them back to Transylvania. That's where we are going: Castle Constanta, the home of the vampyr.

"I want to kill the monster that damned me before I surrender this godforsaken life. I want to see his kind driven from the earth, sent back to whatever hell they came from. I want to make sure nobody else has to suffer as our friends and countrymen have suffered. But be warned, all of you, I doubt any of us will get out of Transylvania alive. Our mission is a suicide mission, plain and simple. Make peace with whatever god you believe in, and prepare yourselves mentally for the end. I'll be back in a few minutes with our transportation."

THE JOURNEY TO Transylvania was long and not without incident, but we saw little sign of the vampyr en route. Eisenstein had a Red Army truck take us to Rumania, driven by a surly soldier called Smirnov. He had been part of a smert krofpeet unit before they were disbanded. Rather than join a deep knife squad commanded by a vampyr, Smirnov had volunteered to rejoin his old penal company. Eisenstein had found Smirnov and five other convicts on the outskirts of Berlin, clearing a minefield. The six men gladly volunteered to help him fight the undead, since the job had a higher life expectancy than their current task. Eisenstein sent the others ahead on a different route to Transylvania.

"They're collecting some supplies on the way," he said cryptically.

The path from the German capital to Sighisoara was strewn with devastation and despair, stark evidence of the horrors war had inflicted upon the peoples of Europe. Constanta and his kind might be the worst monsters to stalk the battlefields, but there was no shortage of other horrors, other monsters in that war. In the long years since the events of which I write, more horrors have been perpetrated: genocide, ethnic cleansing, torments and tortures that would have done the vampyr proud. I'm still not sure what is worse: the obvious, palpable menace of the undead, or what humans have done to each other since in the name of religion, national pride or political beliefs. Such debates are best left to philosophers, not soldiers.

Our trek to Transylvania took days, giving me plenty of time to question Eisenstein about his escape from Gottow. At first he refused to talk about it, but eventually I wore him down. Bit by bit, I dragged the truth from him. Once I knew it all, I understood why he'd preferred to stay silent. The tale of his survival was grotesque and horrific, like so much else about our dealings with the vampyr. Truly, his soul had been damned by the undead.

Gorgo had sliced Eisenstein's skin and flesh to ribbons, broken most of the bones in his body, and given him a beating that would have killed any normal human twice over. But Eisenstein had ceased to be a normal human when he was bitten by Constanta three years earlier. The vampyr taint gave him a thirst for human blood, but it also made him stronger, more resilient, and vastly accelerated his natural healing abilities. When Gorgo set fire to the underground laboratory and sealed Eisenstein inside, the Rumanian had boasted how the facility would be my friend's tomb. Eisenstein had come to the same conclusion and quickly realised there was only one way for him to get out alive. He had to embrace the curse he'd been fighting since Leningrad. He had to give in to his blood lust.

"I crawled over to Dr Rainer's body. He was dead but his corpse was still warm, his blood still fresh," Eisenstein told me one night after we stopped to eat and rest. "I tore open his neck and drank the blood from his veins. It disgusted me, but I rejoiced in the taste too. It felt like I was giving in to a desire that had burned too long in my body. Constantly fighting the vampyr taint is corrosive; it eats away at your soul, Victor."

Once he'd sated himself on Rainer's blood, Eisenstein could feel changes seeping through his system. By then the fires Gorgo had started were raging beyond any control, threatening to destroy everything in the underground chamber. One corner of the space was filled with tanks of highly flammable gas. The blaze engulfed these, superheating the metal cylinders until Eisenstein could hear them creaking and expanding. When the first one exploded, the shrapnel from its disintegration would create a devastating chain reaction.

"I could see only one way I'd survive," he said. "Some vampyr are able to change their shape, transform into different creatures: wolves, bats, who knows what else? But I'd also seen Constanta and a few others become insubstantial, turn into a mist, a kind of transitional state. I'd no idea whether I could achieve that but it was worth a try.

"You know sometimes when you're dreaming, it's as if your spirit has left your body and you can float free, totally weightless? I closed my eyes and tried to imagine myself doing that... I was part of the air, lighter than everything around me. Just as I felt myself coming apart, the first gas tank exploded." Eisenstein grimaced.

"That's when I lost my thumb and fingers, the skin and hair. But it could have been worse. I wasn't a mist when the laboratory blew apart, but I wasn't whole either. The explosions hurt me but didn't kill me. It must have been hours, maybe even a day or two, before I regained my senses. The vampyr taint was already healing my body, repairing the damage Gorgo, the fire and the explosions had done. The blast destroyed the laboratory, but it also levelled the building overhead, giving me a way out.

"I climbed up into the daylight. It stung my skin, but didn't burn me. Drinking Rainer's blood made me more like a vampyr, but it didn't complete the transition. I don't know why. Perhaps because I didn't drink living human blood, or perhaps the explosion purged some of the infection from my body. Or maybe my faith kept some tiny part of me pure. I don't know, and it doesn't seem to matter. I can still walk in daylight but now I can

also move unnoticed among vampyr. They see me as one
of their own, whereas I recognise them for the monsters
they are. I have a rather unique viewpoint; one foot in
both worlds."

By my calculation at least ten days had elapsed
between Eisenstein's escape from Gottow and his timely
intervention at Berlin. I couldn't help wondering what
he'd been doing during that time.

"Preparing for this journey," he said. "Our enemy is
remarkably candid about their plans when they believe
no outsiders can hear them. I've been busy this past
week gathering intelligence. At first what I learned filled
me with dread, especially when I heard Gorgo had delivered the blueprints for Rainer's bomb to Constanta. No
matter how hard I tried, I could never get close to the
vampyr lord. He was always surrounded by bodyguards
and knew my face. Besides, until his blood-sire is
destroyed, Constanta can always resurrect himself, and
I'll still be eternally cursed. But, as I learned more about
what the undead have planned, I realised there was still
an opportunity to stop them, to save mankind and
myself. We have one chance to strike back, to stop the
blood war before it starts."

"How?"

"All we have to do is destroy the most powerful
vampyr on earth."

The Vollmer brothers returned from helping Smirnov
fix our truck's engine. Ralf marched across to Eisenstein
and demanded to be told the mission objective.

"Our driver knows more about the target than us!"

"Smirnov needed to know," my former mentor replied,
"so he could steal the right kind of transportation. But
you're right; everyone should hear what we're up
against. Where's Mariya?"

"Here," she said, emerging from the darkness. "I was
counting the crates of ammunition in the back of our
truck. Where did you find so much silver?"

"While the Wehrmacht was busy teaching the rest of Europe the meaning of Blitzkrieg, their Nazi masters were looting each country as it was conquered, taking fine art, jewellery, gold and silver. The vampyr are not above theft, either. They discovered where much of this treasure trove was stored in Berlin. Unsurprisingly, they wanted nothing to do with the silver, so I had my associates visit that cache. Sometimes it pays to have thieves and murderers on your side."

"Tell us about this grand plan of yours," Ralf said. "What's our target in Transylvania?"

"The father of all vampyr; a creature the Rumanians fear so much they will not even speak its name aloud after dark," Eisenstein replied.

"The Sire?" Hans asked, his eyes widening.

"Precisely. According to legend, it has slept beneath the mountains of Transylvania for a thousand years, waiting to be awakened. Through all that time the Sire's presence was protected by the family Constanta. Centuries ago they were humble goatherds, until one of their number, Vlad, fell into a deep cave while searching for a lost animal. The herdsman came face to face with evil incarnate and survived, but only by selling his soul. In exchange, Constanta became all but immortal. He was made vampyr by the Sire, giving him power over all other undead. He was also able to bend others to his will, accumulating immense wealth and power.

"The people built their new master a mighty castle, near the mountains where his master slept. Little was known or heard of the vampyr outside Transylvania for centuries. There were tales about a fearsome, terrifying warrior fond of driving a stake through the heart of his foes. Some called him Vlad the Impaler, while others claimed he drank the blood of enemies to make himself stronger. In another story, Constanta visited England in the last century, using an old Rumanian name as an alias: Drac. His exploits there are said to have inspired a novelist called Stoker. How much truth there is to these tales, who knows? All I do know for certain is that most people in Rumania had all but forgotten the Sire and his unholy kin, until someone started drilling for oil in the Transylvanian Alps."

"You think they woke the Sire?" Ralf asked, making no effort to hide his scepticism.

"Yes, I do. The lord of all vampyr decided the time had come to claim the earth for his own kind. He sent forth his blood-spawn to bring this about. That's why the vampyr chose to fight on the Ostfront, as you Germans called it. They wanted to prepare themselves for the next war, the war upon humanity. Now that conflict is about to start."

Hans was rubbing a finger across his lips, deep in thought. "Our brother stayed at Castle Constanta in 1941 when it was a rehabilitation centre for German troops. He heard about atrocities committed against Russian prisoners of war at a nearby POW camp. Soviet soldiers were being drained of blood and their bodies burnt afterwards. Klaus was told the blood was taken into the mountains for 'purification', but he also heard dark mutterings about a lake of blood close to Castle Constanta. It seemed hard to believe when he told us, but after everything we've seen…"

Eisenstein nodded. "The lake of blood exists. It is where the Sire slumbers, waiting to rise again. According to other vampyr, the Sire resembles a gigantic bat with a wingspan in excess of thirty metres and a face that's half-human, half-jackal. When the time comes, the Sire will fly out of the lake and sweep across Europe. It is said devastation follows wherever his shadows falls. Nothing mortal can survive: not animals, not plants, not humans. If the Sire rises, mankind will be nothing more than cattle, farmed as sustenance for the vampyr." Eisenstein grimaced. "The coming conflict isn't a war, it's genocide… Unless we stop it."

"How?" Ralf demanded. "There are only a few of us to fight an army of vampyr. If this Sire is so powerful, what hope do we have of stopping it?"

"I have secured a weapon that – if properly delivered – can strike a killing blow against the Sire. But we need time to make that happen. Most of us will embark on a suicide mission into Constanta's domain as a diversionary tactic. When his castle is properly defended, an army would struggle to penetrate the walls. But a small squad can break in via the tunnel you and Hans found last August. Those who make it inside must find the set of blueprints Gorgo took from the German laboratory near Gottow. With these the vampyr could build a bomb that would turn day into night for weeks on end. I don't need to tell you what that would mean. Finding and destroying those blueprints is important, but the attack is essentially a ruse designed to draw out the Sire."

"Then what?" Ralf asked.

When Eisenstein explained the rest of his plan, even Ralf had to admit it might work.

# Two

WE ABANDONED THE truck twenty kilometres from Sighisoara and marched the rest of the way, carrying the heavy crates of ammunition between us. I hadn't seen any other soldiers since we crossed the border into Transylvania, and certainly no vampyr. The war had long since moved on to other regions as the noose tightened round Hitler's Third Reich. Civilians working the fields glanced up as we passed but made no comment nor questioned why we might be crossing through their land. War had taught the peoples of Europe to stay quiet if they wanted to survive.

The closer we got to our destination, the fewer civilians we saw. No birds flew in the sky and no animals moved on the ground. It felt as if we were walking into a dead zone, an area where nothing grew and nothing lived. I thought back to Eisenstein's description of legends about the Sire, of how its shadow left devastation behind. Had the Sire flown over this land long ago, rendering it uninhabitable? If so, I dreaded to think what such a monster could do to a city like Moscow.

We met the rest of Eisenstein's insurgents at midday about a kilometre north of Castle Constanta. Five men from Smirnov's penal company were waiting for us, each of them fearsome brutes with grim faces and no shortage of scars. There was no doubting their steely resolve for the fight ahead. Eisenstein did not bother with introductions.

"Better we don't share names in case one of us is taken by the vampyr and interrogated. The undead are as fond of using torture on their captives as the NKVD."

Each of us took as much ammunition as we could usefully carry. We would need every silver-tipped round to make our mission work. Eisenstein abandoned his sword and crossbow for a PPSh.

"What lies ahead needs firepower, not finesse," he explained.

Eisenstein said he would have to stay with our secret weapon. "If I set foot inside the castle, my tainted blood would give us away in moments. I need two volunteers to help safeguard the secondary site. Who's with me?"

Nobody replied. I hoped Mariya would raise her hand. Whatever happened to me, I wanted her to have a chance of surviving what was to come.

Eisenstein sighed. "Very well. I'll choose the two to stay with me. Smirnov, I might need your talent with engines before this is done."

The driver scowled even more than usual, if such a thing were possible. I felt Eisenstein's gaze shift towards me. We had been through so much together, rescued each other many times, perhaps he felt obliged to exempt me from the suicide mission. I gave a slight shake of my head, subtly indicating Mariya should be chosen in my place.

"And Mariya," Eisenstein announced. "I need someone with good German as interpreter for the other members of our team. We leave in two minutes. Make ready for the mission."

The gathering broke up, Smirnov saying goodbye to his fellow convicts while I talked with Mariya.

"Good luck," she said, stroking one side of my face with her right hand. "You'll need it."

"We all will," I agreed. The urge to kiss her was strong, but I fought it back. This wasn't the time or place to consummate our feelings for each other, not when we were so close to such evil. Behind us I could hear Eisenstein talking with the Vollmer brothers.

"Ralf, I want you to lead the men into the castle. You and Hans know the way inside as well as anyone. Zunetov can translate your words to Smirnov's comrades, and he knows what the blueprints look like so try to keep him alive if you can. Agreed?"

Ralf nodded.

"Whatever happens, I wanted to say it's been an honour serving with you," Eisenstein added.

"Likewise," Hans replied. "Funny, I never thought I'd be thanking a Russian soldier when Operation Barbarossa began. Four years seems like a lifetime now."

The two groups marched in opposite directions, Eisenstein leading Mariya and Smirnov to the east of Castle Constanta while the rest of us went west. I kept looking over my shoulder at Mariya, certain I would never see her again. When she was out of sight, I concentrated on recalling what I could about the castle's layout. The dungeon, dining hall and concealed staircase that linked them were burnt into my brain, but the rest of the interior was something of a blur. We'd seen and done so much since then that it was difficult to recall specific details. Both Ralf and Hans had also been inside the castle. Between the three of us we should remember enough.

To my relief, Ralf had little trouble finding the low ditch leading to the hidden tunnel. All eight of us crawled half a kilometre along the ditch, staying low to keep out of sight from the castle battlements. The tunnel's entrance was open and an uneasy smell of rotting flesh seeped from the entrance. Ralf led the way into the dark, narrow space, crawling along the floor of the tunnel while pushing his MP38 ahead of him.

There was barely enough space for each of us to shimmy along one at a time. I let two of Smirnov's comrades go next before following them into the cramped tunnel. The rest of the convicts came after me and Hans brought up the rear. I could hear my countrymen whispering to each other in Russian, one of them praying that the tunnel didn't collapse on top of us. The thought haunted me for the rest of our long crawl.

Finally, after what seemed like hours of inching our way forward, Ralf whispered to us that he'd reached the hatch to the dungeon. When he opened the small wooden door, the smell of rotting corpses surged along the tunnel, filling our nostrils and choking our lungs. Ralf told the rest of us to wait while he lowered himself into the dungeon. I lay in the darkness, breathing as shallowly as I could, straining to hear what was happening ahead of me. I could see faint glimmers of light from the dungeon but nothing else.

"God in heaven!" Ralf whispered hoarsely. "I'd forgotten how bad it was in here."

I heard careful footsteps then the creaking of a door. Good, that meant we had a way up into the castle. If the dungeon door had been bolted shut from the other side, we would have been forced to retreat back along the tunnel and faced the near impossible task of finding another way inside.

"It's safe," Ralf quietly told us through the hatch. "The floor is still covered with bodies but some of them look fresh. The vampyr must be using this place as a larder."

The two convicts ahead of me crawled to the hatchway and pulled themselves out. I followed close behind, not wanting to spend any longer in that narrow, dirt-lined tunnel. Ralf helped me climb down into the dungeon. Diffuse light leaked into the chamber through greasy windows, providing meagre illumination for the horrific interior. It was much as Ralf had described, with corpses fresh and old strewn across the floor. At least these bodies were not writhing with maggots as they had been on my last visit to this hellhole.

The convicts were examining the bodies, pulling open mouths to peer inside. I saw one of the men grinning as he ripped a gold-filled tooth from a corpse.

"Leave them be," I said. "Haven't they suffered enough without you robbing their bodies?"

"They're already dead, why should they care?" he retorted.

By then the rest of our raiding party was inside the dungeon, Hans closing the hatch after him before climbing down. Ralf drew his pistol.

"Zunetov, tell that thief to leave the corpses alone, or else he'll soon be one of them. That goes for all of Smirnov's convict friends. Tell them!"

"I wouldn't worry if I were you," a German voice replied. "You'll be dead soon enough. Let the thief have his fun."

We spun round to see Karl Richter waiting for us in a corner of the dungeon standing behind two vampyr.

"Traitor!" Hans shouted, opening fire with his MP38.

The two vampyr burst into dust and ash but Karl had transformed himself into a thin white mist, the mocking outline of his features still visible in the centre of the cloud.

"As you can see, my Lord Constanta has rewarded my loyalty by making me a full-fledged vampyr. His elite cadre has suffered several losses lately." Karl let himself solidify for a moment. "You should never have come here. All that awaits you is doom." He snapped his fingers and the corpses around us slowly rose from the floor. They were not dead – they were the undead, and we were to be their next victims.

"Kill them," Karl ordered.

"Fire at will!" Ralf shouted, sweeping his machine pistol from side to side, spraying the vampyr with silver-tipped bullets.

The rest of us followed his example, emptying our weapons into the chests and heads of the advancing creatures. Those closest to us exploded first, then the next line of vampyr, and then the next. But there were simply too many of the fiends, forcing the eight of us together in a tight ring so we were standing shoulder to shoulder as the vampyr encircled us. When one of us ran out of ammunition, he stepped back into the centre of the circle, giving himself a moment's grace to reload. But still the undead pressed closer until there was no room left within the circle, no sanctuary from the monsters.

The convict who had stolen the tooth died first, talons raking across his throat as he tried to reload, cutting open his jugular. He fell forward, crimson spraying the air, unable even to scream because his vocal chords had been severed. The convict to my right died next, then the convict on my left succumbed to the vampyr onslaught.

I heard a Russian scream for mercy behind me, suggesting that another of Smirnov's comrades had perished. Still our circle shrunk, each lost man falling forward to the floor. After a minute of this bloody combat, a voice called for the vampyr to cease. They stopped where they stood, a circle of undead perhaps a metre away from us.

We used the respite to reload and catch our breath, the air around us filled with dust and ash, our senses assaulted by iron and cordite, the twin scents of gunfire and bloodshed. I could see Constanta in the dungeon doorway, signalling to Karl. The turncoat hurried to his master's side, receiving instructions from the vampyr lord. Karl smiled as Constanta pointed towards our group, but I couldn't hear the words passed between them.

The brief pause gave me a chance to notice who was standing on either side of me: Ralf at my right, Hans on my left. A glance over my shoulder confirmed that the surviving convict was behind me.

"What are we waiting for?" I whispered out the side of my mouth to Ralf. "There's no reason for us to stop shooting."

"Good point," he agreed and opened fire once more, his weapon dispensing silver-tipped death to the vampyr five-deep around us.

We all joined in, determined to take as many of the undead with us as possible. Karl bellowed an order to his brethren but the words were drowned out by our gunfire. So much shooting in such a confined space made a deafening cacophony.

Suddenly one of the vampyr launched itself over the top of the others, diving full-length at Hans. He kept firing but his bullets missed the creature's heart and head. It fell on top of him, breaking the circle and scattering the rest of us. The remaining undead leapt forward, recognising their opportunity. I was pinned to the floor, my weapon knocked away, my arms held down by two of the fiends. One of them twisted my head sideways so I could see Hans dying, his neck ripped open, an arterial spray of blood turning the air above him pink.

Ralf saw this too and howled with rage, somehow finding the strength to throw off his attackers. He got back to his feet and tore through the vampyr ranks, smashing the creatures aside with the butt of his weapon or firing point blank into their faces. Ralf raged across the room, screaming and bellowing like a madman. He got within a few metres of Constanta before he was swamped by vampyr and overwhelmed by sheer numbers. I twisted round on the floor, trying to see what had happened to the last of the convicts. He was already dead, his face awash with blood, creatures lapping at his neck wounds.

I closed my eyes and thought of Mariya, picturing her face, her beautiful eyes. A sharp, stabbing pain invaded my mind and then all I knew was blackness...

IT WAS RALF'S screaming that brought me back to consciousness. I came to with the sound of his torment ringing in my ears; animal cries of pain echoing around the dungeon. The only corpses on the floor now were those of Hans and the five convicts. Diffuse light filtering in through the windows cast a queasy pallor across the room. I was chained to a wall, my wrists pinned over my head while my ankles were spread apart beneath me, the balls of my bare feet resting on the cold stone floor. My arms were cold and numb, suggesting that I'd been in this position for some time, perhaps an hour, maybe longer.

A fresh cry of pain snapped my head to the right to see what was being done to Ralf. He was chained to the wall beside me, but his clothes had been stripped away, leaving his naked torso exposed and unprotected. Constanta was sat opposite us in a high-backed wooden chair that resembled a medieval throne, one leg folded across the other, his hands forming a steeple in front of his face. A metal canister rested across his lap. The vampyr lord watched appreciatively as Karl tortured Ralf by using the tip of a bayonet to gouge out chunks of flesh. Karl would flick the pieces of human meat on the floor where several of the undead waited on all fours like eager dogs. They fought each other for the morsels, fangs gnashing and voices growling.

Karl stabbed the bayonet into Ralf's body, eliciting a fresh scream of pain, and then twisted the blade inside the wound to get another. Blood poured from every wound, forming a scarlet pool on the floor underneath the German soldier, mixing with the other fluids that dripped from his tormented body.

"Tell us what we want to know, otherwise it will go the worse for you," Karl warned. "If you think this is pain, imagine if we choose to make you undead like us. Then I could come here and torture you every day for years, even centuries, if I wished."

"I'll see you in hell first," Ralf spat out, blood dripping from his swollen lips.

"You're already in hell," Karl replied. "Or hadn't you realised?" He gave the bayonet a fresh twist before pulling the blade free to lick it clean. "For a tough old bastard, you have the sweetest tasting blood. Quite exquisite."

"There's nothing you can say or do that'll make me say what you want," Ralf vowed.

"Perhaps not. So why don't I entertain you both with a story?" Karl asked.

Ralf snarled abuse at the vampyr, but it didn't stop Karl from telling us about his betrayal and murder of Gunther in the Führerbunker. He rejoiced in describing Gunther's death, taunting Ralf with every last detail.

"Your friend soiled himself before he died," Karl added, looking down at the stone floor beneath Ralf's legs. "Much as you've done."

Ralf started screaming again, but this time he was also whipping his head from side to side, twisting it violently until I could hear the bones grinding against each other.

"What are you doing?" Karl demanded to know. "Stop!"

But Ralf ignored him, mania filling my comrade's eyes. He wrenched his head sideways towards me and something snapped inside him. Foam spat from his lips as the last breath left his lungs. Ralf's head slumped forward, all life gone from his broken body.

Karl cursed in frustration, stabbing Ralf's corpse repeatedly with the bayonet and slicing the torso apart until severed intestines oozed out through ragged flaps of skin.

"Enough," Constanta commanded, rising from his throne and holding the canister in one hand. He approached Karl and whispered something into his ear. The torturer nodded, smirking at me before marching from the dungeon, calling the other vampyr after him. They scuttled out of the chamber, still pretending to be animals on all fours.

Then the only sounds that could be heard inside the dungeon were my terrified gasps for breath and the dripping of blood from Ralf's cooling corpse.

Constanta regarded Ralf dismissively. "Impatience is never a virtue during torture. Still, that's why I always like to keep a spare."

He moved sideways to stand in front of me. "You will tell me what your comrades are doing outside, or else I shall make what happened to your comrade seem like a blessed relief compared to your suffering." The vampyr lord smiled broadly. "I have lived for close to a thousand years. I am nothing if not patient."

"I don't have any comrades outside," I said quietly.

Constanta slapped me hard across the face, the movement so fast it felt like a whip crack. Once I'd recovered, he held the metal canister in front of my face.

"I've no doubt you came here looking for this, the plans and blueprints for Rainer's weapon. Alas, this is as close as you'll ever get to them again." He bent down to retrieve the bayonet Karl had discarded. "A crude instrument of torture, but effective enough for this situation." He rested the tip of the bayonet against my throat, the metal cold to the touch on my skin. "I repeat: what are your comrades doing outside? Deny what we both know to be true and I will have the woman brought here to be violated in front of you until her body gives out. Is that the last thing you want to see before I have your eyes removed? Is that the last image you want imprinted on your brain for eternity?"

I'd like to believe that I could have withstood torture as well as Ralf had, even denied my tormentors the triumph of ending my life. But somehow Constanta had seen through me and discovered my greatest weakness: my love for Mariya. Until that moment I hadn't even realised that I did love her. But now I knew I would sacrifice anything to save her, even my soul. Praying for a chance to redeem myself, I told Constanta what I knew about Eisenstein's plan.

When I finished, he waited a full minute as if expecting to hear more. Eventually he realised that I'd told him the whole truth, at least as much of it as I knew. Constanta started laughing, his enjoyment making my admission all the more galling. I felt my heart sink further, if such a thing were possible. When his mirth had exhausted itself, the vampyr lord stepped close enough for me to smell his putrid, sickening breath.

"I already knew about your ridiculous weapon. Did any of you fools honestly believe strangers could walk through my dominion without me being aware of it? Did any of you think I wouldn't notice such a device being assembled so close to my master? I've sent Karl there now with orders to attack at dusk. My brethren will annihilate your comrades."

Constanta snapped his fingers and another of his kind appeared, clutching a set of heavy metal keys. The vampyr lord gestured towards me as he strode from the dungeon.

"I am weary of this fool. Release him from those chains and then escort him from the castle. Let him run to his friends in the futile hope that he can save them. Let his cowardice be his companion!"

Ten minutes later I was sprinting away from Castle Constanta. The fate of humanity rested on a hillside overlooking a lake of blood. Either Eisenstein's plan would defy the odds and destroy the Sire, or we would all be dead by nightfall. In the distance I could see the sun dipping towards the horizon, part of its circumference already behind the black, brooding peaks of the Transylvanian Alps. I prayed Constanta was wrong and I still had a chance to redeem myself.

# Three

Mariya, Eisenstein and Smirnov had reached their destination about the same time as we entered the tunnel. The trio had marched into the hills behind Castle Constanta, slowly making their way up to a rocky bluff overlooking a crimson lake. Waiting for them there was a single German scientist, nervously clutching a pistol.

"God in heaven, where have you been?" he wailed. "Twice I thought I'd been discovered. A colony of bats flew overhead, circling the lake for several minutes before they went back towards the castle. It almost felt as if they were doing some sort of surveillance…"

"Don't be ridiculous," Eisenstein said. "Bats are flying vermin, nothing more. Don't let superstitious nonsense distract you from the task in hand." He introduced the frightened man to Mariya. "This is Doctor Werner, a rocket scientist I discovered at the Gottow facility. He's in charge of our vengeance weapon, our Vergeltungswaffe, as the Germans like to call it. How's the masterpiece coming along, doctor?"

Werner stepped aside, giving Mariya her first good look at what Eisenstein planned to use against the Sire. It was a Reichenberg, a piloted V1 missile identical to the flying rocket known as the Doodlebug but with a cockpit mounted atop the fuselage in front of the pulse jet engine. The weapon was impressive in size, stretching nearly eight metres in length from nose to tail with a wingspan of more than five metres.

The Reichenberg was resting on the upslope of the bluff, its nose at the top of the cliff almost protruding over the edge. At the other end the missile was held in place by a metal trolley, a starter device attached to the fuselage. Werner quickly outlined how this provided the missile with pressurized air and electrical power prior to launch. When the time came, the Reichenberg would be catapulted into the air, igniting the jet pulse engine. The warhead contained close to a thousand kilos of high explosive.

"Bojemoi," Mariya gasped. "When you described this thing, I thought it was a long shot at best. But this... Do you honestly believe anyone can fire this missile at the Sire with sufficient accuracy to destroy our enemy?"

"We have to," Eisenstein said simply. He looked at the sun as it began a slow descent towards the Alps. "How long before this thing's ready to fly?"

"I've made all the pre-flight checks," Werner replied. "All that's left is fitting the nose cone. I couldn't do that on my own because it weighs too much."

"The nose cone?" Mariya asked.

Smirnov pulled aside a tarpaulin painted with camouflage colours. Underneath was a pointed cone of gleaming metal. "It's pure silver, or as pure as we could make it in the primitive smithy we had to use for the job."

The quartet spent the next two hours fitting the nose cone to the front of the missile, all the time nervously glancing towards the crimson lake stretched out below them. No birds landed on it and no fish broke the surface.

The only movement came from gusts of wind creating brief ripples and a steady stream of bubbles rising in the centre of the lake. Nobody needed to speculate what was breathing inside the lake of blood. They knew all too well.

Once the nose cone was fitted, Eisenstein became increasingly agitated. He marched back and forth at the foot of the bluff, his eyes scouring the surrounding hills for movement.

"There should have been a signal by now... Some sort of indication that the others have penetrated the castle," he fretted. "Even if they've been taken, I'd expect Constanta to send some of his brethren here to capture or kill us. It'll be dusk soon. We don't want to be here when that comes."

"How would they even know we're here?" Werner asked innocently.

Mariya grimaced. "Nobody could survive torture at the hands of the vampyr for long. They would die or they would talk. It's that simple."

Smirnov climbed to the top of the bluff for a better vantage point. "There's no movement at the castle." He turned back to the others and all colour drained from his face. "They're here!"

A dozen vampyr were racing up the hill towards the missile and its guardian while another six appeared from higher ground. All wore hooded cloaks and gloves to protect themselves from the setting sun. Eisenstein was quickest to react, opening fire with his submachine gun. The first shots tore through the undead, exploding most of them into dust and ash. Mariya was almost as fast to pull the trigger, dealing with four more of the vampyr. Werner scrambled backwards towards the missile, his trembling hands unable to steady the pistol he was holding. Smirnov stayed where he was, using his elevated position as a vantage point to pick off the vampyr before they could get close to his comrades.

"There's more coming!" He shouted down to Eisenstein. "I can see them swarming up the hillside!" Smirnov was so intent on his targets that he never saw Karl floating up behind him, his cloak fluttering in the breeze like the wings of a bat.

"They're not the only ones," the traitorous German growled in his victim's ear.

Smirnov spun round to shoot, but it was too late. Karl gorged himself on the Soviet convict who thrashed and flailed at his murderer. The convict's weapon tumbled away down the slope, forgotten in the slaughter. When he'd finished his feast, Karl tossed the corpse into the lake below. He studied the Reichenberg appreciatively, careful not to touch the silver nose cone.

"Marvelous workmanship," he said snidely. "Such a shame you'll never get to use it."

Mariya swung round, about to fire at Karl, but Eisenstein knocked her weapon aside. "Don't! If you hit the missile it could detonate the explosives inside!"

It was Werner who fired the first shot at Karl, his shaking fingers finally locating the pistol's trigger. The bullet flew wildly by the vampyr as Karl marched down the slope towards the scientist.

"Now, now, doctor, didn't you hear what the daywalker said? You should be more careful with that gun. It might hurt somebody."

The other vampyr surged forward once more, forcing Mariya and Eisenstein to concentrate their fire elsewhere.

Werner got off three more shots. The first two went harmlessly into the air but the third passed through the right side of Karl's collar. He stopped, glaring at the hole in his uniform.

"I do believe you're finding your aim. A few centimetres to the left and you would have killed me." Karl smiled at his prey. "Now it's my turn."

He flung himself at Werner, his talons closing round the scientist's neck, grinding the bones together until they snapped. Eisenstein heard what was happening but reacted too late to save Werner. Karl threw the body aside, his talons already reaching for their next target: Mariya.

I SAW THE VAMPYR swarming up the hillside ahead of me but was too far back to intervene. I sprinted up the slope as fast as I could, watching as Mariya and Eisenstein slaughtered wave after wave of the undead. When I finally reached my comrades, less than twenty vampyr were left. I saw a discarded PPSh on the ground and was crouching down to grab it when I heard Mariya cry out. Karl was closing his hand round her throat, his lips drawing back to reveal his bloodstained fangs. I fired at the fiend, cold fury making my arm true.

Half a dozen bullets punctured the vampyr, two punching holes through his skull. He staggered backwards, releasing Mariya from his grasp. She collapsed to the ground, choking and gasping for breath, her lips blue. Eisenstein and I finished off the remaining vampyr, each of the fiends turning to ash before our eyes. Once they were dead I tossed my weapon aside and ran to Mariya. She had stopped breathing and my trembling fingers could find no pulse. I pinched her nostrils shut, closed my lips over hers and blew hot air down her throat, willing her to come back to me. Again and again I repeated the action, intent on reviving her. Then, when I'd almost given up hope, she started coughing and choking. I rolled her sideways so she could breath easier.

Eisenstein was dealing with Karl, his right knee pinning the vampyr to the ground, the barrel of his PPSh digging into Karl's chin. "How do we summon the Sire?"

The German laughed at us, black liquid gurgling from his mouth. "You don't summon the Sire. No one but Constanta can do that. He's the Sire's only surviving blood-spawn. But if you want to see the father of us all, you won't have to wait long…"

"Why's that?" Eisenstein demanded. "Why?"

Karl's eyes rolled back in his head, looking towards the Transylvanian Alps. "He will rise as soon as the sun sets. From tonight mankind will know only... darkness..."

Karl's body burst into flame, scorching the grass beneath it before burning away to nothing.

Eisenstein had hurriedly stepped away from the vampyr as it caught fire. He threw his weapon aside. "I won't be needing that anymore." He climbed the slope beside the Reichenberg, clambering up to the top of the bluff.

"Zunetov! Come and look at this!" After ensuring Mariya was better, I scrambled up to see what Eisenstein was pointing at.

The centre of the lake was alive with bubbles, steam rising from the surface as if something was heating the blood from below.

"Bojemoi," I gasped. "It's coming, isn't it?"

Eisenstein nodded, his face ashen. He glanced across at the mountain peaks where the last glimmers of daylight were fading fast. "We've got a few minutes at most. You have to get the missile flying. Werner showed me what to do as a contingency." We slid down to the starter device and Eisenstein hurriedly explained how to operate it. Twilight was falling with frightening speed and we had no time to lose.

Mariya had recovered enough from Karl's attack to come and help. Between us we got the starter device activated. It began feeding pressurized air and electrical power into the Reichenberg; a humming sound growing louder as the missile grew ready. Eisenstein clambered up to the cockpit and got inside. Mariya and I climbed up on the wing to talk with him.

"Even if you don't hit the target this is suicide," she said to Eisenstein.

"I'm dead already," he said with no trace of regret in his voice. "I was dead the moment Constanta sunk his fangs into me at Leningrad. It's long past the time I should have let the afterlife claim me."

"Are you sure about this?" I asked.

"As sure as I've been about anything in my life, Victor." He reached out a hand to shake mine, his face splitting into a broad smile. "Wish me luck. I'll need it to fly this damn thing!"

I couldn't reply since my throat was too choked with emotions. I went back to the starter, determined to ensure all was ready. I saw Eisenstein hand something to Mariya who accepted it gratefully.

A moment later the air was filled with a screaming unlike anything I'd ever heard before. It sounded as if the earth was about to crack apart, so loud and violent was the wailing, like a thousand jagged knives stabbing into my mind. I clamped my hands over my ears trying to block out the noise, but realised the sound was inside my mind. Mariya tumbled off the wing of the Reichenberg and rolled down the slope, just as badly afflicted by the inhuman screeching. She crawled across the ground towards me, shouting to be heard above the noise.

"What is that?"

Before I could speak the screaming stopped and a new sound took its place: the hissing of steam as if liquid was being boiled in a gigantic cauldron.

"This is it!" Eisenstein shouted. "The Sire. He's coming out of the lake. Get ready to launch!"

I held a trembling hand over the control that would catapult the Reichenberg into the air.

"Ready!" I bellowed to Eisenstein.

He stuck an arm out the cockpit and gave us the thumbs up signal before closing the canopy over himself. At that moment it began to rain blood. I looked past the missile and saw a black shape take to the air, its outline silhouetted against the darkening blue sky. The Sire was much as legend had described it: a vast vampyr bat with an elongated head and evil, glinting eyes. The

# 244 DAVID BISHOP

creature howled at us, each flap of its wings like a thunderclap in the air, its cry tearing through our minds like razors – pure hatred, made incarnate.

"Now!" Mariya screamed. "Do it!"

I slammed my fist down on the control and then flung Mariya and myself to one side, away from the roaring jet pulse engine. Moments later the missile shot into the sky, swerving as it cleared the top of the bluff. Mariya and I clung to each other as we watched the Reichenberg streak towards the Sire. The creature hung in the sky, its wings beating the air, watching the silver arrow hurtling towards it. The Sire roared at the missile as if affronted by this strange object daring to come near. Still the Reichenberg raced at its target, flying straight and true. Perhaps realising the danger, the Sire twisted sideways in the air, turning out of the missile's path.

"Bojemoi," I whispered. "He's going to miss!'

The V1 jerked sideways, desperately trying to follow the Sire. I watched, horrified, as one of the wings came away, sheared off by the sudden change of trajectory. The cataclysmic failure threw the missile out of alignment, sending it tumbling end over end through the air. The Sire looked back to see what had happened and, in doing so, its torso twisted round slightly.

Grigori Eisenstein flew the V1 into the über-vampyr's chest, embedding the silver nose cone deep in the monster's heart. The impact detonated the fuses packed around the warhead, and the missile exploded. Night turned to day as a blazing white light engulfed everything within twenty kilometres. Next came the sound of the explosion, accompanied by an unearthly howl of torment. The last thing I remember was Mariya and I tumbling over and over as the concussion wave threw us across the hillside. After that was only darkness.

# Four

MARIYA AND I woke the next morning to find the landscape around us utterly changed. It was as if the explosion that destroyed the Sire also lifted the curse from the countryside. Green shoots were poking up from below the ground and we could hear birdsong for the first time in days. Both of us were covered in scratches and bruises and Mariya bore angry red marks around her neck where Karl had tried to strangle her, but we were otherwise unhurt. I climbed up the bluff to see if there was any evidence of what had happened to the vampyr. No trace of the Sire remained, but the lake was now merely dark, murky water instead of a vast blood pool. Perhaps the Sire's presence had kept the lake as pure blood. Whatever the reason, the water was returning to its natural state.

I climbed back down to Mariya. "It's over. Grigori did it."

She smiled. "I know. Somehow I can feel it." She rested a hand on her chest. "In here."

I noticed something metallic glinting in her grasp.

"What did he give you?"

Mariya opened her palm to reveal the Star of David emblem. "He said it had helped him fight off the vampyr taint. He wanted us to have it no matter what happened."

We walked slowly to Castle Constanta, not sure what to expect. We were still a kilometre away when it became obvious that there was nothing more to fear inside. The building had been torn apart by the explosion; so devastated that not a single stone stood atop another. When we got close enough, I could see even the dungeon had been exposed to the sunlight. There was no sign of Ralf, Hans, or the others. Perhaps their bodies were destroyed in the explosion. The ruins of the castle were filled with hundreds of piles of dust and ash, mute evidence of all the vampyr wiped out by the Sire's destruction.

It was Mariya who found the remnants of the canister Constanta had shown me. The metal had collapsed in on itself and scraps of singed blueprint fused into the melted mess. Rainer's bomb would never be a threat again, that much was certain.

"What about Constanta?" Mariya asked. "Can we be sure he's gone, too?"

I shrugged. "He once told Grigori and me that he could never be completely destroyed; not while the Sire lived. Even if Constanta did somehow escape the firestorm, he is vulnerable now, diminished, possibly even mortal, like the rest of us. He'd have all the curses of being a vampyr but few of the strengths now. I doubt we'll hear of him again in our lifetimes."

"Good."

"There are other vampyr out there, you know. The undead didn't restrict themselves to the Eastern Front. Constanta used to brag about having his brethren and thralls active in other theatres of the war. For all we know they're still out there somewhere. God only knows what those fiends might be planning."

"What should we do about them?"

"Our war's over," I decided. "Let's go home." We walked away from the ruins of Castle Constanta, Mariya slipping her hand inside mine as we left.

"I seem to recall talk about what we might do after all this was over," she said playfully.

"I was wondering if you'd remember that."

"Oh yes. I never forget a promise."

THAT WAS THE end of my involvement with the vampyr. Mariya and I both made it home to Russia, surviving many deprivations and danger on our long trek back to the motherland. Our passion for each other was born in the midst of a horrific war, but our love was strong enough to outlive the horrors we had seen. In time, we had a family, two daughters and a son. Mariya named the girls after our mothers but I took the responsibility for naming our boy. The choice was obvious and little Grigori has grown into a fine man, a brave soldier and a courageous fighter, no matter how insurmountable the odds – just like his namesake.

For decades after the war I did my best not to think about what I'd witnessed in those dark days and nights at Leningrad and Berlin, the comrades I'd lost to Constanta and his unholy kinsmen. Mariya forbade all talk about the war from our modest home and I was happy to respect her wishes. We'd been through too much to spend the rest of our lives resurrecting the greatest horrors we ever experienced. My beloved wife died in 1959, far too young for one so beautiful, leaving me to raise our children alone. Once they had become adults in their own right, all three of them left home and I found myself alone with my memories. At the back of my mind, I still had nagging doubts about what had happened to Constanta in that final, apocalyptic firestorm that destroyed the Sire. Eventually those doubts started to invade my dreams, turning my time of rest into a recurring nightmare of blood and pain and the Rumanian's mesmerizing eyes, staring deep into my soul, taunting me even in sleep.

Finally the nightmares became too much and I decided the only way to purge them was by writing about my experiences during the war. I soon discovered publishers had little stomach for such a fantastical tale, not if it was presented as fact. Try writing it as a novel, one editor suggested – people will believe anything if it happens in a novel. So, I wrote this volume and the book that preceded it, about my experiences during the Siege of Leningrad. My accounts of events may be fictionalised, but the facts are all too true.

To help job my own memories of those long past days, I started attending annual reunions of smert krofpeet units. Mariya had forbade me from taking part in such gatherings while she was alive, but that restriction no longer applied, sadly. Not many members of the vampyr hunting units had survived the war, but those that did gathered every summer near the Baltic to swap tall tales about encounters with the undead. As the years went by there were fewer and fewer of us left but I kept in touch with the families of several former vampyr-hunters and sometimes heard whispers about outbreaks of the undead. I was even sent reports of Constanta resurfacing in other countries, decades after the war had ended, posing as a senior military figure. According to one story, he died in the British sector of Berlin during 1980, but I had my doubts. If Constanta survived the Sire's destruction, why emerge from hiding twenty-five years later?

I was more interested in discovering what the vampyr lord did during the times when he wasn't active in the Great Patriotic War. Slowly I began piecing together a timeline for sightings of Constanta along what Germans had called the Ostfront using intelligence gathered from my brothers in arms, and also from the few former Wehrmacht soldiers willing to talk about their experiences fighting with, and against, the undead. I discovered there were key moments during the war when Constanta was conspicuous by his absence from the Eastern Front. For example, when the Japanese launched their attack upon the American Navy at Pearl Harbour in 1941, the vampyr lord was missing from our battlefront. Several times I'd heard him bragging about the undead's involvement in other parts of the world. Could Constanta have been sent by Hitler to aide his Oriental Axis partners in their savage surprise raid on the US forces?

During June of 1942, undead activity at the blockades surrounding Leningrad fell to an all time low. Maybe Constanta was busy elsewhere, trying to tip the balance in favour of Axis forces at the crucial Battle of Midway? Tales of atrocities committed by some Japanese units sounded suspiciously like the work of Constanta's kinsmen – Allied prisoners of war in captured Pacific countries tortured and tormented by creatures they equated with monsters. One word came up repeatedly in the fragmented accounts I was able to read with my broken English: Kyuuketsuki – the Japanese for vampire, I've since discovered. Could Constanta have create an undead army among the Japanese warriors and unleashed them upon the American GIs and other Allied soldiers fighting in places like Guadalcanal and Iwo Jima?

If that was the case, what if the Rumanian lord had survived the destruction of his blood father, the Sire? Where was Constanta when America dropped its atomic bombs on Hiroshima and Nagasaki? Could his presence in Japan have been the reason such a devastating weapon was unleashed not once, but twice? I don't know the answers to these questions, perhaps nobody does. But I now know I witnessed only a small part of the horrors Constanta and his kind committed during the Second World War. I never saw the vampyr lord after 1945 and for that I am grateful. I pray upon the soul of my beloved Mariya and the lives of my children that I never see the Rumanian again.

## About the Author

David Bishop was born and raised in New Zealand, becoming a daily newspaper journalist at eighteen years old. He emigrated to Britain in 1990 and was editor of the *Judge Dredd Megazine* and then *2000 AD*, before becoming a freelance writer. His previous contributions to Black Flame include *Judge Dredd: Bad Moon Rising, Nikolai Dante: The Strangelove Gambit* and *A Nightmare on Elm Street: Suffer the Children*, as well as the previous two titles in the Fiends of the Eastern Front series. He also writes non-fiction books and articles, audio dramas, comics and has been a creative consultant on three forthcoming video games.

If you see David in public, do not approach him – alert the nearest editor and stand well back.

# GLOSSARY

RUSSIAN WORDS OR phrases, unless otherwise stated. German nouns are usually capitalised. Russian words are written as phonetic spellings.

**Aufstieg** – *Growth (German)*
**bliad'** – *whore*
**bliatz** – *bitch*
**Blitzkrieg** – *Lightning War (German)*
**Bojemoi!** – *My God!*
**burzhuiki** – *free-standing stove*
**Chort tzdbya beeree!** – *The devil with you!*
**da** – *yes*
**dacha** – *holiday home*
**Dämmerung** – *Twilight (German)*
**Djavoli** – *Devil, Devils*
**Doroga Zhizni** – *Road of Life*
**dubiina** – *idiot*
**Feuerzauber** – *Fire Magic (German)*
**gaduka** – *snake, serpent*
**gefreiter** – *Lance-Corporal (German)*
**gymnastiorka** – *shirt or blouse*
**Halt! Wer geht dort?** – *Halt! Who goes there? (German)*
**Hände hoch!** – *Hands high! (German)*
**hauptmann** – *Captain (German)*
**kasha** – *grain porridge*
**kommisar** – *political officer*
**Leningradskaia Pravda** – *Leningrad Truth*
**Leningradskoi armii narodnogo opolchaniia (LANO)** – *Leningrad People's Militia Army*
**Leutnant** – *2nd Lieutenant (German)*

**Mestnaia protivo-vozdushnaia oborona (MPVO)**
 – *local air defence*

**Moisin** – *rifle*

**Narodnyi Komissariat Vnutrennikh Dei (NKVD)**
 – *People's Commissariat for Internal Affairs*

**Obergefeiter** – *Corporal (German)*

**oblast** – *region*

**Ostfront** – *The Eastern Front (German)*

**pilotka** – *cap*

**plashch-palatka** – *rain cape*

**podonok** – *A person that is the lowest of the low*

**portyanki** – *Narrow cloth strips wrapped round
 feet as socks*

**Pravda** – *Truth, a Russian newspaper*

**samovar** – *a metal urn for making tea*

**shapka-ushanka** – *synthetic fur-lined hat*

**sharovari** – *trousers similar to jodhpurs*

**shtrafroty** – *penal company*

**Smert Krofpeet** – *death to blood-drinkers*

**statsionar** – *convalescent hospital*

**svolotch** – *bastard*

**telogreika** – *quilted jacket*

**tselka** – *virgin*

**Tod** – *Dead (German)*

**tovarisch** – *friend*

**Univermag** – *A co-operative store*

**Upravlenie po delam iskusstv (UPDI)** – *Council
 for the Arts*

**ushanka** – *fur-lined hat*

**valenki** – *boots made of pressed felt*

**Vampyr** – *Vampire (German)*

**vospitanie** – *moral upbringing*

**Wehrmacht** – *The German Armed Forces*
  *(German)*
**zasranec** – *asshole*

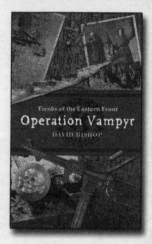